SPECIAL SERVICES

AN ALL OUT
WAR STORY

TAVIAN BRACK

It's important to me that readers remember that this is part of an <u>alternate history series</u>. Thanks to all those who have read the previous stories. Thanks to those who are just jumping on the bandwagon. And, as always, thanks to Panera Bread for the coffee. I hope you enjoy it.

Castle Cornet–Saint Peter Port, Occupied Guernsey, Channel Islands

PROLOGUE

"Ah. Come in, Jackie."

Admiral Roger Keyes tossed down his newspaper and stood up from the chair he'd been sitting in at his office at Whitehall. The man who entered through the doorway took his cap off and shook the admiral's hand. He was dressed in his service dress uniform, which showcased a lean, muscular physique despite his years. The lines on his face were deep, and his exposed skin was almost leather in appearance. A feature that some officers might pucker their brows over. But Colonel John Devereaux was as capable an officer as he was a fighting man. A veteran of the Great War, and half a dozen smaller ones, he'd shaped a career that had once seemed to be taboo in the British Army. Now, with the blessing of Churchill, his unique services were front and center of war strategy.

"Good to see you," the admiral said.

"You as well, sir."

"Please." Admiral Keyes offered the seat across from him, and they both settled in. A teapot sat on the table between them. The admiral poured tea into two cups, giving one to Devereaux. "Darjeeling is your preferred liking if my memory serves?"

Devereaux smiled and picked up the tiny cup. "It is, sir." He took a sip and sighed lightly at the rich flavor. Years spent in India had turned him onto the cuisine, and before leaving the Raj, he'd had a sizeable supply of the tea sent back to his residence in England.

"How's Eve?" the admiral inquired, taking a sip.

"She's well, sir. At home back in Norfolk."

"Well, I hope you got some time with her, Jackie. I'm afraid that we're going to need you in the months ahead."

Devereaux hardly nodded. For most of the last thirty years, he was away from home, only returning to England sporadically after long deployments. Both he and his wife had become accustomed to the life of a career military officer whose expertise too often called him away.

"We've had the last several days. She's, unfortunately, become accustomed to the briefness of our time together." He shook his head sadly.

"So," Keyes began as he sipped from his cup. His eyes scanned Devereaux for a moment, as if he were looking for something before speaking. "We're in a bit of a pickle, aren't we?"

The colonel sighed, rolled his eyes, and put his cup down. "It certainly looks that way, sir."

The last Allied soldier evacuated from France had arrived back in England just yesterday. The tens of thousands of foreign soldiers in the country had done nothing to quell the anxiety that most Britons were now feeling. In the hurry to evacuate the continent in the face of German opposition, a tremor of utter shock had spread across the free world. That shock was no more clear than in Great Britain. Now, as the Allied armies struggled to regroup, preparations were also being made for an invasion of their island nation.

"I don't think I need to tell you we're on the ropes, Jackie," the admiral went on. His voice had turned dreadfully honest. "I met with the IGS yesterday, and I can tell you that there is a lot of knee-knocking going on over there. The consensus is that once Hitler consolidates in France, he'll likely come our way." He paused and looked down at his drink. "And there's not much we'll be able to do about it."

Devereaux gradually nodded. "He might find a bigger fight here than he expects if he does. I don't know what their naval situation looks like, but from what I've heard, he doesn't have near enough boats for an army to cross the English Channel in any great numbers. At least, not yet."

"Not yet is the operative phrase," Keyes replied. "And, of course, the Royal Navy will give the Huns a stiff fight if comes to it. However, we'd be fooling ourselves if we said that we were in fighting shape. We're not. The Army needs time to reorganize, and the Air Force is just a fraction of the enemy's. That Speer character has turned the German industry into a juggernaut. Reports we've gathered suggest that they're outproducing our fighter planes three, perhaps even four to one. I could go on, but I think you grasp the situation."

Colonel Devereaux didn't answer. He didn't need to. He'd been in France when the *Wehrmacht* came rolling through. But unlike so many others who'd been corralled into ports like Boulogne and Dunkirk, pinned to the coast, he and a handful of others had reached the south side of the Somme. He'd made his way back to Paris, then on to Cherbourg before catching a flight back to England. But too many of his friends and colleagues hadn't made it out. Many of them had been killed in action, others missing. Only a handful had escaped, and he knew full well the general situation.

"I'll come to the point of things. I asked for you specifically. We require someone with your, well… career credentials, if you will."

Colonel Devereaux's forehead creased. His expertise in the British Army was that of an irregular warfare type. Similar to the riflemen of the Napoleonic Wars, or the rangers of the American frontier. Small unit, close-quarters types of fighting. An Indian fighter, as he'd once been called by an American friend.

"The Prime Minister has floated about the idea of a specialized warfare unit," Keyes continued. "With half of Europe under occupation, and our resources spread thin right now, he feels the need to have contingency operation in place."

"Contingency?"

The admiral shrugged and grabbed for his cup. "Something outside of the box. A combat unit with the strategic purpose of keeping the enemy off balance, as well as executing certain covert actions."

Devereaux rubbed his bottom lip as he listened to the admiral. It was common knowledge among many of the general officers in London that his personnel file read much more like a biography of a Rudyard Kipling fictional character than that of a more academic nature. He hadn't attended Cambridge, Oxford, or some preparatory school somewhere in England with deep-rooted traditions of scholarly pursuit. As the son of a public school educator, he'd had no such guarantees of social upward mobility. He'd attended university in Cairo, Egypt before earning his commission. His experiences there and in the service during the First World War had set his career on a path that he, and most of his fellow officers, assumed wouldn't go very far.

Following the success of Lawrence and the Arab Revolt in the desert of Arabia, he'd shifted his focus from simple staff duties to making a study of small-scale warfare. Something he took to with great enthusiasm and learned a great deal of. His experiences since those days included infiltrating small bands of guerilla fighters in Afghanistan, Burma, and Malaya and nullifying threats before they got out of control, with no large-pitched battles.

"I see," Devereaux replied. "Infiltration, demolition, sabotage? That type of thing, sir?"

"Precisely."

"Assassination?" the colonel asked him offhandedly. The admiral neither answered nor looked him in the eye. After a moment, the question seemed to fade away, unanswered.

"Some two hundred million people are living under occupation, Colonel. So far as Churchill is concerned, those are two hundred million allies operating behind the German lines."

"Smart way of seeing the situation," Devereaux said in a low tone.

"I think so. And so does the Imperial General Staff. Until the day that we can storm the beaches of France and begin the liberation of Europe, we need to use whatever tools we have in our box. Your record is full of examples of the type of thinking that we need right now."

Colonel Devereaux sat as still as a rock. The Germans were still deeply invested in the process of consolidation and could take years before they had a firm grip on the occupied countries. The small unit raids that he'd successfully employed in the jungles of Southeast Asia and the mountains of Afghanistan might work well under those circumstances.

"It could work, sir." His mind was already beginning to stir. "But we're going to need many volunteers. And they would need to be volunteers, not men pressed into service. Men from all walks of life. Any missions would be of a highly compartmentalized nature. Life expectancy would be short, under the circumstances. This would have to be optional for recruitment."

"Agreed. Which is why I've asked you here today." He leaned in toward Devereaux and smiled. "So I can look you in the eyes and ask you if you'd volunteer for just such an assignment."

Devereaux grinned at the question. "Would I have a choice, sir?"

"Absolutely not. You're an officer and a gentleman in His Majesty's Army." He chuckled lightly. "You have options, but never choices." Both men laughed at the statement. "In all seriousness, Jackie, I need you. I can't think of a better man to put together something like this."

"I appreciate that, Admiral."

He'd spent the previous nine months on glorified desk duty in France, seeing to the training of that nation's Garde Nationale. Before that, he'd been in Malaya, training locals to supplement the British forces before the war broke out. Both duties he'd excelled at, but had found the former to have been quite challenging. And since the French regular forces had collapsed, he'd seen it as a failure as well.

With the highly static political situation in the world before the war, his area of expertise had been abandoned by higher circles in favor of a more traditional approach. But under Churchill, things were changing, and the British Army was changing to adapt.

"Don't get too appreciative," Keyes told him bluntly. "You may curse the assignment before too long." He paused dramatically for a moment. "We're backed up against the wall. It'll take something just shy of a miracle if we survive the next few weeks." The cup seemed to weigh heavily in his hand. "We could use a bit of breathing room. A win right now would go a long way."

"I understand," Devereaux replied somberly. "Is there a specific aim that you had in mind?"

Keyes shook his head. "Not precisely. You'll have to figure that out when you reach your new command. I've put in the necessary clearances for you so that you'll have access to our intelligence."

"I see. And do I answer directly to you, sir?"

"For the time being, yes. Though, that'll probably change. Brigadier Laycock has already been tasked with a similar assignment in Egypt. He may take eventual overall charge."

"Is that Robert Laycock?"

"You've met him?"

"Only once. At a conference in Bombay. Capable officer."

"Well, he's a good man," Keyes told him. "And well connected. The success of this entire endeavor will depend much on the success of your operation,

Jack. If it succeeds, we could well form additional units. The Prime Minister is banking on it."

Devereaux lifted his teacup and emptied the last of his tea. "I see. Well, I don't wish to disappoint the Prime Minister. So, what's our designation?"

"Your designation is First Battalion, Special Service Brigade. Churchill's already taken to calling your new unit commandos."

Devereaux's eyes squinted at the name. "Commandos?"

Admiral Keyes looked back at him and rolled his eyes. "Don't ask me where he gets these things. He's Winston bloody Churchill, and he says the damndest things some days. But, he's the boss." He noticed Devereaux's empty cup. "More tea?"

"Thank you, no, sir."

"In that case," Keyes put down his cup and hoisted himself up from his chair, Devereaux following suit. "I'll send you off with my support." The two men shook hands. "My assistant will have all the details that you need to get started sent over to your new command. We're setting up an office for you in Inverness, something low-key. Good luck, Jack."

"Thank you, sir." Devereaux started for the door.

"You think you can handle it?"

He turned back to the admiral. "What's that, Admiral?" Devereaux asked. He just wanted to hear the answer. "Form an elite unit of men, save Britain from imminent disaster, and bring a swift end to the war?"

Admiral Keyes gave him a friendly smile. "That's about it. Yes."

Colonel Devereaux smiled broadly. "I don't have anything else planned for the next few days." With that, he gave a salute and left the office. The thick wooden door clicked shut behind him.

CHAPTER ONE

It was wet outside. A steady drizzle had been coming down all morning. The skies were turning grayer by the minute, and off in the distance was the echo of thunder. Under the gloomy sky, a company-sized formation stood at ease in an empty parade ground that was slowly turning into mud in the dampness, with only small patches of thin, weedy grass here and there. The formation had been standing there for nearly an hour now, with not so much as an officer or non-com to come and greet them. The men had been ordered into formation just as soon as they'd arrived at, well...wherever they were.

Willoughby shifted his eyes around to see if he recognized any regimental badges in the crowd. So far as he knew, he'd been the only soldier from the 1st Battalion of the Irish Guards who'd volunteered for this assignment. There were men from all different units gathered about. Shoulder badges representing the Northumberland Fusiliers, Cheshire Regiment, Royal Sussex, Coldstream Guards, and a dozen others were in attendance; an impressive mix of soldiers from all over the British Army.

They'd brought in the assorted group from points all over. None of them had been told where they were going, only that it was somewhere along the western shores of Scotland. Their end destination was a ruined old castle just off the North Channel between Scotland and Ireland. They'd placed them next to the old stone keep and built a camp for them. The castle itself was a gutted old structure, housing only birds and small animals. Outside, its walls were covered in moss, and its roof had long since caved in.

Around it, several small structures sat in the open fields. The Army had erected a stout two-story wooden building near the edge of a cleared field, with two metal chimneys at either end. Near it, facing the old keep, was a smaller stone-walled house with an old granite roof. A shoulder-high brick wall surrounded the entire property on all four sides, beyond which was a wooded area. To the east and west, there were two lakes connected by a canal to the north of the grounds, making the area around the encampment a peninsula. It was out of sight and out of mind; miles away from anything more than the tiny farms that dotted the area.

Willoughby, like everyone else, stood silently in the courtyard, just as the corporal who'd met them at their arrival had ordered them to do. And there they'd stayed. Silent as the grave. He could hear his belly grumbling, and he wasn't the only one. He hadn't eaten since the evening before, and he was feeling it now.

"*Ten-shun!*" a voice called out.

The hundred-man company clapped their heels to attention. He could hear boots plodding through the wet ground somewhere. The mud pulling on them made a suction sound as they moved. Four bodies came to a stop in front of the formation, one of which then stomped up a pair of wooden steps onto a small dais that was placed between the company and the tiny house with the granite roof.

The man had a swagger stick under his left arm and the chevrons of a sergeant major on his sleeves. His plump cheeks could have just as easily been made of polished stone, and his cleft chin stuck out under his mouth. Under the sides of his cap, his head was smooth shaven. The sergeant major stood there for a moment, looking out at the half-wet group of soldiers standing in a square in front of him. Below and in front of him, Willoughby could see the heads of three others facing the men.

"Well, well. Aren't we the sorriest-looking bunch?" the sergeant said, shaking his head, which seemed to turn left and right almost mechanically. "I've seen sepoys that look better than you lot." He paused a moment. "Those are Indian soldiers, for those of you who don't comprehend." His gruff voice echoed. "I'm Sergeant Major Mosely, the drill master at this camp. I have the displeasure of being here with you buggers. And you have the pleasure of my magnificent tutelage while you are here. You'll eat when I tell you to, wake when I tell you, and do as I say."

Willoughby's stomach growled again at the mere mention of food. The men who'd come over from Aberdeen with him had been repeatedly told they'd be fed when they reached their destination. That had been two hours earlier, and no food had been forthcoming. Instead, the men had stood at parade rest while someone carelessly tossed their bundles into a pile just in front of the two-storied building. The corporal who'd greeted them had then abruptly left without so much as an order.

"I've been informed that you have not yet had your breakfast." He grinned happily, and his pointed ears seemed to perk up as if he had been reading Benton's thoughts. "Good. Means we're going to find out just what you beggars are capable of on an empty stomach. As you can plainly see, this is some very fine Scottish weather we're having, and we'll be training in it." He rolled his sleeve up and looked at his wristwatch. "From here, we'll form you into sections. As I read your name off, you'll fall in with one of the training corporals. You'll have ten minutes to grab your gear, stow it in the barracks, and report back here. Battledress uniform, gentlemen. You don't want to get your bits caught up on something." He pumped his feet up and down under him and then shouted, "*Move!*"

One at a time, each man fell in as his name was called. By the time Willoughby fell in, the light drizzle had become a steady rain. It took only minutes to break them down into sections with a corporal marching each off to the barracks as soon as they'd finished.

The corporals gave each man only seconds to find his bundle, then hurried them along through the wooden double doors of the two-story building that served as billets. The men stomped their way through the wood-floored halls of the structure, choosing bunks and putting away personal items. Willoughby grabbed a bunk in the center of the first floor, just paces from the main door. It was warm inside, and there was a pair of small iron stoves at either end of the room.

"You're Willoughby?" the man with the bunk beside him asked. He was dressed in the kilt of a Scottish Highlander. His thick hair was curly and bright red.

"That's right," he said, and the two exchanged handshakes.

"MacAvoy. Seaforth Highlanders. I heard about you. Norway, right?" Willoughby gave a nod. "Didn't they pluck you out of the harbor? Saved a platoon of riflemen, didn't you?"

Willoughby sighed. He hated it when others asked him about that. "Not quite."

"So what was it?"

He didn't want to answer, just shook his head and shrugged.

"Oh. Didn't mean to pry," MacAvoy said after realizing his questioning was making Willoughby uncomfortable. "I recognized your name on a list when we came in. Just curious was all." MacAvoy had only a trace of an accent. He sounded more like someone who might have grown up in Lancashire or somewhere in the north of England. Certainly not someone who hailed from the Scottish Highlands. Besides his name, his bright red hair was the only suggestion of his heritage.

"It's all right," Benton said apologetically. "What about you? Where are you from?"

"Ross-shire," MacAvoy said, pointing to the stag patch on his shoulder.

"Ross-shire?"

"It's farther north."

"Well, I don't even know how far north we are now. Seen action?"

"France. Such as that was. About near broke our backs at Arras," MacAvoy said, shuddering at the memory. He kicked his boots off one by one before reaching into his kit bag for his trousers. "A slaughter, mate."

"Well, friend, Norway was no picnic either. Barely made it out of Narvik. Picked up a couple of souvenirs on the way out too." He used his thumb to indicate his rear.

MacAvoy's eyes flashed, and his lips curled into a grin. "You're joking? Hit in the backside, were you?" He laughed. "Well, I suppose if you're going to get it, that's probably the best place to get it in."

"I suppose so." Willoughby chuckled. "Too many other boys got it in a lot worse places."

"That's a fact, mate." MacAvoy unbuttoned his kilt and put one leg into his trousers, then the other. "Willoughby. It's English, isn't it?" Benton nodded. "How'd an Englishman end up with the Irish Guards?"

"Grew up outside Belfast," Willoughby said. "When the war started, I showed up at the recruiting office and signed up on the spot. I didn't much care where I was sent off to."

He opened the trunk at the end of the bunk, tossed his kit bag in, and let the lid slam shut. Others were finishing up their hurried changing and heading back toward the double doors. MacAvoy buckled his trousers up and laced his boots just as a corporal came bursting through the doorway, screaming and yelling.

"Get your worthless tails in motion!" the man shouted as he walked down the row of bunks. His shrill voice sounded more like a teen who was trying too hard to over-impress.

The high-pitched corporal herded everyone back out into the courtyard with time to spare. The last man fell into position just as the sergeant major counted the last seconds on his watch and blew a whistle hard. He had cloaked himself in a faded lime-green groundsheet, as were two of the corporals. The rain was coming down steadily now, forming puddles in front of the dais where he was standing.

Behind the dais, Willoughby could see lamps on inside the stone-walled house, and a steady smoke was piping out of the chimney top. Through the pane glass, he could make out the sight of people periodically peeking outside at the men standing in the rain.

"Time's up!" Sergeant Major Mosely shouted over the sound of rain. "The time is now eleven hundred. You and your empty bellies will go through that gate there. You will double-time it down the road behind Corporal Carney. Any of you who fall out during that run will repeat the entire thing if I must run you until midnight. So do yourselves a favor and don't fall out. Corp, take them out."

"Yes, Sergeant! Company, by the right, quick march!" The company turned to the right and moved toward the front gate. "Company, form up in two ranks!"

The soldiers double-timed it toward the front gate, their boots splashing through the puddles in the path. As they reached the gate, another man emerged out of the guard shack, pushed the gate open, and let the men through in two parallel lines. The sound of the rain was the only thing that could be heard apart from the muffled commands of Corporal Carney.

Benton was standing in the middle of the courtyard when the last man came staggering through the double gate. It was MacAvoy. The Scottish Highlander was desperately out of breath by the time he reached the rest of the company.

It was still dark outside. The only light in the muddy courtyard came from a single large bulb outside of the officer's quarters.

MacAvoy joined next to him in formation. His face was as bright as his red hair was, and he was panting for breath.

"Guess I'm not in the shape I was," he said between breaths.

The rain had stopped, but the thick, dark clouds still blotted out the sun. It must have been close to fourteen hundred hours when the company finally assembled. Not a single officer or non-com was around when they got back, except for the corporals who had led the exercise. The men lingered under the light until the door of the officer's lodgings swung open and three individuals emerged.

"*Ten-shun!*"

Two men in officer uniforms stepped outside, followed closely by Sergeant Major Mosely. Benton was still out of breath, and his legs wobbled under him. In front of him and to the right, another private was heaved half over as if his belly were about to explode. Nobody had eaten, and their exercise in the rain had become an hours-long affair. But he stood there, in the center of the formation, back rigid, eyes front, and chin up, staring at the back of the head of the man directly in front of him.

He caught a glance of the officers inspecting them. The first was Captain Zahlman, the man who'd recruited him into this little venture. He didn't recognize the lieutenant, who was the second one.

The two then turned to one another, and after a minute of a hushed conversation between them, the captain gave a nod to the sergeant major who had taken to standing in front of the formation.

"At ease," the sergeant said in two drawn-out syllables.

The captain stepped up onto the wooden dais and looked out over the company. He was a tan-skinned man with a lean physique. Under his peaked cap, he had thick, black hair and a thick mustache to suit. His eyes were deep, and his face was sharp. Despite the gloomy wet weather, his uniform was as neat as the rest of his features.

Zahlman was known to Willoughby, having visited him at his unit weeks earlier. He'd been familiar with Willoughby's record from the matter in Norway the previous year. The captain had been rather candid the day they'd met, when he'd made him an interesting offer.

"Command is putting together a new fighting unit," Zahlman had told him. "I'm in charge of one of them. We're a specialized unit within the Army, and I'm looking for volunteers. You'd be gone for weeks at a time, operating behind enemy lines. It's a highly dangerous assignment, and the likelihood is that you'll end up dead within six months. I can't give you any more information than that right now. But if you're interested, I'll leave you with my information."

Benton had accepted the offer right on the spot.

His injuries in Norway had been far from severe, and his motivation to be an active part in the fighting had been overwhelming. Not that he was eager to kill anyone, he wasn't. His experiences in Norway had left a foul taste in his mouth. Literally. Killing did not sit well with him, but sitting out of the war while his mates fought and died was even worse. Besides that, his only living relative was his grandfather, and his grandfather had taught him since boyhood to live by a strict moral code.

He'd returned to the Irish Guards after that, where he'd remained until receiving new orders just days ago. He'd thought the matter had been dropped until Captain Murphy had called him into his office and informed him of the transfer. Effective immediately. The next thing he knew, he was on a train headed for Glasgow. From there transported to, well...wherever they were now.

"My name is Captain Zahlman." His voice was a deep baritone. Despite his physical attributes and his name, his English accent was perfect, laced with a classically educated upbringing. "I am the commanding officer here. This is Lieutenant Claymoore. Lieutenant Claymoore is my second. By order of the Prime Minister, our purpose and aim is to conduct operations against German-occupied territories. This is a specialized unit. That means volunteers only, and anyone who does not wish to remain here, may go through those doors over there and put in for reassignment. No questions will be asked. Those of you who choose to remain shall endure some of the most challenging training conditions you may ever undertake, only to be tested against the most brutal, real-life situations. We are not—I repeat, *not*—conventional army here. Our mandate is to strike behind the lines, to cripple vital enemy centers of command and communications, to keep the Germans off balance, and to carry the fight to the enemy without him ever knowing we were there.

"For the next few weeks, you will be trained here, drilled night and day under the most arduous circumstances. We'll teach you everything you need to know to accomplish our mission. You'll learn to do things while you're here that you never thought you were capable of. And before you're unleashed on the enemy occupiers, you'll have the full knowledge that you go forth as the most highly trained, professional group of soldiers anywhere in the world." He paused dramatically. "So, for those of you who are willing to put your names and lives on the line for your country, and also for an additional three shillings a month, I welcome you." A low ripple of laughter went through the assembly.

"Sergeant Major Mosely is the drill master. His word is law." He looked up at the dull sky. "For those of you who are not a Scotsman, you may have realized that the weather here is rather dreary. We will train under these conditions. From here, you'll go back to the barracks. I want every man of you showered, changed, and back on parade in one hour. Schooling begins today. Do you understand?"

"Yes, sir!" the company said in unison.

"Sergeant Major Mosely, move them out."

"Sir!" Mosely said in a voice that could only be that of a drill instructor in the British Army. He gave a quick, perfect salute, then turned toward the formation as the captain stepped down from the dais. "All right, you bunch of misfits. By section, you'll report back to barracks. I want you back here by fifteen hundred. If you're lucky, I may even let you eat at some point today."

With that, the man to Willoughby's front and right hunched over, and out of his mouth came what little there was in his stomach. He wasn't the only one either. Two others up-chucked. To their credit, not one of them lost their balance after such a grueling run on empty stomachs.

"Welcome to Special Services." Mosely's face twisted into an almost grotesque smile. "Company, *dis-missed!*"

CHAPTER TWO

Exhausted, Willoughby pulled off the straps of his rucksack as he strode through the double doors toward his bunk, letting it fall from around his shoulders. The metal buckle scraped across the wood floor as he walked. The rest of the troop stomped sluggishly through the barracks, with hardly so much as a word. They each tossed their dirty sacks next to their bunk. Small chunks of dried mud littered the floor as they left behind what was stuck to the bottoms of their boots or Bergen rucksacks.

He tossed his filthy pack onto the floor next to his storage chest and dropped himself down on his bunk. He was tired. In fact, he was absolutely exhausted. That simple fact, that he was physically drained, was not something he was used to feeling.

He'd worked on his grandfather's fishing boat since age eleven, which had taught him a lot about hard work and long days. From dawn until dusk, they'd be out there pulling in their catch before they made port. But the work didn't stop there. The hold would need to be unloaded and cleaned out thoroughly before the day was officially over. That routine would go on through the beginning of winter before calling the season over. When he'd joined the Army and gone off to training, he'd found the daily routine there almost relaxed and effortless. Recruit training now seemed like a breeze when he looked at it in the rearview mirror. Even his combat experience in Norway was a relatively straightforward affair. Other than wrestling around on the ground with a German soldier twice his size, whom he'd been forced to kill by biting into the man's throat. But it had been little more than ranged shots and a brief close-quarters fight.

But the routine had become most challenging for a week and a half now. The training had started tough and became progressively tougher. Sergeant Major Mosely seemed to have no end to the obstacles he'd throw in front of the troop. Eight of the one hundred men who'd started the training had left after the first forty-eight hours. After the mold had broken, a dozen others had dropped out successively.

"Bugger me," MacAvoy whispered, and Willoughby could only nod his head.

He reached down and unlaced his boots. Every part of his body ached, and he could feel his wet feet, drenched in the sweat of his socks. It was now only zero-nine hundred hours. They'd begun the morning four and a half hours earlier with a five-kilometer run to an obstacle course that had spanned across the narrow canal just to the north of camp. A network of toggle rope bridges crisscrossed above the canal. Traversing the rope bridges had been the simple part. Climbing up the trees that linked those rope bridges to either side hadn't. Particularly with rucksacks weighing an additional sixty pounds on one's back.

Then there had been the mortar fire. Pre-positioned underwater explosives had gone off at intervals, meant to imitate mortar fire. Tall geysers of water covered them each as they crossed the flimsy, makeshift concoction. More than one man had to be fished out of the water after losing his footing. Willoughby himself had almost taken a dip.

They'd ended their morning exercise by taking a mock enemy observation bunker that had been set up in an empty field. But it had cost them almost half their number to take it. One of those casualties had been Willoughby himself after he'd inadvertently crawled through a disguised minefield. He'd been retired from the exercise, and forced to wear the bright red sash of a dead man around his neck.

He pulled his boots off one and a time, looking at the small pool of water at the bottom of them as he took them off. He rolled his socks off, ringing them out over his boots. His feet were raw and pruned.

Benton looked at MacAvoy, who was sitting on the edge of his bed. His uniform was soiled from the waist down. He'd been one of the fortunate ones who'd survived the training exercise and taken the position. But the umpires had called today's drill a failure after the element of surprise had been lost and so many casualties incurred.

Perhaps failure was the greatest teacher, as the saying went. If it was, it didn't sit well with Willoughby, or anyone else, that they hadn't succeeded. For some boys, those who'd fought in France and been forced to retreat, it had been only a subtle reminder of that hectic event. No one liked to lose.

"Fifteen minutes!" a voice called from the open door before it slapped shut.

Willoughby walked over to the window with his boots, swung it open, and upended his footwear, draining the water outside.

The drilling never seemed to end. Morning, noon, and night, it went on. Mess time was quick, and physical fitness and schooling filled most of the day. The short time in the afternoon or evening allotted to them for personal matters was typically filled with reading up on lessons and hygiene. Cold showers didn't seem to bother most of the other men after a long day in the field.

"Wonder what they've got for us this afternoon," he muttered. He unbuckled his belt and rolled his trousers down, grabbing another pair out of his chest. It was go, go, go all day long, leaving very little time to keep up with things like laundry.

"All I know is whatever they're serving up for lunch stinks to high heaven," MacAvoy said as he peeled his trousers off, clumps of mud falling on the floor. "Did you smell it as we passed the mess tent?" He shook his head, and Benton laughed at the observation.

"I did. I'll let you know what's on the menu." He pulled a new undershirt over his head and then reached his arms into his tunic. He grabbed his green beret and put it on before walking back out the double door toward the mess.

The cookhouse was a flimsy tent pitched in the corner of the grounds to the right of the main gate, away from the officer's quarters. It was rarely ever full, as men usually had little time to eat. Troops would go in, quickly grab what they could, and then be back on their way to the training grounds in but minutes. Today was no different.

Willoughby grabbed a tray and made his way down the line. Food workers scooped servings of food onto his plate. He took a seat with another of his mates. Donald Abernathy was with the medical troop. The tall, bulky man was hard to miss, as he stood almost six and a half feet tall. An orderly with the Royal Army Medical Corps, like so many others in the camp, he'd been with the Expeditionary Force in France and had seen the result of the German blitzkrieg.

"Another tough day?" Abernathy asked him, looking Willoughby up and down. The two troops were training at opposite ends of the camp.

"When isn't it?" Willoughby said, poking at the slab of meat on the center of his tray, then ruffling his nose. It smelled like a burned tire. He poked at his cut potatoes and put one in his mouth. He looked around the tent. It was half empty. Men ate quickly around here. The only thing worse than the enlisted food was the noise corporal instructors made if someone showed up late for training. "What about you?"

Abernathy nodded his head and swallowed down a mouthful of steamed carrots. "I didn't expect a walk in the park," he said. "Won't lie, though. I find it hard to keep up sometimes." He shrugged. "But I guess I'm not expected to know what you lot do." He patted the red cross on his arm. "I don't go fooling with explosives and heavy machine guns."

"There's that, I guess. Though when the show begins, you'll have to keep right along with the rest of us, won't you?"

Abernathy nodded. "Well, that's not a problem. Keeping up with you a lot." He looked at the faces of three others as they walked past, settling down on the table across from the two. One of them gave Abernathy a cynical look.

"Who's that?" Willoughby asked.

Abernathy looked back at the other man, then back at Willoughby. The man put his tray down and took the seat directly across the aisle from them.

"His name's Hawkes. Came from the Buffs, I think. Can't recall now. Real chip on his shoulder." He took his fork and poked at the tender meat, then took a bite of potato. "But if you want something, he's the bloke to see."

Benton looked at Hawkes. He wasn't any taller than Benton was, but he had as chiseled a look as he'd ever seen on a man before. And he'd grown up on his grandfather's fishing boat, where fishermen were seldom soft characters. But Hawkes also had some old scars on his face. The damaged skin was smooth and pink.

"Why's that?" Willoughby asked him.

"He knows how to get things. Used to run a sort of black market for himself before the service snatched him up. Bit of a rogue." Abernathy bit into the cut of meat.

Willoughby caught Hawkes's eye and stared at him briefly across the tent for a moment. He looked like a bit of a ruffian.

"How do you know about that?" Willoughby asked Abernathy.

The other man pushed the half-chewed meat out of his mouth and back onto his plate. His face then turned disgusted.

"God, that's awful." He took a drink of water and swished it around in his mouth before swallowing. "Umm. We were in the lorry together on our way up here. He and a few others. After five hours in the back, you hear a thing or two. He's a Londoner. Army grabbed straight out of the clink. Escaped with the rest of us out of Boulogne."

Willoughby poked at his overcooked carrots. "Really? The clink? Jailbird, eh?"

"Aye. Not sure what he did to end up there. But his attitude hasn't improved any. You see the two with him?" Willoughby nodded. "Ramsay's the short one. He's not too bad. On his own, that is. Put him with Hawkes and he's a real follower. Does everything Hawkes tells him to."

"And the other?"

"Nooke. Don't let the good looks fool you, either. He's a cruel one. Another lad told me he cut up a girl down in London for saying no." Willoughby blinked. Army camps were rumor mills anyhow, and he didn't always believe the first thing he just heard swirling around.

"Stories, probably."

Abernathy shrugged at the suggestion. "I could've believed that. But-" he stopped and threw a cautious look over his shoulder at Nooke, "-he and Hawkes beat one lad the second night here. The boy fell out of line during a run. The corporal made everyone run the whole damn thing a second time. Hawkes wasn't too happy about it. The kid was one of the first to resign. Two others got beaten down in the last few days. One of them's out. Left the day before yesterday. I treated his wound. The eye socket was swollen, and a finger was broken. When I asked him what happened, he told me Hawkes wanted him to smuggle some food into camp from one of the local farms. When he said no, well…"

He listened to Abernathy's warning for a minute, then poked at the tender piece of pink and brown meat before deciding to himself it wasn't worth taking the chance. Instead, he filled up on vegetables and potatoes and a thin wafer of wheat bread. You never passed over a chance to fill your belly whenever the opportunity presented itself. But whatever animal that meat had been cut from, it certainly wasn't worth risking one's health over. The last thing anyone needed, besides a visit to the clinic, was the runs.

"Well, who's to say what really happened?" Willoughby said. Though the look of Hawkes said a lot about the man. And his confession to Abernathy that he'd been picked up by the Army straight out of jail might track with just such a person. "Though, in my experience, men will sometimes say just about anything."

The parade ground was sunny and dry for a change. The break in the normally dark weather was a welcome reprieve. Two sections worth of men—in this case, twenty-four—stood at ease in a square in the center of the yard, facing the dais. Captain Zahlman stood atop the wooden platform. Willoughby stood in the center of the front row.

Below the dais stood a sergeant in a short-sleeved khaki drill uniform. Above his shoes were leg wrappings, and he wore a dark-colored turban on his head. The glistening roundel of his native 35th Sikh Regiment was clasped in the center. He had a dark, thick beard that was peppered with flecks of gray. His eyes, though; they were piercing. Almost intimidating. Willoughby could swear the sergeant was staring straight at him.

"Today," the captain said, "you'll begin the hand-to-hand combat training course. Here, we'll teach you the skills you'll need to know to save your life, in the event other weapons are unavailable to you." Zahlman looked down from the dais and held out an open hand at the man standing in front of him. "This is Sergeant Major Singh. He'll be instructing you on the techniques you'll need to master. Believe me, you can ask for no finer instructor."

Sergeant Major Singh stood like a statue. His thick beard blew gently in the afternoon Scottish breeze, but that was his full movement. In his right hand, rather than the crop that so many other sergeants carried, was a tall, thin bamboo stick.

"The sergeant major is a veteran of the First World War, and he's spent most of his life on the Northwest Frontier of India." He paused and looked at the faces staring back at him. "Sikhs are regarded as some of the best fighters anywhere in the world, and you should be honored to have him as your instructor." From his hand, he held up a double-bladed knife so everyone could see it. "A Fairbairn-Sykes. The preferred fighting knife of the Special Service Brigade. You'll practice with it, and you'll master it before you leave. When your rifles run dry, this little beauty may just be what keeps you alive. This, and your wits.

"Behind you, there is a crate. Each of you will draw one of these. I hope you had a hearty lunch, gentlemen. You'll be here until you learn to handle one of these. Take charge, Sergeant Major."

The Sikh stomped his boot on the ground and brought his bamboo stick up. He waited for Captain Zahlman to leave the ground before uttering a word.

"Group, fall in line." He had a heavy Indian accent, but his English was perfectly clear. "Take a knife and then form a semi-circle. Now!"

Each man in line took a single knife and then formed a wide half-circle in the middle of the courtyard. When the entire formation had gotten into position, the Sikh sergeant major stepped into the center. He had no knife, other than some kind of ceremonial dagger, which hung on his waist. The fingers of his right hand held the thin bamboo, and he gave each of the surrounding men a hard gaze.

"Whatcha think of this bloke?" a voice to his left asked in a low voice. Willoughby looked over. It was Nooke, the one Abernathy had pointed out to him. To Nooke's left was Hawkes. Hawkes grinned and rolled his eyes, and the two men chuckled almost inaudibly. Hawkes caught Willoughby looking at him, and the two exchanged looks for a few seconds.

Benton brought his attention back to Sergeant Major Singh, who was standing perfectly still and seemed not to have heard the comments. His feet swept back and forth in the dirt, the muscles in his neck protruded, and his knuckles cracked as his grip on the bamboo stick tightened.

His eyes looked around before settling on a trainee. "Attack me."

"Me, Sergeant?" the man asked. He was standing three positions down from Benton.

"Yes, you. Attack me with your dagger." The words ended so abruptly and casually, that it felt almost as if he were telling a poor joke.

Willoughby looked at him. The man blinked, gulped visibly, and then started toward Sergeant Major Singh. He gripped his knife from the top and brought it up as he moved toward the Sikh, who, Benton noticed, hadn't moved a centimeter. The private stepped in toward the Sikh sergeant. He lunged forward, bringing his knife up and then down at the sergeant major.

In a single, fluid motion, Sergeant Major Singh took half a step in as the private moved at him, raised his left forearm, blocked the attack, and then drove the tip of his bamboo stick into the private's neck. In a second move, his forearm brushed the private's knife hand aside, wrapped his fingers around the man's head, and pulled him forward.

"You're dead!" Singh shouted, his voice popping. He looked around and pointed at another private. "Attack me."

The second private came in, more cautious than the first. He held the knife from the bottom, his fingers gripping the hilt. He held his free hand up as if he meant to use both to attack. Singh's feet swept back and forth as the man approached. When the second private got to within two or three feet, he hesitated, then lunged forward with the knife, extending his blade outward in a single stabbing motion.

Almost faster than the eye could see, the sergeant major's left hand reached around, grabbing the private's wrist, then twisted it back, and once again drove the tip of his stick into the other man, this time getting him squarely in the chest. With his right foot planted behind the attacker, he pushed him down to the ground.

"You're dead!" Singh shouted again. He looked down at the private and gave him a curt nod. Both of the attacking trainees fell back into the circle. The sergeant major's gaze swept around the circle. Suddenly, there was a deep quiet that fell on the group. Willoughby looked around at the group. The eerie grin Hawkes had had on his face was now gone.

"You." Willoughby exhaled when he saw the sergeant major was looking right at him. "Attack me."

His fingers gripped the blade, and he took three steps toward him, breathing through his nose, trying to contain his nervousness. He stopped three paces away, squeezed his grip, and spread his stance out with his left foot ahead of his right. With an exhale, he lunged, bringing both arms forward. His knife hand struck toward the sergeant major, and his left arm came up to block the bamboo stick.

Sergeant Major Singh brought his stick upward sharply, then suddenly back down as Willoughby stepped into him. He blocked Willoughby's knife with an inside deflection, pushing Benton's arm out, then grabbed him with both hands by the torso. Using his body weight, he fell backward, pulling Willoughby over him as his back fell to the ground. Singh's leg lifted him clear through the air and sent Benton falling over him, landing on his own back with a thud. The Sikh jumped up, then came down again, leaning on his chest with his knee, sticking the tip of the bamboo into his throat.

"You're dead!"

With the wind knocked out of him, Willoughby remained on the ground for a moment, trying to catch himself. Sergeant Major Singh promptly stood back up, dropping a hand to help him back to his feet. He pulled Willoughby up and motioned for him to fall back into position.

Winded, and with a sore back—and pride—Willoughby limped back into the circle of men. He glimpsed Nooke, who had a smirk on his face, watching him. He dusted the dirt off his trousers.

"Not bad, mate," the lance corporal standing to his right whispered to him. "Almost got the bugger."

Sergeant Major Singh went back to a relaxed stance in the center of the half-circle. "Almost is not good enough," the Indian sergeant said, his eyes circling around him. The lance corporal, who probably thought he hadn't been heard, turned flush. "The blade is not the weapon. You are the weapon. The blade only follows where you lead it." He dropped his right leg back, putting himself in a traditional fighting stance, with the end of the stick held like a knife. "Treat it as a part of yourself." He thrust the stick forward. "As an extension of your body. As a builder swings a hammer or a fisherman casts a rod."

Willoughby watched the Sikh move in a series of moves, waving and thrusting the stick around like a master chef handled a cutting knife. He moved left, and then right, then kneeled before coming back up swiftly, like a boxer delivering an uppercut. Then he ended just as he'd begun. With not so much as a flicker of emotion, he stood still, with his bamboo stick clenched between the fingers of his right hand.

"Now, we will begin."

CHAPTER THREE

"Are you all right, lad?" a voice echoed down the side of the flat rock face.

Willoughby blinked hard. A dull pain went up his lower back and down his legs. He blinked again, looking at the faces of the others standing above him. It took him a few seconds to realize he was lying on the rocky ground and looking up. At the top of the rock face, the fuzzy image of Sergeant Major Mosely came into focus. His large, bulbous head was staring straight down at him as if he were only feet away.

Another man dropped his arm down and helped to pull Willoughby back up on his feet. A sharp pain went through his tail as he put his weight on it.

"You good?" the other private asked him. Willoughby took a moment and then nodded.

He'd taken a fall, and in doing so had learned a hard lesson that you didn't need to fall from a great height to hurt yourself. His belaying partner, a man named Morris, had the good sense to tighten the rope when he dropped, which had softened the blow. But as he rubbed the small of his back, he realized it hadn't softened it enough.

He unstrapped the rope from around his waist.

"Fall out of the course, Willoughby!" the sergeant major said. Willoughby nodded up at him and limped off the training course.

Across from the rock face, on the opposite side of a dried-up stream bed, half a dozen other men were gathered under the trees. More injured and bruised men, who'd taken a tumble from the cliff climbing.

He sat down on an upturned log of wood, grunting and groaning. Another man poured a tin of lukewarm tea and offered it to him, which Willoughby gratefully accepted. He looked down at his boots. They were beaten, and inside, his feet were blistered as all hell. His ankles were aching, and his fingers had worn raw.

Repelling down the side of a cliff was easy. Climbing back up that rock had been damn near impossible. He'd fallen three times. Hard falls too. The first time he'd come crashing down while only six feet off the ground, landing on his heels. The next two times, he'd fared better, making it only ten feet before losing his grip and tumbling back to the ground. Lucky for him, Morris had softened the drop, but he'd landed hard on his tail that third time.

He sipped away on his tea and tried to let go of his frustration. The training here had never been easy, not at all, but after three weeks, the exhaustion was really beginning to show through. Thirty percent of the recruits who'd arrived that first day had been written up as RTU. Return To Unit was the last thing that anyone in camp wanted to hear. It was the British Army's way of telling you that you just didn't measure up. Recruits were always free to leave of their own accord, of course, but as each day went by, more and more were being sent back because they simply weren't cutting it.

Sitting under the trees, he watched as other men made their attempts to ascend the rocky face. It was only a fifty-foot climb to the top, but few of the others had conquered it. Those who had were typically Scotsmen, who had been raised climbing just such rock faces.

From the great rock face, he could hear the shouts and commands of the training corporals and sergeants. Their voices carried across the distance like bullhorns. As usual, Sergeant Major Mosely was the loudest. When you watched the old veteran soldier at work, it was impossible to imagine the man could be anything but a sergeant major in the British Army. Some people had very specific skill sets. Mosely was one such man. He stood atop the fifty-foot rock, looking down at the rows of men attempting the climb. From there, his voice could shake the very foundations of the cliff.

"What's the matter with you?" Abernathy asked. The medical orderly made his way down the half a dozen men sitting under the shade of the trees. All of them had various injuries from trying to climb the cliff.

Willoughby ignored the question. The pain he felt in the tail of his spine or his sore ankles paled compared to his ego. He'd gotten used to mastering challenges quickly during his time in the Army, and he felt wholly dissatisfied with himself when he couldn't.

Abernathy walked up to him, tapping his boot, which was stretched out over his knee.

"You all right, Benton?"

Willoughby looked up at him. He took another drink of tea and swallowed it in a hard gulp. "I'm fine."

Abernathy looked him in the eye. "It's not fine," he said. "Where's it hurt?"

He hesitated for a moment. "My pride." His tone was gritty. "I've had injuries before. I'll be fine."

"Yeah. Shot right in the bum, he was," another man said, and some others laughed.

Stories always seemed to spread around the barracks like a heavy wind through an open window. He'd told that story to MacAvoy on their first day here, and that had been all it had needed, he guessed. Of course, it could have come from anywhere, he supposed. More than one other trainee had noticed his name on the rolls and had brought up the subject of Narvik.

The tall Abernathy towered over Willoughby and cast a shadow through the light that shone through the tree branches. His bright teeth showed when he looked at Willoughby and chuckled along with the others. Willoughby ran his tongue along the inside of his cheek and nodded at the laughter.

"So where does it hurt?" He stooped down.

Willoughby didn't answer, just nodded his head toward his ankle. The other man gestured to his boot.

"Mind?" he asked Willoughby, who nodded. Abernathy wiggled the boot off and then the sock. His fingers probed the ankle. Willoughby winced in discomfort. "Just a slight sprained ankle. Not bad," he said, but his words struck Willoughby as not the least bit sympathetic. He looked at Abernathy, who gave him a dismissive shake of his head. "Get off it, mate. You'll live."

"I'll live," Willoughby said, "but I don't think my ego will ever recover."

"It's just a cliff, mate." Abernathy stood back up. "How many times did you have a go at it?"

"Three."

"Fourth times a charm, then. Stay off it for a little while. You're not alone. Half the company's got one injury or another. Get back to the hospital and put some ice on that." Abernathy pulled out a yellow paper, scribbled out a note, and handed it to him. It was his permission pass to sit out of training for a few hours. He tapped Willoughby's knee and walked off to the next man.

The sergeant major's loud voice boomed from the top of the cliff as yet another trainee came tumbling down. His belaying partner fed the rope so that the man made a soft landing on his rear, but down was down. Swimming with packs full of gear, running 10 kilometers before dawn, or navigating live-fire exercises, all seemed easier than climbing some damn rock in the middle of nowhere.

"You lazy bastards!" Mosely shouted. "You can't even make it up fifty feet of rock. How the bloody hell do you think you're going to scale a wall when there are mortars going off around you?! Move! Move!"

Willoughby got up from the log he'd been seated on and moved off toward the castle beyond the trees. He put some weight on his right ankle, flinching slightly at the sharp pain, and limped away. It took him half an hour to limp back to the main gate. When training was going on, it was expected that everyone would be on the proving grounds, save for anyone on excused duty.

The guard at the front gate stopped him, and Benton handed the yellow paper to him. Trainees were not allowed back to the barracks during exercises, but they were allowed access to the hospital. There were always men to be found there, suffering from any number of injuries sustained while training.

"Go ahead." The guard gave him a nod, and Willoughby walked through.

Behind the officer's quarters, there was a small building nestled under a pair of tall oaks, about a hundred feet from where the old, dilapidated castle stood. Behind that, the paths that used to run through the estate were overgrown with vines and thickets. Interweaving branches and roots twisted and wrapped around one another.

He walked up to the door facing the castle keep, and just as he was about to turn the handle, something caught his eye. He swore he saw movement from the corner of his eye. The branches at the end of the building shook, scraping against the walls of the hospital as if they'd been disturbed. There was no breeze and no sign of any birds. Then he heard the distinctive sound of a twig snapping in half. Willoughby let go of the handle, looked over at the guardhouse to see who else might be around, then walked the broken brick path.

The vines that connected themselves between the trees covered the bricks. He stepped through them and pushed away the tangled branches. The walls of the castle keep were covered with that same overgrowth so thick its doors were completely obscured. He thought for a second about trying to pull one open, but continued on. They'd been specifically ordered to not go into the castle. Anyone caught doing so would be brought up on disciplinary charges, perhaps even RTU'ed for disobeying the standing order.

Beyond the castle, there was a brick wall with a high archway through which the path wandered. A door had once been there, but all that was left now were six rusty old hinges drilled into the brick. The field beyond it was filled with knee-high grass that went for a hundred yards to a line of trees.

He looked around but saw nothing except for an empty field. He waited and watched for a minute, then turned and walked back the way he'd come when he saw no sign of anyone.

The hospital was empty except for a single nurse. The middle-aged woman was finishing up her duties when Willoughby showed up. He handed her his yellow pass.

"Another sprained ankle. Seems like half you lot are here on any day." Her expression was dismissive. She handed him back his note and then crossed the room to an ice cabinet. "Sit." She picked away at the ice, put the shards into a thin cloth, and tied it off. "Take your boot off. Put this on your ankle for a while."

She put the cold cloth into his hand and gave him another glib look. He did as he was told, putting his foot up on a stool and putting the cold press on it.

"What's your name, Private?"

"Willoughby."

She jotted the name into a logbook and put it away. "I have to make a run to the guardhouse." She looked at her watch. "Stay here. I'll be back in just a few minutes."

"Yes, ma'am."

She gave him a thoughtful look, then pulled her key from around her neck and locked up a small closet near the desk.

"Don't touch anything," she said before grabbing a white satchel off the back of a chair and leaving.

"Old battle axe," he muttered after she'd gone.

After a couple of minutes, the cold cloth soothed the sharp pain in his ankle. His entire foot—both feet, actually—felt like hell. Willoughby and half the barracks seemed to spend their evenings puncturing small blisters from the bottom of their feet. He sat for a while with the cold press on his foot, so long that he drifted off. He was tired.

The door creaked back open. Willoughby popped open his eyes, not wanting to be caught resting in the hospital by the sullen nurse who'd shown no care for trainees she thought to be shirking. But it wasn't the nurse who came in. Instead, it was two men dressed in the plain brown battle dress. He recognized the first man as soon as he stepped inside. His face was marred by a pair of scars along his left cheek. Hawkes gazed around for a moment, looking to see who else was around. The second man was Nooke. He'd seen both of them in the mess tent.

"The nurse isn't here," Willoughby said as Nooke closed the flapping door behind him. Neither of them said anything for a half minute. Willoughby could see neither man seemed to have any injury.

Hawkes's eyes settled on him. He had dark brown eyes, and he seldom blinked. "Not here to see the nurse." He had a hoarse Cockney accent. "Wanted to have a word or two with you."

Willoughby didn't like how that sounded, but he didn't make a move. Hawkes got closer to him while Nooke crossed behind the nurse's desk, peeking out the window between the blinds.

"With me?"

"Aye." Hawkes picked up a chair, turned it around, and straddled it backward, facing Willoughby. "I know who you are. Willoughby. Irish Guard. You know who I am?"

"Hawkes," Willoughby said. The two locked eyes.

The Londoner licked his thin lips and gave a cold, hard stare. "Word 'bout you, Willoughby, is you're a fighter. Stories 'bout you in Norway are all around camp. I reckon you've heard 'bout me?"

"From the Buffs," Willoughby said. Nooke, across the room, stepped away from the window, attempting to open drawers and cabinets carefully. All were locked.

Willoughby looked at Hawkes, and Hawkes at him. The man had a fiendish grin on his face, showing just a hint of slightly browned teeth under his thin lips. His pink scars seemed to become even more pink when he smiled. Willoughby had seen such looks before, typically on men of disreputable character. Then there was Nooke, the taller of the two. He was lean and muscular. He'd seen him on obstacle courses during the training, and his slim physique was almost contrary to just how much strength he had. Like Hawkes, Nooke too had a look in his eye that was ice cold.

There had been a rumor around camp about a trainee who had been RTU'ed during the first week of training. The man had gotten himself involved with a gambling debt to Hawkes, and when he couldn't or wouldn't pay, Nooke had followed him to a lavatory where he'd kicked the fellow half to death before urinating on him. Willoughby never thought much of rumors; they floated around camps like pneumonia. However, in Nooke's case, he believed the stories.

"Aye. From the Buffs. But now, I'm here. I suppose you've heard other things as well?" Willoughby only shrugged lightly. "That's okay. That's all right. Don't want to answer. Don't want to get your hands dirty. So, I'll do the talkin'. My friend Nooke here, and a couple others, have a little sideshow goin' on. I reckon you heard 'bout that." He rubbed his chin. "Could use a man who's got a reputation for being a fighter."

"Oh? For what?" The question drew a strange grin from Hawkes. The grin quickly flipped into a serious scowl. Hawkes was as strange as a character out of some book he'd read once. *Doctor Jekyll and Mister Hyde*. His stare was peculiar, even a little unnerving, and his mood seemed to change with a snap. Abernathy had mentioned Hawkes was a man who could get things. Willoughby had been in the service long enough to know exactly what that meant. Items, usually army-issued items, were sometimes 'lost' for no apparent reason. For time and memorial, such things happened in army camps.

"I'm never one to miss an excellent opportunity." Hawkes grinned again. It was a strange grin. "You've got balls, Willoughby, I'll give you that. Big ones. Whatcha say? You come in with me and I'll give you a nice cut of any profit."

Willoughby gave Hawkes a stern, singular shake of his head. "No thanks. You do what you will, Hawkes. I don't want any part of it."

The grin on the other man's face disappeared, and his expression immediately turned to displeasure. His dark brown eyes seemed to get even darker at that moment. He was an odd sort. His pale face turned even paler, and he suddenly looked colder. It was enough to make even Willoughby shudder slightly. He thought of the action in Norway, defending the Narvik evacuation, and the German soldier that day who'd had the same coldness in his eyes, too. The look on his face as he was trying to choke Benton to death was almost like the look on Hawkes's.

"You're sure 'bout that?" Hawkes asked him. There was a retort in his tone.

"I'm sure."

"I see," Hawkes said. "Well, fisherman, if I were you then, I'd keep my mouth shut. Accidents occur around here. One good fall from a cliff and...uh, well..." He smirked at Willoughby. "Stay out of my way. Understand?"

"You two do what you will," Willoughby said. "I don't give a damn. Stay away from me, and I'll stay away from you."

Hawkes stood up, moving the chair aside and stepping toward Willoughby. He got so close that Willoughby instinctively raised his hand up to keep him from getting any closer, but Hawkes pushed the hand away just as quickly as it had gone up. Nooke moved in from the side but didn't make any aggressive moves.

"You just keep out of my way," Hawkes said, coming close to poking Willoughby in the chest with two fingers. "You don't want to cross me." He sneered and, for a few moments, the two stared at one another.

Finally, Hawkes stepped away, gave him a gentle pat on the cheek, and the two made for the door. Willoughby sat there, watching them go. He felt a flush of anxiety coursing through him. He waited until the door clicked shut, then sat back down and put his boot on again. Men like Hawkes and Nooke weren't the types to just let things go. He knew what he'd seen and what he'd heard. And he knew types like that didn't just go away, nor did they forget.

CHAPTER FOUR

There was a downpour outside. Colonel Jack Deveraux steeped a tea bag into a cup of piping hot water, turning one eye out the window to watch as uniformed bodies sprinted through the rain outside. Typically, summer weather in Scotland was an unpredictable event. Wild and wet one minute, clear and beautiful the next. Through the single-open window pane, droplets of water fell inside, dotting the windowsill. He put down his pipe, picked up a small cloth and wiped it dry, closing the pane, then walked back to his chair.

He looked at the tiny clock above the hearth. His appointment was running late. No doubt the weather was responsible.

Next to his chair was a large table with green file folders stacked on top of it. Deveraux had been poring through them for the last two days straight, getting himself up to speed on the training. Paperwork was hardly his first love, but years spent as a staff officer had made him used to it.

He sat in his chair, reading, and smoking for several more minutes before it came. There was a gentle knock at his office door.

"Come in."

The polished oak door opened, and his secretary stepped in. "Captain Zahlman to see you, sir."

The colonel picked his pipe back up, used his lighter to puff it back to life, and gave the man a nod. "Thank you, Sergeant. Send him in, please."

The man stepped into the small office. His cap was tucked neatly under his arm, and his uniform, as usual, was immaculate, though slightly wet. For such a young man, he wore several decorations for distinguished service and gallantry on his uniform, including the green and purple General Service Medal for his actions during the Arab Revolt in Palestine. But unlike many other young officers Deveraux knew, this one didn't wear such things to flaunt. In fact, despite his accomplishments, he'd struck Deveraux as one of the more modest British Army officers. That was exactly why he'd requested the young man be assigned to him.

"Apologies, sir," Zahlman said. Deveraux stood from his chair. "The weather practically washed out the road."

Most senior officers, including him, looked kindly upon punctuality. But he understood, and he didn't bear Zahlman any ill intent. Besides this, there was hardly a veteran officer in any army anywhere in the world who hadn't run late because of inclement weather.

"I had a feeling. You think this is bad?" Deveraux pointed to the torrent of water outside. "You should have been with us in Malaya in thirty-six. Ha. Talk about rain. I couldn't make a mile a day through that jungle. Pneumonia, malaria, ear infections galore." He shook his head at the memory. "Have a seat, Saul."

"Thank you, sir." Zahlman pulled out the only other chair in the tiny office, beside the table with the green file folders, and sat down.

His eyes ran around the cramped room, hiding an expression of surprise. The colonel saw this and chuckled lightly. Zahlman had never visited his headquarters before. The tiny office looked much more like something a librarian might work in than a full colonel. The old country house had been donated to the British government by its owner, some Scottish MP, for official use. On paper, the modest house was occupied by a small, and relatively insignificant, British Army training command that instructed field units on the proper use of radio equipment. But the truth was far more than that.

Four battalions were being trained at camps around Scotland for the very purpose he and Zahlman had been precisely selected for. From thirty-thousand feet, it would appear to many as just an inconsequential training unit. But to those cleared to know, it was far more than that.

Deveraux crossed the room to a cabinet and pulled out a bottle and two glasses from the bottom drawer.

"Something to warm you up on such a dreary day." He put the two glasses down on the table and poured.

"Oh, that's all right, sir." Zahlman's voice indicated he was just playing the professional officer. It made Deveraux smile as he poured.

"Nonsense. Don't make a habit of it, but behind closed doors is behind closed doors." He pushed one glass forward and took the other, dropping back into his chair.

The heat from the small fireplace was just enough to battle the dampness seeping through the old windowpanes. The house was an old eighteenth-century Georgian. Small breaks in the outer walls and archaic windows did little to nothing to keep the damp and cold out on certain days. Since the building housed a unit that was supposed to keep a low profile, he was quite certain repairs would not be forthcoming soon.

Zahlman took the first sip of the drink and made an approving face.

"Macallan. Nothing better on a day like today," Deveraux said. "So, Saul, tell me what your feelings are. How's the training progressing over there?"

"We're right where we expected to be at about this point, sir. For one reason or another, about a third of the trainees have left. As for the rest of them, it's beginning to take a toll. Physically anyway."

"The physical exhaustion always seems to precede the mental. You're just over three weeks in now. You must be getting a sense of who's cutting it and who isn't?"

Zahlman shrugged slightly, letting the Scotch flow down his throat. It was damn good Scotch. "There are several who have real potential. I've been submitting steady reports, sir."

"Yes, I see that." Deveraux waved a hand at the stacks of folders across the table. "I've had to play catch up. Meetings in London and Edinburgh have kept me away. It seems like all I've been doing the past couple of days is catching up on reports. Makes for some interesting reading. Damn interesting. Some of our trainees, not just at your camp either, are exceeding set standards. I tell you, Saul, things are coming along at a pace better than London had expected." He turned toward the small fireplace. The pinks embers were dying out I the dampness. He reached down and tossed in a small log.

"And you, sir? Did you think the program would make such progress in such a short period?"

"Hmm. I'm a different story. I have spent much of my career building armies out of mountain tribes and jungle dwellers. Not a simple business, but once you realize you can train anyone to do just about anything, things become easier. Much easier. The answer to your question, however, is that I had the utmost confidence in the program from the start. It's a necessity, given the circumstances, and I think the timing is right. If we can train Pashtun tribesmen in the mountains of Afghanistan to fight for us using irregular tactics, I don't see why we can't do the same with our own countrymen.

"The War Office, however, is eager to put the program to the test. Dill himself has exhibited some skepticism about it all. He thinks no litmus test can be given without just sending the boys out and seeing the results. I told him all we can do is train for specific missions as best we can, and then watch and see the results. Churchill feels optimistic about it all, though. That much I know."

Zahlman cleared his throat. "You've spoken with the prime minister?

"Good lord, no. He's got bigger things to do with his time than mingle with a lowly colonel. But I was a staff officer for years. Many of my old comrades have moved up the ladder with consistency. Word gets around, unofficially. Whenever you know something, the higher-ups think you don't know, Saul, deny it fervently. It pleases them to no end to think they know something you don't." He laughed and took a sip. "Anyway, Churchill supports the idea. He's quite eager to put things to the test."

"I see," Zahlman said, suddenly feeling the strain. He'd only ever seen limited action, and that had been nothing more than a quelled rebellion. The idea of taking a handful of specially operating men behind enemy lines, against an enemy that vastly outnumbered them and had swept aside the BEF just two months earlier, was enough to give anyone pause, no matter how uniquely trained those men might be.

"Which brings me to my next point," the colonel said. "We're already coming up with a list of potential targets in which to make our first trial run. MI6 has identified several possibilities. Putting together an operation will probably take us another few weeks, but I'm confident I'll have something by the time you've finished." He studied Zahlman's face as he told him, noting an almost imperceptible flush in his color. "Does that trouble you?"

"No, sir," Zahlman said immediately.

"Good. I understand your feelings, however," he told Zahlman. No officer, no matter how much training and preparation they had, looked forward to leading a group of men into battle.

"May I ask you a question, sir? Off the subject?"

"Of course."

"We're hearing a lot of rumors in camp. There's a lot of chatter about. Hitler landing a cross-channel invasion and all that. I don't normally get distracted by such things, but certain people, people I know and trust, have suggested such a thing happening."

Deveraux sipped his Macallan, giving the junior officer a sympathetic nod. "As you say, try not to become distracted by such things, Captain. Our job is to meet the enemy no matter where he is or may come from. I can tell you this, off the record. If the Bohemian corporal wants to try his luck with such a thing, he might find us better off than he thinks. He's not the genius he claims to be."

"No, sir."

"But, getting back to the original topic of conversation." He pointed his finger at a brown folder sitting at the bottom of the stack on the table. "Be so kind and grab that file." Zahlman pulled the folder out. "Open it. It came across my desk a couple of days ago. It concerns a recruit up at Achnacarry. He's having a bit of difficulty, I'm afraid. Or rather, some people up there are having some difficulty with him."

Zahlman scanned through the pages, moving his lips as he read through the lines.

"He's with Captain Marble's group right now, but you can see his specialty."

Captain Marble was training men for a specialized reconnaissance force at a different camp. Zahlman nodded slowly as he read the man's biography. His eyebrows flared at one point.

"Yes, I see you caught that," Deveraux said, reading the other's facial expressions.

"Explosives and demolition?"

"Hardly a good fit for a recon force," Deveraux said, and Zahlman nodded in agreement. "Keep reading."

Zahlman skipped through the record. His forehead creased in confusion, but he continued to read on, and his eyes widened. "He's South African? Says here he volunteered for service with us."

"He was serving with the South African Corps, but he had some disciplinary problems. Because of that, the South Africans won't allow him to serve in combat. He was on their chopping block because of it. But his expertise was too good for us to pass him up when he requested service." He saw Zahlman flinch ever so slightly. "The unfortunate byproduct of his specialty and his heritage has made some in camp, well, uncomfortable."

"I see," Zahlman replied softly. He took another sip of scotch. Zahlman had had his share of discrimination during his career, hell, his entire life. A Jewish officer, born in Palestine, was bound to run into racial discrimination during his life.

"Normally, I don't give a damn whether soldiers are comfortable with one another, but in this case, it's unfortunately led to an incident."

Captain Zahlman nodded again. "Yes, I see that. Brawl with another trainee. *Tsk, tsk.*" He read further. "Says here he put another recruit in hospital."

"Hmm. Broke the man's nose. Could have been worse. Anyway, Captain Marble was ready to bounce him from the program. However, based on the report you have, it wasn't he who started the incident."

"But he ended it." Zahlman finished the statement, drawing a smile from the colonel.

"He did indeed. He's a volunteer both to the program and to the Army itself. In fact, he'd been granted a remittance because of his civilian occupation back in South Africa. They considered him essential to the war effort, but he volunteered anyhow. Then volunteered for Special Services when that came along."

The file ended, and Zahlman closed it back up. "Sounds like the type of person we might not wish to lose."

"Precisely my thinking. I spoke with Captain Marble last night. I'm going to have him reassigned to your command, Saul. I feel, given your background, you might be a better fit for him. Besides that, you'll be commanding a raiding unit. An explosives expert would make more sense in a unit like that. It would also round out your command. I've put in the request. I expect he'll be out of Achnacarry by the end of the week."

"Provided he doesn't break any more noses. His file doesn't indicate any disciplinary problems." Zahlman had had his share of discrimination during his career—hell, his entire life. A Jewish officer, born in Palestine, was bound to run into racial discrimination during his life. Deveraux didn't reply to the comment. Zahlman knew he didn't need to either. "I look forward to having him, sir. He'll certainly add to the internationalism of the command. I've got Canadians, Australians, Dutch, even a Czech. He'll be the first South African."

"A true Imperial force." The colonel upended the last of his Scotch. "Led by a Palestinian Jew." He chuckled. "A motley crew. Off to save the empire."

Zahlman laughed along with his commanding officer at the irony. He held up his nearly empty glass in salute, then downed the last in one.

CHAPTER FIVE

Willoughby ran through the gaps between bushes, scraping his hand along a jagged branch as he went. Only feet ahead of him, Private Scarborough cleared the last line of shrubs and dove onto the mound of dirt beyond. Behind Willoughby, came Corporal Mansfield and Private Zeleski. One by one, they joined Scarborough on the ground behind a low-lying mound just beyond the bushes.

A handful of seconds later, the last man came crashing through behind them. He was taller by half a head than any of the rest. But he was slower as well. The tan-skinned South African, whose name now escaped Willoughby, was a bull of a man, with long, thin legs, but a wide torso, where most of his weight was placed. He fell to the right of Scarborough.

Two hundred yards straight ahead, their target sat in the center of a large clearing. That target was an old barn house that was supposed to serve as a German Army headquarters, inside which was held their objective. At the perimeter of the clearing, there were makeshift guard towers overlooking the approaches. Two were on the northern and eastern sides, and a third was on the southwest side, high in an old windmill.

Several men outfitted as German soldiers were patrolling the area around the barn. Two large double doors faced southward, but on either side, doors were cut into the wood planks.

"How many?" Willoughby asked Scarborough. The other man was peering through a single-lensed monocular.

"I can see seven - no wait! There's two more around the corner, on the north end." He moved the small spyglass around, covering the end with his hand to avoid the sun's glare. "I can see Team Two. Northeast side. They're moving toward the field."

Willoughby looked in the distance at the knee-high grass surrounding the property on three sides to the north. That's where most of the enemy patrols were concentrated. He checked his watch. 1122 hours. The assault was set for 1125. "Three minutes," he said. But as soon as he did, the entire plan instantly went to hell.

A voice screamed out across the clearing. It came from the northern side of the building and was followed immediately by a popping of rifles.

"Dammit!" Scarborough cursed.

The gray uniformed troopers around the barn unslung their rifles and ran to the north. Willoughby watched them go, which left only the man standing guard atop the windmill. His rifle was out and ready. Next to him, Corporal Mansfield unslung his rifle and uncapped the scope. He zeroed in on the man in the windmill. The corporal was a first-class shot and carried a specially fitted scope on his Lee-Endfield.

"Wait!" Scarborough halted him, holding up a hand.

The double barn doors swung open, and a half dozen more men came running out. The last one pushed it closed behind him.

"Six more," Scarborough said. "I could see two inside, right before he shut it. But there might be more."

"That's seventeen," Zeleski said. "I thought there was only supposed to be twelve?"

Willoughby watched the soldiers on the north side run out into the field, firing their rifles away toward the high grass. "Change of plans," he replied. "You got him, Corp?"

"I've got him," Mansfield replied, peering at the remaining guard in his sights.

"Take him," Scarborough told him.

Corporal Mansfield pulled the trigger. A half moment later, a rubber bullet hit the man up on the platform. The man swore loudly at the impact. Then, the five men jumped up and charged across the stream to the other side. Willoughby and Scarborough covered the main door as they moved, and Mansfield and Zeleski kept their guns on the western edge of the barn. The

South African brought up the rear. Despite his long-legged stride, his colossal frame slowed him down.

The dash to the barn was a grueling hundred meters, and Willoughby felt his breath leaving him by the time he hit the southwestern wall. The barn was a deteriorating old structure with planks of wood for walls. But for the sake of the exercise, the planks were considered being concrete, and the barn was a bunker.

From the north, the sound of rifle fire echoed. Team Two was the decoy unit, meant to draw the patrol away from the barn. Willoughby listened to the sound. German Mausers made a smoother sound, more like a light popping. The British Enfields were louder by comparison. An experienced soldier could gauge who was on the winning side of a fight by the sound of those rifles.

Hugging the side of the barn, Willoughby tapped Corporal Mansfield on the shoulder and gave him the signal to move around the corner. Mansfield peeked around the corner and then ran out to cover the western wall. He gave a quick nod that the coast was clear.

The side door was halfway down the western wall. Zeleski took point, covering the north, while Scarborough put his hand on the door handle, ready to yank it open and storm through. Willoughby looked around, worried that another part of the plan would come unraveling at any moment. If there had been seventeen guards when there were supposed to only be twelve, then anything could have changed.

His eyes drifted along the field and to the west side of the barn.

"Wait," he said, putting his hand on Scarborough's. He nodded toward a stack of hay halfway down the side of the barn, behind which he saw a small opening. "There! Check that out."

Zeleski moved up and pulled the haystack away, revealing a wooden window-well hidden behind it. He put his head down and pushed the window open, looking underneath the building.

"It's clear. Some sort of root cellar."

"That's our new way in," Scarborough said. "Go!"

Zeleski squeezed himself through the window first, followed by Willoughby. The room was dark and dank, and it smelled of animal dung. Above them, through the planked wood floor, he could make out small shafts of light and hear the floor squeak from the footsteps of the men above.

Scarborough came through the window, and then the South African. His long legs easily touched the floor before his head was even through. Corporal Mansfield came down last, pulling the hay back into place behind him.

"That way!" Scarborough told them, pointing to the other end of the cellar. "Van Dekker, in the rear." He ordered the South African.

Van Dekker, Willoughby repeated back in his head. He filed the name away.

Zeleski took the lead. He pulled open a thin wooden door that led up a short flight of steps. They came out in the barn's rear, behind a stack of boxes and bales of hay. Above them, it was clear twenty feet up to the rafters.

Willoughby covered the opening between boxes, rifle level, and ready. Just feet away, he could hear muffled voices. The rear wall was just five paces away, and the double door would be forty on the opposite end. In between was a small maze of hay stacks.

Scarborough, the acting mission officer, gave the order for Mansfield to scale the hay. Mansfield pulled himself up to the top and crept forward to get a view down into the center of the barn. He gave a hand signal down at them and swiped two fingers to the left and one more to the right. He descended back down without a sound.

Scarborough gave a hand signal, and Willoughby nodded his acknowledgement. Ten seconds. He and Zeleski crept around to the left. Scarborough, Mansfield and Van Dekker went to the right.

Willoughby hid in the shadows behind the last of the tall stacks, with Zeleski right next to him. In the middle of the room, he could see two figures in German clothing, pistols in hand. There was another voice coming from out of sight. In front of the double door, there was a single body tied down to a chair. That was their objective.

He mentally ticked off the seconds, holding up the last five with his hand. As the last one ticked, he and Zeleski rushed out from behind the haystacks and into the open. At the same moment, Scarborough and Mansfield stormed around the right side of the barn.

"Bang!" Willoughby shouted, pointing his empty rifle at the man standing directly in front of him. Behind him, Zeleski took the other two. "Bang. Bang."

"You're dead," Willoughby told them.

The three startled men in German uniforms went still. They also fell silent as they were effectively 'dead' and stood in place without making another sound. Willoughby looked at the double doors, and the two on either side. For a moment, he wondered why they hadn't been covered.

"Do you what you came to do," Scarborough told Van Dekker. He pointed at Willoughby. "You take that thing on the way out."

The tall man put his rifle down and unstrapped the bag from his back. Van Dekker was the fresh addition to the troop. He'd come in just two days earlier from another unit as an explosives expert. The man went straight to work putting the mock explosives together at the base of the haystack.

The three 'dead men' stood around quietly as the team gathered themselves together. Willoughby was untying the dummy. Just then, something struck him.

"You hear that?" he asked aloud.

The group stood silent for half a second, listening. "No gunfire," Scarborough noted. Outside, the fighting was over. "Let's move!"

Van Dekker shook his head in reply. "I need half a minute," he answered, with a distinguishable accent.

"Quickly!" Zeleski snapped. He looked at Van Dekker, and then at Scarborough, who held up a finger. "Finish damn you."

Van Dekker ignored him. His hands worked over the mock explosive without taking his eyes off the work.

It was all being done by the book. Too much by the book, so far as Willoughby was concerned. The manual said it took so many seconds to prep and arm the explosives, and the rules said they had to wait out those seconds. Finally, after a very long twenty seconds, the South African finished.

"Done."

Willoughby untied the stuffed puppet and tossed it over his left shoulder.

"About damn time," Zeleski muttered, exasperated.

"Let's go!" Scarborough said. He motioned for Zeleski to take the lead and pointed at the western side door.

Zeleski opened the door slowly. As the old door creaked halfway open, a spring recoiled, and there was a loud snap like that of a mousetrap. Above the door, hidden behind a wooden beam, a small pail of water emptied onto him. The others stood there momentarily, stunned at what had just theoretically happened. Zeleski had tripped a booby trap and was now dead as well.

Scarborough shoved Mansfield toward the main door, and the rest followed behind them. The corporal pushed the double door open just wide enough for the rest of them to get through. What was left of the team made it halfway across the field toward the stream before a loud whistle blew.

"Time!" Sergeant Major Mosely roared. He and Captain Zahlman were standing off to the south side of the yard, watching the exercise play out. "That's time lads!"

Willoughby dropped the dummy on the ground. A minute later, the entire group gathered together in the yard in front of the barn, including the decoy team and men dressed as Germans. MacAvoy, who'd been the one Mansfield had hit with a rubber bullet, climbed down from the windmill. Captain Zahlman and Sergeant Major Mosely moved into the center of the men.

"Well," -Zahlman began, slowly looking around at the men- "that went better than the last exercise. However, it ended the same way." He zeroed in on Scarborough, who had acted as the officer in charge of the rescue team. "Scarborough, what happened?"

"Moved too slowly, sir."

"I'd dare say so. Where was the hang-up?"

Scarborough hesitated, but finally threw an aggravated look at Private Van Dekker. "The explosive charges took too long to set. Our window of opportunity ran out in the meantime."

Captain Zahlman studied Scarborough's face. He looked at Private Van Dekker and then at Corporal Mansfield. "Is that your assessment as well, Corporal?"

Mansfield looked at the captain but shook his head. "No, sir."

"Why not? You're a corporal, you've led men before. Why don't you agree?"

"Private Van Dekker moved just as quickly as I think he could have with planting the charge, sir."

"So what went wrong?" Zahlman inquired further.

The corporal shook his head. "I don't know, sir. Maybe we should have moved a little faster."

Zahlman made an approving look. "Perhaps you should have." He looked at Zeleski in his wet uniform. "What happened there?"

"I sent Private Zeleski to secure our escape route. He tripped a booby trap."

"Did you kill all the guards inside?"

Scarborough gulped. "Yes, sir."

"When you rescued your hostage, did it ever occur to you to keep one guard alive to question about traps like that?"

Scarborough sighed heavily. "No, sir. It did not."

Zahlman's nod was almost a soft, non-verbal reprimand. "The lesson here is to not kill everyone in sight simply because you can. Remember, officers make valuable hostages themselves. Even if you can't take them with you, you can question them. Here, a few seconds of questioning may have not cost you a man. How many of the decoy team were lost?"

"We lost two of them, sir." Sergeant Bowvers answered. Bowvers was in command of the decoy team.

Zahlman swallowed hard and nodded. "Losing men is never easy. But you can't hold up an entire war when you do. Infiltration and rescue was the mission, and the mission is always paramount. The decoy team did their job and provided a diversion for the rescue team to infiltrate the bunker. Any success there was your success as well. Their failure was because of the decisions made once they were inside. By the way, whose idea was it to enter through the cellar window?"

"Private Willoughby's, sir," Scarborough answered.

Captain Zahlman gave Willoughby a considerate look for a moment and nodded approvingly. "Not the original plan that you came up with, was it?"

"No, sir."

"What made you consider that, Private Willoughby?"

"Because it wasn't the obvious route, sir."

The faintest of grins touched Captain Zahlman's features. Zahlman had been the one who'd recruited him into the unit, and had made such an impression upon him following Norway that Benton had signed up immediately, without reservation.

"Good thinking, Willoughby. Sometimes, the best road to take is the most unexpected one, and a little unconventional thinking is a good thing. Had you gone through that door, you'd have been dead like Zeleski. A brief word of advice to all of you, though; know your surroundings. The more you know of what's around you, the better your chances of success. Understood?" They all nodded. "The drill was against you from the very beginning. The odds of success were slim to none. If you'd gone through the side door to begin with, you would have triggered the trap and the exercise would have been over. Since, as you noticed, the fighting outside was over, the easiest and quickest route was to go out the main door. Once secrecy is no longer at stake, you must adapt to change. Do you all understand?"

"Yes, sir," they unanimously replied.

"Very well." He gave the sergeant major a nod.

"All right, you. Get yourselves back down the road. We'll be going at this again this afternoon. Those who were German this morning hand off those uniforms. You'll be back in brown this afternoon."

The field training was several kilometers from the camp, right in the middle of Scottish farm country. Just down a dirt road, there was an assembly area set up. The sight of men dressed in German attire must have confused some of the few civilians in the area when they saw them walking by. One older man, thinking they were German soldiers, threw a few choice words at them, making the men laugh.

"Off to the stockade, you go," one man said, playfully pushing one of those dressed like a German.

MacAvoy fell in next to Willoughby. "That shot hurt," he said, rubbing his chest where the rubber bullet had smacked him.

Willoughby shrugged. "Sorry, mate. It was Corporal Mansfield that got you."

"Wait until I'm back in brown and you're wearing this," he joked, tugging at his German tunic.

The group walked down the road for a half kilometer to a clearing where a small tent was set up and what passed as food was being doled out. A second troop of soldiers was already there, finishing up with their meals, and getting ready for their own run at the hostage rescue.

"I've got to get out of this damn thing," MacAvoy said, making a beeline for the trees behind the line of vehicles and taking the gray uniform off.

Willoughby followed behind him. Hawkes, Nooke, and Ramsay were there. Only Ramsay was in British browns. He found the sight of the other two dressed up as Nazis almost more befitting. The Londoner's reputation among the trainees was becoming more and more notorious every day that went by. It was disturbing to Willoughby that none of the non-commissioned officers had caught on to him yet. Usually, sergeants could smell trouble in their sleep.

When he got to the clearing, he kicked his boots and rolled his wet socks off. His feet had become raw and white from all the training in the wet and the rain. It was a miracle that they weren't more blistered than they were already. The calluses that he'd gained in recent days had toughened, and he barely noticed them anymore. It was hard to keep oneself in tip-top condition when there was hardly any time that didn't include training.

But it was all paying off now. The midnight marches, the mock raids, and the constant survival training had taken their toll, but the results were showing. Half the company they'd begun with had left. But the ones who'd remained more than made up for losing numbers.

"Hey now! Have a lookie here!" Willoughby turned his head toward Hawkes. Hawkes gestured curtly as the recent addition approached the rear of the clearing. Private Van Dekker strode into the clearing, undoing his kit and letting it slip gently to the ground. "The man of the hour," he said mockingly. The South African didn't reply. "What's the matter with ya'? Not chatty?"

The tanned South African openly sneered and rolled a cheek.

Hawkes jumped up to his feet. "You want to say something?" He leveled an open hand at Van Dekker. "This is what you get when you let a damned Boer into the Army."

"Where are we getting our recruits from these days?" Nooke asked crudely.

Van Dekker paused just long enough to return the hard gaze that Hawkes was giving him. The South African had a thick torso and long arms, but Hawkes was the better conditioned of the two. The two men locked eyes.

"You got something on your mind?" Hawkes pressed, clearly trying to provoke a reaction.

"Yeah, I do," Van Dekker replied. He dropped his rifle to the ground and stepped toward Hawkes, who grinned fiendishly. The South African paused, as if he wanted to see if Hawkes was going to hit him. But Hawkes didn't budge. In an instant, Van Dekker shoved him in the chest, and the brawl was on.

Hawkes came back with a left jab, then a cross to his face. Van Dekker grabbed Hawkes by the neck, and the two grappled with one another.

"Whoa, whoa!" Willoughby shouted, jumping in to help peel them away.

Behind Hawkes, Nooke and Scarborough motioned toward the brawlers. Corporal Mansfield jumped in and squeezed himself between the two. After a few seconds, and a big of commotion, the two were forced apart, with Van Dekker suffering a punch to his eye.

"That's enough of that!" Mansfield hollered. He stood in between the two. "Knock that rubbish off. That means you too, Hawkes."

"Anything is more than what you've got," Willoughby said to Hawkes, drawing eyes from the others.

"Knock it off, he says," Hawkes mocked. "You okay with this here, Corp?" He waved a finger over at Van Dekker, who just stood there, staring back.

Willoughby knew just what he meant by the question, and it had nothing to do with setting off a mock explosive.

"He joined up, same as the rest of us," Mansfield told him.

"Blew the God damned exercise," Scarborough shouted.

"That's not true!" Van Dekker snapped back.

"Why don't you just shut it!" Willoughby found himself telling Hawkes.

The Londoner turned his eyes at him and gaze him a nasty look. "What's that, fisherman? Speak up now if you got something to say."

"Yeah, I do. Shut it!" Willoughby repeated. "I think we're sick and tired of your mouth."

The men around went deadly quiet. Hawkes raised his brows, and his little cadre appeared shocked at the sight of someone challenging him so brazenly. Hawkes pushed Mansfield away from him, then looked contemptuously at the South African, and his eyes seemed to turn darker. Then he turned back to Willoughby, licked his lips, and came to within a pace of him. Willoughby didn't back down, and the two men held a long gaze at each other.

"Bullocks. We're recruiting damn savages now." He spat on the ground next to Willoughby and then turned, shaking his head as he walked away.

Willoughby watched the back of his head, thinking the man was a pig as he stomped off.

"Let's go, lads," Hawkes said. He grabbed his brown blouse, threw down the German tunic, and stomped off with Nooke and Ramsay in tow. A few others walked off also, including Private Scarborough.

"Nasty cuss," MacAvoy said about Hawkes.

Van Dekker didn't utter a word, though he gave an approving nod at Corporal Mansfield and Willoughby, which was returned. Willoughby sat back down, reached into his kit, and grabbed a new pair of dry socks. He put his boots on and went over to the South African, who had walked off to sit under a tree.

The man wore a weathered look. He had lanky arms that swung heavily when he walked. His face was pitted, and lined with creases, and his fingers were thick and tough, not unlike those of fishermen who'd spent their lives laboring hard under the weather. Something Willoughby could certainly relate to.

"May I sit?" He asked him. The South African nodded. "I'm Willoughby. Irish Guards."

"Van Dekker." He had a thick Boer accent.

"You can call me Benton if you'd like."

"Dole," Van Dekker replied. "That one?"

He gestured to Hawkes. "Hawkes? He's just a damn fool. The Army's full of them, unfortunately."

"Not you though?" Willoughby just shrugged in reply. "Been in action yet?"

"Some," Willoughby replied. "Norway. You"

Van Dekker just shook his head. "No. Worked in the mines in South Africa before I volunteered for service."

"You volunteered?"

"Then I volunteered for the British Army when it came up."

"Damn me, mate. You're either brave or foolish to do that much volunteering for the British Army."

"Much better than the South African," Van Dekker rebuked him. "Have you been to South Africa before?"

He shook his head. "No."

Van Dekker gave him a forgiving look. "Then you'd understand if you had." He grinned, but didn't say another word, but his eyes spoke volumes.

Willoughby felt stupid for a moment. He might have inquired further but kept his mouth shut, suspecting just what the other man might say in response about his native land. He chose not to press him on the issue. The term Boer didn't carry with it a positive image for many Britons.

Before he could reply, Willoughby was startled by the deep voice of Sergeant Major Mosely. The thickly built sergeant trudged through the area. "Chow down, lads! I want every man back up that road in thirty minutes."

"Benton," MacAvoy called over. He was dressed back in brown and pointing his thumb over at the cookhouse.

Willoughby nodded back at him. "You feel like joining us?"

Van Dekker looked at MacAvoy standing there. "With you two?" Willoughby nodded back.

"The only thing worse than the sound of Sergeant Major Mosely's voice is the food here. But the company is agreeable." The tall South African grinned, bearing his bright white teeth. He gave a firm nod. "All righty then."

They stood up and walked over to MacAvoy.

"You better put this on," the Scotsman said, tossing him the German uniform he'd taken off.

Willoughby's nose wrinkled at the suggestion. He held up the worn tunic and calf-high boots. "Do I have to?"

MacAvoy shrugged and nodded. "Afraid so. I did my bit."

Willoughby frowned at him. He looked at the tan South African.

"Wouldn't look as good on me," Van Dekker said.

"Looked better on Hawkes," Willoughby replied. "More natural."

CHAPTER SIX

Marie Lecèsne wet her lips with the tip of her tongue as she approached the guardhouse that sat at the end of the causeway that led to the castle overlooking the bay. It wouldn't do to have dry lips when she got to where she was going. Not at all. There were two guards at the checkpoint, and the gate was down. It was drizzling outside. One guard was standing inside the tiny guard hut smoking a cigarette, the other was outside, his rifle slung over his shoulder. He saw her approach and cracked a disgusting smile.

She'd been through this two dozen times now, and she knew which of the guards were okay and which ones weren't. *Okay?* She thought. It was a strange way to describe a foreign occupier. Given the circumstances, though, some of the German soldiers were better than others. The soldier standing outside was a pig of a man. Almost as bad as the man she was going across to see.

"Halt," he said as she got to within ten feet. She saw the man inside the hut looking out the small window, giving her a sympathetic stare as she stood outside in the rain. The first guard took three steps forward and looked her up and down. "Open your shawl."

Around her shoulders, she wore her white shawl with pink and blue flowers. It matched her dress. She spread it open for him the see. Her dress came down below her shoulders, exposing her delicate white skin. The top two buttons were undone enough to let her cleavage show. The tight dress accentuated her curves.

The pig smiled at her as his eyes drank her in. She could almost see the disgusting thoughts running through his mind right now. But he never once flinched.

"Seen enough?" she said to him in her native French, flashing a soft smile.

He got closer to her, close enough that he could touch her without the other soldier seeing. The fingers of his right hand ran around her waist, slipping them in between the buttons of her dress. In the back of her mind, she pictured his dead body on the ground. It gave her the strength to put up with the harassment.

"Seen enough?" he said with his harsh German accent. Some soldiers spoke decent enough French. "I'll let you know when I've seen everything that I want." His teeth were mostly white, with light-brown stains. All the Germans on the island seemed to smoke. "Maybe I'll do more than look." His fingers ran down, stopping between her legs. That's when she pulled back, pulling her shawl back over her shoulders.

"You?" She scoffed. Her eyes turned away, looking around to see who else might be watching. Both German occupiers and island natives gave it little attention. "You get a promotion. Maybe then we'll talk," she said. "I only fuck sergeants and officers."

He looked at her for a minute. His face contorted in such a way that she knew she'd gone too far. Behind him, the other man stepped out of the hut.

"Problem?" the second one asked.

"No problem," the first said. "Sergeant Buhler's *guest* has arrived."

There was a long moment of silence. "Then let her through," the second one finally said. He was an older soldier, and gentler than many of the others.

"Go ahead," the first soldier told her, cranking his neck for her to go. The second soldier lifted the gate, and she walked around the man and toward the causeway. The second man gave her an almost friendly nod as she passed by him and across the bridge. She feigned a smile and batted her eyes at him when she went by.

By now, Marie was used to being harassed by the occupying Germans. Though it had only been a month since the first of them landed on Guernsey, it seemed much longer already. The people living on the island had fallen into a monotonous routine. The soldiers did their thing, the people did theirs, and they tried to stay out of one another's way. Most freedoms the people had enjoyed had been curtailed. No large groups could gather, banks were closed, and civilian homes and some buildings had been confiscated. But above those things, the people were free to do most of what they pleased. Except for leave, of course.

Castle Cornet sat at the end of the long causeway. As usual, soldiers patrolled the high walls that overlooked Saint Peter Port. The old fort had been turned into the heart of German activity on the east side of Guernsey. Large guns were still being installed inside the fort and around the port. Some were long and pointed out to sea, others smaller, meant for airplanes.

Marie had been out there enough times to have put together a good plan in her head of what the fortifications were. One day, she might observe a new bunker going up, and the next, perhaps, new troops coming and going. She knew where the living billets were, and where the lookouts were posted. Little by little, she observed everything.

She watched as a line of gray uniformed soldiers marched past her, the officer glancing at her briefly. Her frequent visits had made her almost unnoticed. So much so that some men walked right by her without so much as a word or a look.

She crossed over the end of the causeway bridge and onto the graveled surface around the old fort. An iron door facing the entrance was pushed open, and three Germans came out. They barely noticed her. The last one held it open long enough for her to go in, then pushed it shut behind her.

Through an archway that led to the middle of the castle's courtyard, she branched away, down a single flight of stairs, to a hallway beneath the fort. A soldier sat in a small room at the bottom of the stairs, a cigarette clenched between his fingers. She could hear the crackling of a radio as she went by.

"Stop!" a voice called through the echoing hall. Her feet immediately stopped. An unfamiliar soldier came out from a room off the hall. "What are you doing here?" His voice was so hard that it took her back for a moment.

She was thrown off by the question and gulped hard.

"I asked you a question," he said, grabbing her by the arm. He was strong.

"I... I was..."

"Who let you in here?" he asked angrily, squeezing her arm. He spoke German, and her German was rusty.

"She's here for Sergeant Buhler," another voice said. It was the man who'd been sitting in the tiny radio room. He was sticking his head out into the hall. "That's his little plaything."

She looked at the man holding her arm and tried to make a smile, but his grip was painful. Marie batted her eyes at him softly. Slowly, he let her go and looked at her exposed legs.

"Plaything, huh?" He shook his head. "Common whore, you mean." He sighed loudly.

"She's here all the time," the radioman told the other.

The soldier gave her a disdainful look. "I don't like it. Just marching around here like some Parisian prostitute."

"Please, monsieur," she whispered. "I'm going to be late. The sergeant hates it when I'm late." She put her tiny hand over his. "He gets mad."

It was a lie, but Sergeant Buhler was an ugly oaf of a man, the size of an ogre. Mad or not, he was quite intimidating.

Finally, he relented. "Go."

She smiled and continued down the hallway. It was dank and smelled of dirty water. The third door from the end of the hallway creaked open after she knocked. Buhler smiled at her, and she smiled back. His tunic was unbuttoned and hung open, exposing a white undershirt and a bulging belly. An uncorked bottle of gin was in his hand, and he grabbed her with his other, pulling her into his quarters and kicking the door shut.

He smelled of alcohol, and his whiskers were rough against her skin as he kissed her neck. The sergeant was a good foot and a half taller and must have weighed two hundred and fifty pounds, mostly in his midsection. He was old too. Old enough to be her father. His nose was flat from where someone had broken it years earlier. A picture on the dresser near his bunk was that of his wife back in Saxony. Sometimes he made her look at it when he did what he did.

"My little bitch," he said to her, pulling her by the hair. He slobbered on her neck with his tongue. She looked at the picture of his wife and wondered whether the woman missed him or had been happy to see him go.

After a minute, he pulled away and took a swig of gin.

"Will you pour me a drink?" she asked him. He smiled at her, then took a glass off the dresser and poured her a generous drink. The gin was the only thing that got her through these brief sessions of his. She'd found out early on that if he drank too much, he'd usually just pass out. But other times, it made him more abusive.

"So, Maria," he said to her incorrectly. He ran his hands up and down her body as she drank. "What should we do today?" he asked, grabbing her rear.

"Slow down, lover," she said to him in French. One thing about the fat fool was that he at least spoke her language, which was strange since they were both on an island inhabited by English speakers. "Let me get my shoes off first."

Marie downed a large gulp of alcohol and kicked her shoes off. She smiled at him, and he kissed her. His tongue went into her mouth. It was only the taste of the gin that got her through the unpleasant experience.

The fat sergeant took his coat off and threw it on the back of a chair as he kissed her. She faked her way through it, as she always had. When her drink was empty, he poured her another. Together, they kissed and touched for nearly an hour. In that time, they'd both polished off half the bottle. Well, truthfully, he drank most of it. She knew how to slow it down enough to keep a clear head. But when he'd had enough, he grabbed her and turned her around, bending her over the desk.

"Gentle," she said to him. He was always gentle at first, but never remained that way.

She unbuttoned herself, taking her bra and undergarments off before he took his cock out. He kept his trousers on, but his shirt came off, exposing his immense belly. He grabbed her and put himself inside, bouncing her back and forth against the wall. His moaning was the most repulsive sound she'd ever heard, and hated it when she heard it. When he got close to the end, he grabbed her, turned her around, and finished in her mouth.

"Ahhh." He let out a long, relieved sigh.

She didn't look up at him. She might not live to make it out of the fort if she saw his fat, disgusting face after that. The urge to kill him was already too much.

He staggered back and fell onto his bunk, laughing. Marie grabbed his shirt and wiped her mouth with it before he saw her. He laid back onto the mattress, and she straddled him. She knew he would pass out shortly. But that's usually when he became chatty.

"Satisfied, lover?" she asked him.

"Oh, my dear. You have no idea." He laughed. "If my wife could only fuck like you do, I would be home right now." He laughed again and waved his hand toward the picture on the dresser.

"Soon, you'll be home," she said to him. "Soon."

"Not soon enough, my dear." He reached for the bottle, sitting at the edge of the small table next to the bed, spilling some of it on himself as he drank from the end. "After this, perhaps I'll go home for a while."

"After what?" she asked, taking the bottle and holding it for him.

He laughed again. "You're a sweet girl, you know?"

"Thank you. What were you saying?"

"Oh, nothing. Just some fool visitors we have to contend with. Again!"

"Oh, you poor thing," she said to him, soothingly. He chuckled as she teased him with her fingers around his neck. "Someone special?"

"Agh! Everyone who comes here is special. And none of them are." She poured a little more into his mouth. Just enough to keep him drunk, but conscious. "Oh, no. My dear, that we have guests coming once again. Another damn SS visit. Those fools in Berlin are always making our jobs harder. Word came over the machine yesterday." He dozed off for a moment until she roused him with a gentle nudge.

"Machine? What machine?"

"Hmm? Just something we have. It's a code machine, my dear. Oh, my head is spinning."

She nuzzled his head. "Ooh. Sounds mysterious. Are you the one in charge of that?"

He rubbed his head with his hands. "Only one," he said back. "I think I'm going to sleep now."

Marie ran her fingers over his torso. "Tell me, my love," she whispered. "Where is this machine?"

At first, he seemed to nod off, but then a sharp inhale through his nose brought him back to consciousness. "It's called Enigma," he drunkenly whispered back. And without even knowing what he was doing, he rambled on for the better part of fifteen minutes on the matter. Marie knew which buttons to press and how to keep him speaking.

It was less than an hour after she'd first arrived that she casually left the fort. The normal jeering looks were given to her by some as she passed by the gate at the end of the causeway. It was still drizzling. Marie strolled through the streets, making her way to a church just outside of Saint Peter Port. A priest stood outside, bidding farewell to a parishioner.

"Good day, my child," the priest said in greeting. "What can I do for you today?" He was an older man, hefty around the midsection. But he had a friendly smile on.

"Father, I wish to make my confession."

"Of course. Come in. Come in." The priest gave a good look around as he let the young woman in and closed the door behind them. "Were you followed?"

"No," she said. They exchanged cautious looks and walked into the church toward the altar. Two small confessional booths were to the left. She went into one, he into the other.

"How are you, my dear?" he asked her genuinely. The priest and she had been in contact for weeks, and he understood just how she came about the information she passed along. Or, at least, had a good enough idea.

"I'm fine, Father." She crossed herself. "God forgive me." She could hear him sigh heavily. "The fat one was particularly drunk today."

"I'm sorry, my child. You should not have to do what you are doing." He said a brief, quiet prayer. "So, what is it you have to share today?"

"More SS are coming to the island in the next couple of weeks."

"Good God."

SS officers had come shortly after the island's capture, and it had been a terrible experience for everyone. They'd taken many people away with them. They'd also imposed strict order on the remaining inhabitants. Many of them had been detained and questioned. Some of them had met unfortunate ends. The thought of another round of deportations was not welcome news.

"But there's something in the castle he told me about. He called it Enigma."

"What's this?"

"They use it to send coded messages back and forth. The pig talks when he drinks. I doubt he'll even remember telling me when he wakes up. All he wants to do with me is—" She stopped mid-sentence. "Well, it's in the fortress. He told me where."

"Did you write it down?"

"Of course not," she said. "But he tells me things and I remember."

The priest nodded. Marie had been going to the fort three or four times a week for the last several weeks. All that time, she'd carefully observed the citadel and the garrison inside. She had a very detailed memory and had previously recounted the layout of the different rooms in the passageways beneath. Marie could draw a map with her eyes closed once she'd been somewhere enough times.

"Good," he said to her. "Very good, my dear. You know the routine. I'm very sorry, Marie. Sorry that you have had to, umm…" He couldn't finish.

Marie was silent. She couldn't say it either and didn't even wish to think about it. Outside, in the nave, the thick door creaked open. She straightened her back at the sound of heels clicking along the wooden floors.

"God, the father of mercies…" The priest gave a brief and loud absolution. Loud enough for the other person in the church to hear it. When the two emerged, there was an older woman wearing heels standing in the middle of the aisle.

"Thank you, Father Arthur," Marie said.

"Go in peace," he told her. She crossed herself and made her way out the door of the church.

* * *

The bulb hanging from the front of the officer's quarters cast a light from its front door for twenty paces out. There was no light outside the trainee's billets. Only at the front gate and at two watchtowers along the outer perimeter were there any other lights, none of which was anywhere close to the barracks.

MacAvoy yawned deeply as he paced the length of the building. It wasn't yet 0100. The worst time possible for one to have drawn guard duty. In truth, there was never a good time for guard duty, but midnight had to have been the worst possibility of any. Armed with nothing more than a hand torch, he slowly walked down one side, made a right turn, and marched half a dozen paces between the barracks and the clump of trees in the corner of the parade grounds.

In the shadows of the barracks, out of sight, he stood facing the stone wall behind the building. He unzipped himself and drained his bladder, listening to the crickets chirping in the night.

Finished, he reached down to zip himself up, but in an instant, both of his arms were pulled back behind him. One foot kicked him in the back of the knee, and he collapsed forward. Before he called out, his face was planted down into the dirt he'd just soaked with his piss. He tried to push and squirm out of the hold they had on him.

"Stop fighting," a voice said in a rough whisper.

MacAvoy kicked his legs out and tried to turn his head to call for help, but a pair of hands grabbed the back of his hair and buried his face in the dirt.

"Shut up!" the voice said. "Shut up or I'll bury you face down."

"Shh."

MacAvoy twisted and turned, but he lost any strength he had after only a few seconds. He stopped moving around and tried to turn his head just enough to get some air into his lungs. Then, the hand holding his face down yanked him up forcefully, and he gasped for breath.

"Listen to me," the man holding his head whispered. "Shut your bloody mouth or I'll cut you."

He felt a coldness against his throat. His gaze drifted upward at the man hovering over him, and he glimpsed the man's eyes—dark brown. MacAvoy nodded just enough for the other man to see. He had wet dirt on his face and the smell of piss in his nostrils.

One man bent down and thumped the back of his skull.

"That's better," the voice said. It only took MacAvoy a moment to recognize it. Hawkes. "Listen to me, you Scottish bastard. Your friend, Willoughby, is a snoop and a bit too clever." Hawkes took MacAvoy by the face and squeezed his cheeks until his mouth opened, then stuffed a balled-up piece of cloth in. Hawkes shoved it in so far that MacAvoy gagged on it. "If I were you, I'd be a good little friend and tell him to play friendly and leave things that aren't his business alone. Understand?" Hawkes stood up straight. "Let him go, boys."

The other hands released their grip on him. For a moment, he just lay there, trying to catch himself. He thought about pulling the rag out of his mouth, then thought better of it. If Hawkes saw him move, he might think he was going to scream for help. So he stayed still, breathing through his nose.

"Let this be a warning to you," Hawkes said and spit on him, then drew his boot back and kicked him in the face. The other two laid into him as well. They kicked him in the ribs and the groin, over and over. Hawkes stepped on his face with the heel of his boot. MacAvoy let out a muffled cry. When the kicking finally ended, he writhed around in pain.

"If they ask you who did this, you tell 'em your friend Willoughby did it. Understand me?"

MacAvoy didn't roll over until he knew the three of them were away and waited a few seconds more. He slowly pulled the rag out of his mouth and held his injured stomach with both hands. He stayed there until someone found him, lying in a patch of pissy dirt with the taste of blood in his mouth.

* * *

It was right before Reveille when someone poked their hard fingers into Willoughby's side. His head snapped up from his pillow and turned toward the hand still on his shoulder. His vision was hazy from sleep, but cleared up quickly. Sergeant Major Mosely was standing over him, his enormous head hanging menacingly above him. Another man stood behind him.

He sat up and rubbed his eyes, then launched himself from his bunk. "Sergeant Major."

"Private. Get yourself together, lad. The corporal here'll escort you to the CO's office."

"The captain's office?" He looked confused.

Mosely put his hand on Willoughby's shoulder and squeezed slightly. "It's all right, lad. Best you hurry, though. The captain will explain."

Mosely turned and walked off. The corporal, wearing the white belt and cross-strap of a provost guard, stood by while he put his uniform on. His eyes drifted around the barracks while everyone else was sleeping. He noticed MacAvoy's bunk was empty. He followed the provost corporal to the officer's quarters. The provost opened the door and motioned for him to enter, and then let him into a small side door leading to a tiny room. The provost closed the door silently behind him but didn't enter.

Willoughby marched into the center of Captain Zahlman's small office. He came to a stop, stomped his feet on the floor, and saluted. Captain Zahlman sat behind the small desk, his tanned face covered by his hands. Only his eyes peeked over his fingers. He let Willoughby stand there for a while before finally saying a word.

"At ease. Willoughby, your record to date has been spotless. You've excelled since coming here. Your marks are higher than most of the rest of the company. Your reputation with your former unit CO was exemplary." He paused for a second. "Until now, it seems."

Willoughby stood there, his face wrinkled in confusion. His eyes squinted, and he looked over Captain Zahlman. The officer sat back in his chair and gave him a hard stare.

"Have you had any unreported incidents since you've been here?"

Willoughby looked unsure. "Sir?"

"It was a simple question, Private. Have you had any friction with any of the other trainees?"

"No, sir."

Captain Zahlman pushed himself up from the desk and came to within an arm's length of Willoughby, carrying a file in his hands with him.

"You're friends with Private MacAvoy, aren't you? Reports here are that you two have become rather chummy." He waved around the thin file. "Sergeant Major Mosely claims the two of you have become constant companions."

"Yes, sir."

"Do you know whether he's made any enemies here? Someone he may have gotten involved with?"

Willoughby delayed speaking for a moment. Only one name came to mind, but to his knowledge, MacAvoy had had no dealings with the person in mind.

"No, sir. I'm sorry, sir."

"I see," Zahlman said, biting his lower lip in thought. "Private MacAvoy is in the hospital. He was brought there very early this morning."

"Sir?" Willoughby's brow furled and his jaw dangled in shock.

"He was attacked during his guard shift last night." Willoughby audibly inhaled sharply. "Someone must've had it in for him. Do you know any such person who might have had it in their mind to do such a thing?"

"No, sir. I don't. May I ask something, sir?" Zahlman nodded. "Is he all right? I only ask because—"

"He'll survive," the captain said. His voice became a little coarser. Willoughby let go of a relieving breath. "But his injuries are severe enough. Broken rib, broken nose, multiple contusions. You have no idea who might have done this?"

He shook his head. "No, sir. Isn't he talking?"

"Private MacAvoy isn't saying much of anything. Claims he didn't see the faces of his attackers. As his friend, I was hoping you might shed some light on the subject for me."

The captain stared him in the eye. A dozen thoughts went through Willoughby's mind. Hawkes was the most likely subject after his encounter with the man the day before yesterday. But that had been his encounter with Hawkes. So far as he knew, MacAvoy had no dealings with him.

"I'm sorry, sir. I don't know."

"I see. Unfortunate." He moved back behind his desk, dropping the file. He pulled open his top drawer, grabbed at a cigarette case, and then lit one up. "Since you can't provide me with anything relevant, let me just leave you with this bit of warning, Private. This is not a playground for schoolboy antics. We're a training center, and this is serious business. If one of ours was the culprit here, we'll find out about it. I won't have operations here interrupted for the personal reasons of anyone. Do I make myself clear?"

"Yes, sir."

"Good," Zahlman said in between a wisp of cigarette smoke. His eyes studied Willoughby up and down. "He's in the hospital. Perhaps you can jog his memory for us. Dismissed."

"Sir!"

After leaving the captain's office, he went straight across the yard. What was called the hospital in camp was nothing more than a converted old garage that had once housed automobiles. The estate had shuddered back in the Twenties, and the buildings had fallen into disrepair. The garage, however, had been gutted and turned into a makeshift clinic for the trainees.

MacAvoy was one of two patients in the room when he walked through the main door. He snatched his cap off, saw the nurse look at him, and gave her a courteous nod. MacAvoy was bandaged around his right forearm and in the middle of his face. Small dots of red soaked through the gauze around his nose. His eyes were shut when Willoughby approached, but at the creak of his walk along the wood floor, they fluttered open.

"Hey, mate." He looked MacAvoy up and down. He was in a pair of hospital pajamas, cloaked in a flimsy-looking striped robe that had seen better days—standard issue for Army hospitals.

MacAvoy's mouth curled back in a grin. He had bruises on his cheek where his lips seemed to twitch.

"Am I a sight or what?" MacAvoy whispered.

"Yeah. You've looked better, Dunk. What happened?"

MacAvoy's eyes blinked heavily, as though he were fighting some pain. "They got me," he said to Willoughby. "Got me last night outside the billets."

"Who?"

"Hand me some water." His mouth and lips were pale.

Willoughby looked around him. There was half a pitcher of water on the table behind him and an empty paper cup. He filled it and put the cup in his friend's hand. MacAvoy sipped slowly on it.

"It was Hawkes." Willoughby swallowed hard and shook his head. "Hawkes and his cronies."

"Jesus. Why didn't you just tell the guards what happened? Why didn't you tell them who did it?"

The Scotsman smiled. "He wanted me to say that you did it," he whispered. Willoughby looked over at the nurse, taking the other patient's temperature. Her back was turned, and she didn't show any sign of hearing the conversation going on. "He said that you're too damn much of a snoop. He wants you to stay out of his business."

Willoughby sighed. "I'm sorry, Dunk. You shouldn't have gone through this. It's my fault."

"I think the bastard wants you out. Figures if he hurts me, you'll get the message and quit." He tapped Willoughby's hand with his.

"Maybe I should," he whispered.

MacAvoy shook his head in response. "No, mate. Then you'll just have given in. Besides, it's not in your nature. And I don't want to be here stuck with someone like that bastard."

"You didn't answer my question. Why didn't you tell the guards who did it?"

"The damage was already done. He'd sent his message." He held up his good hand and touched his bloodied face. "If I'd told the guards or the captain what happened, that they wanted me to finger you for it, it would've come down on your shoulders. Besides, how do we know one or two of the guards aren't in on it, hmm? The man's a lowlife. I heard he ran a black market before. Probably knows who he needs to buy off."

Willoughby grunted and nodded. "I heard that too. All right. So we'll keep it between us."

He looked back at the nurse. She was finished with taking the other patient's vitals and jotting them onto her record. He looked back down at his friend, whose mouth was still awkwardly twitching at the end, and patted him lightly on the chest.

"I'm afraid I'm going to have to ask you to leave now, Private." She wore the green service dress uniform of a field nurse and on her left lapel the rank of a sister nurse, the equivalent of lieutenant. "Private MacAvoy should get some rest."

Willoughby nodded. She had a tone of authority in her voice. "Yes, ma'am. Get some rest, mate. Are you going to be back on the training ground, or..." He just looked at the rest of MacAvoy's body.

"There's no *or* about it," MacAvoy said. "A broken rib and a busted nose isn't going to keep me away." He looked up at the nurse sister, who gave a double nod of her head. "I'll be seeing you."

CHAPTER SEVEN

Colonel Hoth paced around the dock with his staff, waiting. In the distance, through the morning fog, the dull drone of a bullhorn sounded. The ghostly outline of the expected ferry began to break through the mist and head into the harbor. Hoth looked up at the yellow-gray sky and the orb of the sun trying to break through. It was only 0600, and it was expected to be a pleasant day outside at some point.

His junior officers were reflexively quiet, and the senior ones were impatient. Not one man present held these moments in high regard. In only seven weeks of occupation, they'd had an inordinate number of so-called 'special visits' by SS and Gestapo officials. For an island that only boasted several thousand residents, they'd hosted half a dozen former envoys from Reich Security already and deported hundreds of undesirables back to mainland Europe.

No part of German territory was immune to the leash of Berlin.

The ferry signaled again, its engines began to reverse, and the double-decker started to slow. For a backwater of the Reich, it seemed to get more than its portion of visitors. Unlike previous visits, which came via sub or small plane, this one came by a ferry from Saint-Malo, carrying more than just its high-ranking officials but half a company of engineers as well, bearing some much-needed construction supplies.

Hoth glanced at Captain Gerhardt, his chief of staff, and nodded curtly. Gerhardt ordered the rest of the staff into positions. An honor guard squad formed behind the assembly. It never hurt to show the SS a courtesy or two, even if was only done for appearance's sake.

One final blow of the horn, and the ferry came coasting in. Its engines went into full reverse, and the boat came to a stop in the middle of the short pier. In the distance, Castle Cornet watched over the inlet.

A gangplank was rolled out, and the passengers began to disembark. Unlike he'd expected, the SS officials were the last to leave the ferry. Three men walked steadily down to the wharf. The first two were clearly SS, in the black uniform of their service. The third man wore a *Wehrmacht* uniform, his presence something of a surprise. As they approached the assembly of officers, the first two gave the standard Nazi salute.

"*Heil Hitler!*"

"*Heil Hitler,*" the colonel said, giving the appropriate salute.

The third man, almost unconsciously, prepared to give a traditional military salute, then caught himself in the last second and held his palm straight up.

"*Heil Hitler.*" He bore the emblem of an *Abwehr* officer with a captain's rank.

"I'm Colonel Hoth," he said, shaking the hands of the two dignitaries. "My chief of staff, Captain Gerhardt."

"Lentz," the first man said. He wore a major rank on his collar. He nodded at his companion. "This is Ofhoven." His face was demure, and he showed no outward sign of emotion.

"And I'm Captain Hoff. Intelligence." He gave a friendly smile and nodded to the other Army officers present.

Colonel Hoth gave him a curt half-nod. "I was not made aware that the *Abwehr* was sending a representative. What are your orders?"

"Normal inspection duties, sir," Hoff said modestly. "I'm only here to make sure proper security procedures are taken around the more sensitive equipment." He gave an eye to the backs of both SS officers, then went deadly quiet.

Colonel Hoth looked him up and down and gave the man an accepting look. "I don't like being surprised by unexpected visitors. Your orders." He held out a stern hand.

Hoff dug into his coat pocket and produced his orders. Hoth handed the paper to Captain Gerhardt, who reviewed them and then nodded.

"Well, gentlemen. If you come this way, I'll have you taken directly to our command post." Hoth turned and began to walk toward a pair of automobiles waiting for them.

"If it's not too much trouble, Colonel, we'd prefer to go straight to our work," Major Lentz said.

"And that is?"

"Precautionary security review. Reich Security wants to make sure we've eliminated any potential threats to our position here. Remove any undesirable persons from the area."

They reached the cars. Hoth turned to look at Lentz. "We've had several of these reviews already, Major. As Reich Security already knows, over a thousand individuals have already been removed from Guernsey since taking over here. The rest are shepherds, farmers, and seamstresses. We've had no trouble from any of them."

"Not so far," Lentz said languidly. "We intend to keep things that way."

The two men traded looks at one another. Colonel Hoth had plenty of experience in dealing with Himmler's many minions. He knew their methods, though he didn't always approve of them, and he understood the best way to handle them in some ways was to give them what they wanted. Then, to impress upon them that their methods were so effective that the mere rumor of them kept civilian populations in line.

"I suppose," he said with as much rehearsed relenting in his voice as he could put into it. "I'll have Captain Gerhardt here take you—"

"We'd much prefer if you took us around, sir." Lentz's spontaneousness caught him slightly off-guard.

"I'm the garrison commander here, Major. I have many duties to perform."

"One of which is the security of the Reich," Lentz said. He stepped closer to the colonel. His bright green eyes looked strangely into Hoth's, and he bit his lip while he waited for a response. "Please."

Colonel Hoth could not hide his aggravation. It was going to be a long day, and he had little wish to go around all day with these two. He snapped a look at Gerhardt.

"Captain, please take Captain Hoff to wherever he needs to be, provided his absence will not interfere with the major's inspection." He looked at Lentz, who shook his head.

"Yes, sir."

Hoth opened the door and stepped away. "If you would, Major."

Lentz smiled, and both he and Ofhoven stepped into the close-topped Daimler-Benz. Hoth gave Gerhardt a quick look of displeasure and stepped in behind the two SS officers. He shut the door and told the driver to go, leaving his staff behind.

"Thank you, Colonel," Lentz said. "We don't wish to interfere with your obligations, but this gives us some privacy in order to speak freely."

Hoth looked at the SS major. His face and his gaze were friendly enough, but Hoth had known types just like him in Germany. A friendly smile and an innocent comment were often enough to set people at ease just enough for someone to do or say something that would land them in an open investigation.

"What about?" he asked matter-of-factly.

"You command the garrison closest to enemy territory," Lentz said in an almost trivial tone. "Berlin has concerns about the potential of an incursion. The British may try to liberate the island and use it as a forward base against us."

"I see. We have over seven thousand troops based here. Anything of any sort of value was removed or destroyed before the British troops left. I can't imagine what sort of value this place would be to them right now. They've just fled the continent, and they're not in much shape to go launching forays into our territory."

Lentz nodded and looked out the window as the car rounded the corner and left the harbor, driving through the almost vacant streets of Saint Peter Port, the largest settlement on Guernsey. A couple of shops had reopened since they'd taken control, but the vast majority of the population and businesses had remained behind closed doors.

"Perhaps," Lentz said. "It's our job to address potential security concerns. Do you have concerns you wish to voice? Since we're here, anyway."

"I've been over this with your predecessors," Hoth said. "The island is quiet and passive. Anyone Reich Security thought could cause trouble has been deported."

Lentz grunted. Hoth noted Ofhoven was oddly quiet. "Yes, I know. Poles mostly, if my memory serves. Right now, we simply can't trust Poles." He looked back at Hoth and smiled in his discomforting way. "You agree with that, don't you, Colonel?"

"About Poles?" Lentz nodded and Hoth shrugged his reply. "I do as I'm told, Major. If OKH wants Poles deported back to Poland, then I do it. If they want Frenchmen deported back to France, I do that." He turned his head away from Lentz, though he could still feel the other man's eyes on him.

"That's good, Colonel. We just wanted to hear you say it. Don't need another repeat of Krakow." He turned his head away just as Colonel Hoth turned his back to him. He saw Ofhoven, sitting between the two, look out the corner of his eye at him.

"Krakow? What of Krakow?" He let his voice turn sharp. He didn't care for Lentz's accusation. Reich Security be damned.

The SS major looked at him and made an innocent face. "I didn't mean to offend you, Colonel. I just wanted to restate standing orders regarding prisoners and undesirables. That's all I meant. Perhaps in Krakow, you were... unaware of those standing orders."

"I'm well aware of my standing orders, Major Lentz. I don't need to be reminded." He let his gaze move to Ofhoven, who dropped his eyes to his lap. "I did my duty in Poland, just as I was ordered to."

"Really? I thought I'd read of an incident when you'd failed to turn over certain individuals. Perhaps I misread your file."

Hoth sighed audibly. He saw what was going on. "Children. Five and six-year-old children. Speak plainly, Major." He emphasized the rank. "They were isolated from their parents, and I turned them over to the appropriate parties."

"The SS were the proper authorities, Colonel Hoth," Lentz said. This time, his voice was bitter. "All Jewish-born persons are to be turned over. It does not state anything about their ages. Instead, you turned them over to the enemy."

"The enemy?" Hoth looked at him and held his gaze for a long moment. Perhaps he was treading too far, but he didn't care right now. "The Red Cross?"

Lentz didn't reply, but they locked eyes for a time before the colonel looked back out the window at the empty village.

"My apologies, Colonel Hoth. I didn't intend offense. If I didn't do my job, then-", he chuckled, "- Berlin would have me shot. And we wouldn't want that."

"No," Hoth muttered. "We certainly wouldn't want that."

✳ ✳ ✳

Sergeant Major Singh paced through the formation of men on the open ground, just beyond the walls of camp. The Sikh was like a marble statue, even when he moved, observing the men tossing one another around on the muddy ground.

"Use the weight of your attacker. Their momentum can be used against them!"

Willoughby dusted his trousers off and cracked his neck. Corporal Mansfield had thrown him onto the ground for the fifth time, rolling him forward as he'd charged. Mansfield dropped his hand and helped him back up to his feet.

"Five straight bloody hours," Willoughby said in a low tone. He looked over at the sergeant major to make sure he hadn't heard the comment. The Sikh had an uncanny sense of things going on around him and seemed to hear every comment made. But he showed no sign of emotion and remained completely stoic during training.

"Train your reflexes," Singh said. His whole body turned as he mimicked the movements he was trying to instill. "A split-second delay can cost you your life!"

Mansfield picked up the empty rifle, and the two switched places. This time, the corporal came charging at Willoughby. He grabbed the end of the rifle, yanking it away, and in a blink of the eye, sent the corporal down to the ground. Mansfield's forearms spread out to absorb the blow, and he rolled off to the side.

The troop had been at it all morning. Willoughby had reached an exhaustion point about two hours earlier. Except for brief water breaks, they'd been tossing one another around since assembly.

Singh was a merciless driver of men. It was hard not to see it. The Indian sergeant was as strong as an ox and as strict as the stick of bamboo he was always holding onto. More than one man had felt the crack of the inch-thick rod on a shoulder or the rear. Nothing debilitating, but it left a mark as a reminder of what not to do.

They switched again, and Willoughby took the rifle. He let out a long breath before getting ready to make yet another charge. Just as he did, a whistle blew, and the troop came to a stop.

71

Lieutenant Claymoore was standing outside the circle of men, watching the exercise. The young officer blew his whistle a second time before stepping into the center of the formation. Normally, the youthful lieutenant was a part of these exercises, which was welcome for the men. It wasn't often that a man in the ranks got to toss around his commanding officer. But Claymoore was inexperienced in combat, and most of the men respected him for taking part in training right along with the rest of them.

"All right. That's enough of that." The lieutenant took off the whistle and tossed it to the sergeant major. "I'm sure you're all tired of tussling with each other. Let's see how you do with your knives."

Claymoore scanned the group and challenged a man to attack him. A lance corporal from the Grenadier Guards drew his double-sided blade and walked into the middle of the semi-circle. Claymoore took a defensive stance and waved him onward.

The Grenadier lunged forward, stretching his knife out. Willoughby watched him. The man's knife hand was stretched out too far compared to the rest of him. Claymoore caught him by the wrist and pried the blade out of his hand. He feigned a knife stroke and then let the Grenadier go.

"You!" he called to another man. The second man approached carefully, keeping his knife under his free hand. When he came within three feet of the lieutenant, he struck upward. His grip was steady and controlled. Claymoore dodged, but the man pulled the lieutenant by the arm toward the blade. He stopped himself just before the tip touched the lieutenant's ribcage.

"That's a kill!" Sergeant Major Singh shouted as he watched the demonstration.

"Nooke!" Claymoore called, and the tall Nooke stepped toward him.

He eagerly approached Claymoore. His blade was gripped tightly, and he stood just outside of arm's reach. The two men locked eyes for several seconds and then, finally, Nooke lunged. Willoughby watched the move. He was too far out of reach to make a credible attack, and his torso leaned too far forward. Claymoore caught him by the shirt and spun him around, but Nooke stayed on his feet.

"Adjust your stance," Singh told him sternly.

Nooke lunged again, but was still too far out of reach. He was trying to use his lengthy arms to strike from safety instead of closing the gap between them. Claymoore could easily deflect the attack. Willoughby watched as he launched into a third strike. He dipped his whole torso down as he struck out. Again, Claymoore deflected him, grabbing him by the collar and pulled away.

Willoughby had seen Nooke in hand-to-hand combat training before, and the man was a capable fighter. A street fighter by nature. But, here today, he lacked discipline.

He made one more attack on Claymoore, but made the same mistake of over committing himself. He wasn't nearly close enough when he sprang, and the lieutenant grabbed him by the wrist and bent his arm at the elbow. He didn't disarm Nooke, but that was the end of the exercise.

"Do not overextend your attack," the sergeant major said as Nooke walked off. "You lose all momentum when you do." His thick whiskers blew in the wind.

One after another, men took turns with either Lieutenant Claymoore or Sergeant Major Singh. Some failed, but most of them got their blade in at least once. Singh was a master fighter, and those who tried him usually failed. Willoughby tackled Claymoore with relative ease, but lost his knife once to Singh, before getting him on the second try. That alone was a feat, and he felt wholly satisfied with himself for it when the exercise was over.

Just after noontime, they halted for a break. The mess was serving up a beef stew with a loaf of bread for a meal, and it wasn't half bad. A far cry from the normal concoctions they'd been putting together. The cuts of beef were actually fresh. Willoughby found Abernathy sitting at a table by himself and joined him.

"You see this?" Abernathy asked him. He was sitting at the end of the bench with his boot off and a single finger pushing right through the side of the toe. "So damned worn out there's hardly anything left of it."

Willoughby didn't need to be told. His own footgear was wearing thin these days as well. In the weeks past, he'd managed to beat them up so badly during training that he'd had to mend the heel of them to keep the things together.

"Good luck finding another pair," he said. "I made a request a week ago, and I still haven't seen a good pair of boots."

Abernathy tossed a disagreeable look at him and sighed. "Hawkes has some. I know he has. Scarborough's got a fresh pair."

"Hawkes?" Willoughby asked him. He knew the man to be a thief of goods, but fresh boots were like gold. Good footwear was a scarce commodity. "New boots?"

"Aye. That ain't all he's got either, Benton. Sergeant Bowvers was telling me he's been selling many goods to the lads. Socks, cigarettes. Some say he's got a stash of booze, too." Willoughby shook his head and rolled his eyes. "Don't believe me?"

"No, I believe you," he said. "I don't put anything past the man. Anyone caught drunk is asking for trouble. Now what about these boots? You say he's got some to sell?"

"Scarborough's got a pair. So did Matthews. Paid a pretty penny for them too, I heard. But Hawkes is a dealmaker. Buy any pair of boots, get yourself a nice carton of smokes to go along with them. Only twelve shillings."

"Twelve?!" Willoughby shook his head. "Jesus Christ!" That was practically a week's pay. His eyes looked around for Hawkes, but he was nowhere to be seen. "I'm sure part of that goes to whoever he needs to pay off. Somebody's bringing that stuff in for him."

It was hard enough to get certain items, like footwear and fresh socks, from the quartermaster. There was always a demand for such things. And people the likes of Hawkes and Nooke, who knew how to get things, could get fat selling stolen goods like that.

One of the guards, no doubt. He'd suspected someone in camp was helping Hawkes bring in his contraband. There was always someone in any given army camp who could get things, but usually it was simple pleasure items, and not military issue. He'd shrugged Hawkes off a couple weeks earlier when he'd made Willoughby the offer.

"By the way, MacAvoy's back on the rolls," Abernathy said. Willoughby's eyes lit up at the sound of the news.

"Really? That's good to hear."

Willoughby had been afraid his friend might have been shipped off as RTU, but MacAvoy had fought to be allowed to stay. It happened from time to time that a soldier who'd been hurt during training had to start back over with a different unit.

"He's mended up, then?" Willoughby asked. Willoughby had formed a bond with him, and he hated to think the Scotsman wouldn't be around any longer.

"He's back on the line, somewhere," Abernathy said. "Doctor cleared him for duty, and Zahlman signed off on it."

"Good to know."

"You wouldn't be thinking about doing something foolish, would you?"

Willoughby snapped his eyes up from his stew. "What do you mean?"

Abernathy gave him a dubious look. "I think you know just what I mean. Someone put your friend in the hospital, and maybe you want to pay someone back."

Willoughby pouted and sniffed the air heavily. "I would never think such a thing. Never."

He couldn't even convince himself of it. MacAvoy had told him who'd done it. It had come as no surprise. A part of him had been tempted to inform Lieutenant Claymoore, but something had stopped him from doing that. MacAvoy hadn't identified his attacker either.

"So," Willoughby said, "about these new boots. Where do you think he's got them stashed?"

CHAPTER EIGHT

Captain Zahlman stood anxiously, waiting for Colonel Devereaux to finish with his telephone call. Zahlman's eyes ran over his commanding officer as he listened to the person on the other end of the line. His eyes floated around the tiny office, then finally to the window and the rain coming down outside.

"I understand very well, sir. Thank you." The colonel hung up the phone and leaned forward in his chair. He took the file sitting in front of him and tossed it across his desk for Zahlman to look at. The younger officer went through it, grinning like a child reading his Christmas wish list. "We're approved!" Devereaux said, trying to contain his enthusiasm. It wouldn't do to break professional demeanor too much. "Headquarters has green-lit the operation."

Zahlman began flipping through the thick folder. "When do we leave, sir?"

"Eager to go?"

Zahlman shrugged. "Perhaps a bit, sir. This is the first time we're taking these boys into battle. It's an untested unit. I'm eager to see how we do." He paused and gave a shrug. "And I've yet to see combat against the Germans myself."

"Well, this will be one hell of a first time for you, Saul. But to answer your question, there are still some minor details to work out, but Keyes wants us out under the cover of total darkness." He spun around in his chair and looked at the calendar pinned to the wall behind him. "The new moon period begins in seven days."

"Seven days?" Zahlman asked. "Not much time."

"That's the job. We have to be ready to go at a moment's notice. This isn't regular army anymore, Captain. Anyway, as soon as we get the orders in writing, you'll be moving south to Cornwall. You'll need to submit a list of names for this mission. Keep it as tight as possible. This will be your first run, and the unit needs to be small and mobile. Ten names, perhaps twelve."

"Hmm. I assume Lieutenant Claymoore and I are on it, sir?"

Zahlman nodded. "As well as Van Dekker."

"The South African?"

"It's in the brief. He's an explosives expert, and that'll be mission critical. We'll go down the roster and add to it. That needs to be top priority. Any suggestions?"

"A few. Sergeant Bowvers, for certain. He's led men into combat before. That Canadian fellow, Darjan. We should have a top sniper as well. Corporal Mansfield fits the bill."

The colonel gave an agreeing nod. "Fine. I want to have something put together for the colonel by tomorrow. I'll be off to Achnacarry in the morning for an inspection, but should be back by noon."

Zahlman grunted and grumbled as he read the lines of the intelligence report. It would be a hastily put together operation, but the objective was too good to pass up. Though he didn't like the idea of going into a situation like this without more planning, and perhaps even some backup. But time was of the essence.

"I'll have it done by then, sir. I'd like to get Lieutenant Claymoore's thoughts on the matter."

Devereaux nabbed his smoking pipe and puffed it to life with the strike of a match. "What are your feelings about him? Claymoore, I mean?"

Zahlman put the file back down on the desk. "He's a fine officer. Highly motivated. Young and inexperienced, but he has an excellent head on his shoulder. And he's kept up with the training right along with the men themselves. It's earned him some credibility among them."

"That's good," Devereaux said. "Any good officer should be able to lead from the front. There's a big difference between a leader and just another officer in uniform, Saul. So, he's up to the task?"

Zahlman nodded. "Yes, sir. Undoubtedly."

"Excellent. In that case, I look forward to seeing your recommendations for the unit." He pushed himself up from his chair and stood. "You'll stay for lunch. I'd like to discuss some thoughts with you. And besides, this damn rain will only hold you up."

CHAPTER NINE

Willoughby followed a line of men into a small room at the end of the hallway. The tiny room wasn't much larger than a storage closet. There were no windows, and the air inside was stuffy. A waist-high podium stood just inside, and some chairs were in the center of the room. Behind the podium, the paneled wall was covered with a large corkboard. On it were pinned maps, diagrams and enlarged photographs.

The seats in the center were quickly snatched up, and everyone else stood against the far wall. That's where Willoughby was. Looking around the cramped space at those gathered, he recognized about half of the faces present. The other ones must've been part of the group that had come into camp just yesterday afternoon from the camp at Achnacarry. By the patches on their uniforms, they'd been drawn from just as impressive a mix of units as those who he'd trained with.

Present among them were men from the Royal Warwickshire, Ulster Rifles and Scots Guards, among others. The group waited inside for several minutes, chatting quietly away as they waited. Willoughby had just struck up a conversation with Corporal Mansfield when a voice rang out.

"Attention!" someone called, and the group straightened right up.

Captain Zahlman came striding in, with Lieutenant Claymoore right behind. Zahlman went right to the podium, and Claymoore closed the door behind them and placed a small wooden box next to the captain's feet.

"As you were," Zahlman told them.

The two officers had been in closed quarters for two days now, and there had been a steady stream of staff cars coming and going in and out of camp. Then yesterday evening, this new group of men had come in, and the rumors instantly began to swirl that perhaps they were being fast-tracked for an assignment. That was the hope, anyway.

Zahlman shuffled through a sheaf of papers, then cleared his throat heartily. "We've got a mission. The first of many, I hope." Men nodded their agreement. "Headquarters has green-lit an operation and given us a target. This will be a first for us as a unit. Some of you may think this came rather quickly, and, well, it did. But it landed in our laps, and we can't afford to pass it up."

He motioned to Lieutenant Claymoore. The lieutenant rasped his knuckles against the enlarged map. "It's called Operation Doorstep. This is our target: Guernsey, in the Channel Islands. You may not know, but the islands were taken shortly after our retreat from France."

Half a dozen small dots of land graced the map just off the French coast. Guernsey was the northwestern most of the islands, a good hundred kilometers from England.

"MI6 believes the Jerries will most likely use the island as a listening post." Claymoore stepped back and drew attention to the photographs pinned up on the corkboard. "We know from aerial reconnaissance that they've brought in heavy equipment that points to the construction of radar installations and observation posts. If the Germans complete these installations, they'll be able to monitor RAF and RN movements in the vicinity.

"Headquarters has determined they'll have had to set up communications using one of their infernal Enigma machines." Willoughby had never heard the term before. He looked around as heads turned to one another in added confusion. The lieutenant stepped back, exposing a grainy photograph of the device. "They're code machines. Berlin uses them to communicate with their front-line units. They look like typewriters, but they're not. And HQ wants it."

Captain Zahlman picked up a meter stick and stepped toward the map of the island, striking the tip against it. "The mission is to deposit a small force on the island, proceed to the target area, recover this device and the code books along with it, then proceed through a pre-planned escape route. The objective is to get in and out again without raising the alarm."

Willoughby gasped. Around the room, he could hear a low grumble go through the others. He and Corporal Mansfield exchanged raised brows. Some of them had seen action before, as in a straight up fight. That was nothing new. But sneaking into enemy territory and pulling off a stunt like this was something else. Something most soldiers weren't experienced in.

"Excuse me, sir." The voice was Sergeant Bowvers.

"Sergeant?"

"I'm sorry, sir, but won't the Germans have this thing guarded at all times? And won't they notice that it's simply gone, then report that in?"

"That's correct," Captain Zahlman said. He grinned slightly and then continued his brief. "So we must make it appear as if the machine was never stolen to begin with. Between intelligence sources we have and intercepted messages to the German headquarters at Rouen, we're highly certain the target is located here: Castle Cornet."

His meter stick landed on the picture of an old fortress that sat just off the east coast of the island. In the background was a sizeable town. A single causeway connected the fortress to the town just next to the harbor. From ten thousand feet, it appeared like an old medieval citadel that overlooked the harbor, with dozens of tiny dots anchored between the castle and the town.

"Radio antennas present would seem to confirm that intelligence. We can assume that the citadel is well guarded. However, it's miles away from the main occupation headquarters and billets, which are on the western edge of the island. This is a high-priority operation, gentlemen. With the collapse of the French and the withdrawal from European soil, we're the last domino. Intelligence gathered by this might well help us survive what's coming. Am I understood?"

"Yes, sir," the room echoed.

Zahlman nodded. "Very well. So let's begin. Lieutenant." He handed the meter stick to Claymoore.

"The raid will need to follow a very tight timeline. A submarine has been designated for us out of Falmouth in Cornwall. They'll ferry us to our destination, a point one and a half nautical miles southwest of Saint's Bay Harbour. From there, we'll row ourselves onto shore. It'll be a new moon period, so hopefully, that should give us some cover."

Hopefully? Willoughby sighed inwardly. Not a word that inspired soldiers.

"Upon making landfall, we'll split into two groups. Unit One will go with Captain Zahlman. I'll command Unit Two. We'll proceed along two different routes, which you'll be briefed upon once we leave Falmouth. There are two secondary objectives we must accomplish. Once we do, we'll proceed to the target area. Our rally point is just to the south of this town here, Saint Peter Port. Rendezvous must occur by no later than zero two hundred hours."

Willoughby studied the map. The insertion point was right on the southern shore, and the target zone was perhaps three or four kilometers away. In mountainous Norway, they'd traversed that in a couple of hours, with the Germans right on their heels. On a flat island like Guernsey, it should be no problem.

"Vital to our primary objective is to connect with locals," Claymoore said. "Intelligence sources on Guernsey will provide us with the precise location of the machine in question and a layout of the garrison stationed there. Questions so far?"

"Do we know the number of Germans on Guernsey, sir?" Bowvers asked.

Claymoore nodded. "The entire island has a garrison of roughly two thousand, perhaps more."

Another low grumble went through the men. There were ten men in the ranks in the room, and Zahlman and Claymoore made twelve. Those were odds of two hundred to one. And an island that small would be overrun with Germans. Willoughby shuddered at the thought of being caught in a fight, cut off from rescue.

"But keep in mind, that's the entire island. We're reasonably certain the castle itself is only garrisoned by a company at most. But we should be prepared for anything. We also have to assume there will be patrols on the island. Since secrecy is paramount, we must avoid contact with those patrols."

Claymoore nodded back at Zahlman. "Thank you, Lieutenant. Infiltration and recovery are the orders of the day, men. The code machine is in a subroom in the lower levels, underneath the castle. Once we reach our rally point, a small team will infiltrate through an access point. We have the diagrams for the castle from archives in London, so we know the layout. As the lieutenant has already stated, secrecy is paramount; so, the infiltration team will go through the storm drain system that runs under the castle." He indicated the diagram of the fort wall. "They'll enter here and maneuver through the drains."

Willoughby's stomach twisted at the thought of someone going through those drains. Stormwater or not, it would be a tight fit for anyone. He didn't relish or envy the person tasked with that assignment.

"Lance Corporal Wallace will lead that," Lieutenant Claymoore said. "Willoughby and Van Dekker will accompany."

His heart sank instantly.

"When the retrieval is complete, you'll escape back through the drainage system," Zahlman said. "Once the item is in our possession, we'll make the last leg out of the area. We'll make our escape, not through the route we took, but to the north." Zahlman traced the route along the map. "The sub will have circled back and will be waiting to extract us."

Willoughby could feel his heart pounding right out of his chest. For the first time in a long time, he felt uneasy. A difficult thing to accomplish considering the path his life had taken. He'd bitten the throat out of a German soldier out of survival once. But that was different. This wasn't going to be a simple fight in an open field, and there wouldn't be any rescue should they be caught.

"Sir?" Willoughby spoke up.

"Private?"

"Sir, how are we to cross the water to get to that point?" He hesitated, then asked, "And will we be armed?"

"The answer to your second question is no. You'll have your knives, but no firearms. As far as crossing the water, the Jerries have a boom across the harbor. A chain that spans the breadth of the bay. The three of you will have to cross the bay and proceed along the shoreline until you get to the bottom of the stormwater runoff. There's no easy way to do it, so you'll just have to pull yourselves across."

Lance Corporal Wallace spoke up next. "Begging your pardon, sir, but that must be a thousand feet long."

"Fifteen hundred," Claymoore said.

"Nobody said this was simple work," Captain Zahlman said. "That's why we train for this. We do the things others can't. It's that simple." He gave the entire group a hard look. "This is an important mission. Our objective isn't some trinket. It's strategically vital. I wish we'd had more time to train before our first assignment, but we don't. I'm not going to mince words with you men. We're on the verge of invasion. Right now, Hitler is readying his armies to come across the English Channel. I'd be lying if I told you we were ready for him.

"This is our ace in the hole. We retrieve it, we gain the advantage." He pointed at the photo of the Enigma. "It should be the middle of the night watch, and the number of guards on duty should be at its lowest. Our intelligence suggests most of the guards are posted along the causeway, and not on the fortress walls. Once inside, you'll need to maneuver through the lower hallways."

"Pardon me, sir." Sergeant Bowvers spoke up again. "But how exactly are we to convince the Germans this code machine of theirs was never stolen?"

Zahlman nodded. "We were just coming to that." He looked back at Claymoore, who moved next to him at the podium. "Seven low-altitude RAF bombers will act as both a diversionary force and our cover. At a pre-determined time, they'll come in low, and drop high explosive bombs on their targets. Those targets are a line of defenses west and northwest of our objective." He paused and looked around the room. "And Castle Cornet itself."

"Our target, sir?" Willoughby found himself asking after another low grumble of chatter went through the room.

"The bombers will hit the target only after we've made our escape. The RAF assures us the heavy nature of their ordnance will be enough to reduce the fortress to rubble. The lower levels should collapse. That'll provide us with the cover we need for this operation to be a success. If the Germans believe the fort was infiltrated, they'll inform Berlin, and any codes we recover will be worthless. However, if it appeared the equipment was destroyed by way of a bombing strike, then there's at least a chance of overall success.

"But for safe measure, we're bringing along an added guarantee." He pointed to the back of the room, and everyone's head turned to the lone soul standing in the corner. "Private Van Dekker is with us as an explosives expert. While inside, he'll place special explosive charges that will be timed to go off about the time of the bomber strike. It must appear that the castle and anyone in it has died by an explosion. And the machine,"—he reached down and placed the wooden box at his side on top of the podium—"will appear to have been destroyed."

The lieutenant opened the top and tilted the box over just enough for everyone to get a look inside. It was a spitting image of the photo on the wall. From where Willoughby stood, it would have appeared as some sort of strange typewriter, but with a series of mechanical dials and keys.

"A mock-up, of course," Lieutenant Claymoore said. "When it's lying in pieces under a ton of rubble, it would appear as authentic if anyone were to dig it up. Once the real one has been captured, this will be left in its place. Just a concoction of roughly identical parts, really, but it'll do."

Captain Zahlman stepped back in. "Once we're clear of the area, and the bombers have hit their target, we'll escape to the north. The Houmets are a group of small tidal islands just off the northeast coast. That's our extraction area. Once we're away from shore, the submarine will rendezvous with us, and we'll make our way back to England. If, for whatever reason, we cannot connect with our contacts or complete our mission, we'll still make our escape to the north, with the mission having been a failure. Our Royal Navy friends will linger only until zero five thirty hours." He paused for a minute, and the room was dead quiet for that time. "Questions about the operation?" Zahlman asked, and Willoughby raised his hand. "Willoughby?"

"Yes, sir. Do we have backup?"

"None whatsoever. Failure means we're either killed or captured. This unit will be the first of its kind, and headquarters can't risk a full-scale incursion; so we're on our own. The only help we'll get after we arrive will come from those bombers. And they'll be deadly accurate. Time will also be of the essence, so for those who are making the infiltration, I cannot stress enough that you'll need to move fast. The airstrike can't be called off after they've left England, so for God's sake, move quickly. Anything else?" No one uttered a word. "Very well. Lieutenant."

Captain Zahlman grabbed his papers and left through the door without another word. Claymoore gave a look around the room.

"The team roster is as follows: Team One is Sergeant Bowvers, Corporal Mansfield, Privates Belafonte, Ashford and Darjan. Team Two, is Willoughby, Pendleton, Van Dekker, Dodd and Lance Corporal Wallace. Our individual team objectives will be shared once we leave Falmouth. We've secured the water reclamation plant in Ayr over the next two days. We'll be heading there in the morning, where we'll be conducting some last-minute training exercises.

After that, we'll be going right down to Cornwall. Zero-hour will be at exactly fifteen hundred hours on the seventh. Get as much rest as you can between now and then, gentlemen. You're going to need it. Dismissed."

The room began to clear. Willoughby was just about to walk out the door when he was stopped.

"Willoughby." Claymoore waved him over. "A moment, please."

"Sir?"

"I wanted to have a brief word. You're familiar with Private Van Dekker?"

"Yes, sir."

"I thought so. I put you with him because I think you're the best choice to watch his back. Understand?" Willoughby nodded. "He's vital to this mission, and I need someone I can trust to keep him safe. That's why I chose you. Your ability to keep your friends safe."

He looked at Claymoore. The lieutenant's expression was impassive, but the words... For such a young officer, he seemed to play things fairly close to the chest. Whether that was just his nature, or because he'd had suspicions about Hawkes, Willoughby didn't know.

"Thank you, sir," Willoughby said. Though, truthfully, he wasn't that thankful.

"You'll be accountable for him during the mission. Speaking of friends, MacAvoy is a week behind in his training. He won't be with us on this one."

Willoughby nodded. He'd figured as much. The Scotsman was a good soldier, and he liked him. He'd hoped the man would have recovered in time to finish with the training right along with him, but MacAvoy wasn't the only one who'd been set back.

"I want you to know, though, that once he is finished, his place with one of the new groups being formed is assured." That made Willoughby grin. "And, provided we survive this one, yours is as well."

"Thank you, sir."

"Zero eight hundred hours tomorrow. Be ready, Private. Dismissed."

He left the officer's hut. As had been typical, the weather was overcast and gloomy outside, with a light shower that had been coming down for most of the day. He headed for the cookhouse first for lunch. The mess was packed with men, some of which had just come from the briefing he'd attended.

Willoughby wound up eating with a few of the men who'd come down from Achnacarry. One of them, a Private Dodd, had been in Norway and had heard of Willoughby after the Narvik evacuation. They ended up trading stories with one another and discussing their experiences there, and how difficult it had been for the infantry to compete with the better-equipped German *gebirgsjäger*, their elite mountain troops.

Most of the men in camp had been in France when the Germans had come rolling through. A few had never seen combat at all. Until now, Willoughby had been the lone person in camp who'd seen action in Norway. The true fight had been in France. At least, that's how so many of his companions had seen it. With Norway just a minor sideshow. But Willoughby had worn his service there as a badge of honor.

Afterwards, he found MacAvoy. He must've just returned from an exercise. His face was covered with mud, and his uniform was wet up to his waist. He was peeling the clothes off his body outside the barracks. The Scotsman saw him approach, and a friendly grin broke out on his face. "You seem happy," he said to MacAvoy as he approached.

MacAvoy washed his dirty hands clean with water from a bucket. "Heard you're off."

Willoughby sighed. "You heard about that?"

"Aye." He looked around. "It's a small camp."

He shrugged back. "They've got a job for us."

"Hmm." MacAvoy laughed ever so slightly and rolled his head. "Guess they can't hold up a whole war for one man. When do you leave?"

"Couple of days. Claymoore's got us running exercises until then."

"Well...hope you make it back in one piece, mate." The two men shook hands.

"Yes, me too. Wish you were coming with us, Dunk."

The Scotsman nodded, then pointed to his crooked nose and twirled his fingers around in the air. His injuries had healed well enough, but the time lost during training had to be made up for. He'd been a tough one, that had been apparent. Hawkes had sent at least one other trainee packing from broken bones. The Scotsman had been luckier. But in the end, Hawkes had gotten what he deserved. Whether he'd left voluntarily or otherwise, Willoughby didn't know for sure.

"Highlanders must be a tough bunch," Willoughby told him. "You people heal quicker than most."

"Nah." MacAvoy waved it away. "Just foolish enough to not let it slow us down."

"I suppose so. Claymoore told me you'll get an assignment just as soon as you're done here." MacAvoy's smile broadened. "Whatcha say we go off tonight with the lads? Public house in Stranraer, and have a drink."

The trainees were at a point that they could leave camp regularly now. A few drinks after hours in the evening were permitted, so long as it didn't interfere with their training. The men had been gathering at taverns as of late.

"Sounds good. It'll be a proper send off for you."

"Let's hope it isn't the last one."

"Aye. We can hope."

CHAPTER TEN

Colonel Hoth sat at the end of the dining table wearing a freshly pressed service uniform. To his left and right, several of his staff officers were dressed for the occasion. At the other end of the table, almost as if by cliché, Major Lentz sat. A steward placed a steaming plate of lamb and sauerkraut in front of him. In his hand, he stirred the glass of dark French red wine around by the stem, sniffing the vintage and subtly nodding an approval. The man's bloodless lips protruded from the bottom of his mouth.

Hoth couldn't help but stare at him, and he was sure the other man knew he was staring. No visit by Reich Security was a welcome one, but even by previous standards, this was the most uncomfortable visit by far that he'd ever suffered through by SS personnel. As soon as it was over, he planned to have a discussion with his superiors in Rouen.

"I commend you on your command record here, Colonel." Lentz raised a glass at him. The colonel delayed momentarily, unsure what to make of the overture, then raised his own glass and nodded. "I feel I must apologize to you for the comments made when we first arrived. In the car, I mean."

Colonel Hoth's lip pouted slightly, and he hesitated. He had no admiration for the SS and their methods, but sometimes just putting an issue to rest was victory enough.

"I'd forgotten all about it," Hoth said. He sipped on his glass of red wine. He'd stowed away a case of the good French vintage for special occasions. Though in his bowels, he hated the thought of wasting a fine bottle on men like Lentz and Ofhoven. Though, as a seasoned officer, he knew sometimes he had to bite the proverbial bullet for appearance's sake.

"Very gracious of you," Lentz said. "My report to Reich Security will be most glowing of your command here. Very glowing. I'm particularly impressed with how well the men under your command are drilled." He put the glass down and dabbed a napkin at the sides of his mouth. "If the British landed a force here, I believe they'd have a proper fight on their hands."

Hoth grinned unenthusiastically. In reality, defensive preparations were none of the SS officer's concern, and he knew it. Reich Security's considerations didn't extend beyond identifying and dealing with internal threats. Army preparedness was well outside his purview. The man was simply placating. No doubt the generals in Berlin would be voicing their own dissatisfaction when such a report was made. He would be quite happy when the two left the island the following evening.

"Yes. Well, these men are professional soldiers," the colonel said.

"I thought most were conscripts?" Ofhoven said, spooning some sauerkraut into his mouth.

"Professionally drilled," said Captain Gerhardt. Hoth gave Gerhardt a forgiving look. "And led."

"Still, as far as security goes, I have one or two minor concerns," Lentz said.

"And what are those concerns?" Hoth asked, swallowing a bite of lamb.

"Since you asked, my main concerns revolve around your decision to place the Enigma machine so far from your headquarters. Was there a reason behind that?"

Colonel Hoth drank down another gulp of wine, trying to dull the agitation he felt. He licked his bottom lip and wiped his mouth.

"My reasoning behind that?" He shook his head at the question. "Well, I'm not sure how that's any part of your security inspection. However, to answer your question, I placed the decoder where it is because that's where the only transceiver arrays left are located." He tried to put as much authority in his voice as he could. "The British left us with nothing useful. We were forced to commandeer the only one remaining. That was my reasoning, Major."

"I see," Lentz said. "All the same, don't you feel it would be more protected and better secured if it were located closer to your headquarters?"

"Or your headquarters located closer to the port?" Ofhoven said.

Hoth delayed. To his side, Gerhardt gave him a sharp look, which he returned. He didn't like being questioned like this under any circumstances, much less at a dinner with his staff present. His first instinct was to lash back, but his years of experience told him differently.

"Well, those are very good concerns, Major, Captain. Let me explain to you why. First, as commanding officer here, the choice of my headquarters is up to me. Putting it in the west instead of the east of Guernsey was the logical choice, since that's where most of our defenses lie, and because of its proximity to the airfield. Second, as you said, it gives me more intimate command of the drilling of the men. Men, who you just said, were expertly drilled." He smiled at the end of his answer.

Lentz chuckled. His false niceties and compliments were shining through fairly obviously at that point. After days spent on their so-called security review, the man had become like an ingrown toenail to Hoth and his staff.

"I understand, Colonel. Though, I might encourage you to review that decision. Or, at the very least, add extra security around it."

"I'd be happy to do so. I'm expecting additional security to arrive in the coming days. And when these engineers finish putting up new towers, I'd even have the machine moved closer to my headquarters for safe measure. I'm as committed to securing our position as any other officer. Will that satisfy you, Major Lentz?"

"Of course. And at any rate, I'll be highlighting the example of readiness to the bureau personally. Before we leave, however, if your staff wouldn't mind, we'd like to do one last tour of the island. Perhaps tomorrow morning?"

Hoth gulped down a generous amount of wine. He rolled his head around the table at his officers, and then back to the SS major. "Of course, Major, of course. Anything we can do to assist you."

And anything that gets you out of here quicker, he thought.

Lentz smiled down the length of the table. Hoth knew these inspections were as much about the command staff as they were about actually rooting out threats from the occupied population. Now that the German position in the West was secure, the SS had little to do but go from post to post, giving subtle reminders of their authority. It always came with friction, but this Lentz was something else entirely. No security review should have taken as long as it was taking him, and he resented it.

Not that he'd ever say it aloud.

"Thank you, Colonel. We'll call on your officer in the morning." He sipped on the French red. "That is good. Very good. Hmm. I look forward to making out my report."

"Oh?"

Lentz bit into his lamb and nodded. "Absolutely. I can see you're the right man to command here. I think this will be an uneventful command."

Hoth looked down the table at him and chewed his food in silence. He was tempted to ask whether it was his years in combat that led Lentz to that conclusion, but it might have been seen as crossing a line.

"In fact," Lentz when on between chews of food. "I don't see much of anything going on here now that we've gotten rid of all the undesirable troublemakers. Nothing much at all."

* * *

There was a light mist that concealed their approach, and the waves almost guided the two small rubber boats into the cove on the southern shore. As soon as the rafts came close enough to the shoreline, the men disgorged onto the thin stretch of beach.

Ahead of them, a tall precipice looked down on the tiny tract of sandy beach. The men spread out to cover the ridge above, kneeling to keep their bodies as small as they could. Once the last of them had made the beach, Lieutenant Claymoore signaled with his blue hand torch, flashing it several times in the distance. Moments later, a cable tugged on the rafts and dragged them back out to sea.

Above the cove, the banks rose steeply, like walls. Willoughby covered the high ground as the rest of the troop arranged into a defensive ring. On his left, Captain Zahlman checked his watch and then tapped him on the shoulder, giving him the signal to scale the precipice.

Large rocks gave Willoughby more than enough reach to climb with his bare hands. He stopped at the very top, peeking his head above the ridge, and looked over the top. After a minute, he saw no movement, and gave the hand signal for the rest to follow.

It only took a couple of minutes for the twelve to scale the mere fifteen-foot-high bluffs. The field at the top was clear for a hundred paces until it reached a wooded area. A pebbled pathway curved around the edge of the island, feet from the rocky cliffs. One by one, they crossed the pathway and ran into the woods beyond. The only sign anything was aware of their presence was a family of birds scared out of a nearby tree.

"Look out," Zahlman ordered quietly as soon as they'd crossed into the tiny wooded area. Two men covered the pathway and another a field of knee-high grass beyond the trees. "This is where we split. You know your objectives?" The group nodded affirmatively. "The time is twenty-two-forty hours. We're precisely ten minutes ahead of schedule. Lieutenant, I expect when we meet up again on the Fort Road, you'll have the information we need."

"Yes, sir."

Willoughby glanced around the empty island. It felt strange to him that they'd actually arrived. Not because they were about to infiltrate a highly fortified position, but because they were standing in enemy occupied British territory. For a fleeting moment, he thought about the retreat from Narvik and watching the Germans push them from that coast. Now, they were taking the fight into hostile country.

"Very good." Zahlman stretched out his hand, and Claymoore gripped it. "Good hunting, Tom."

"You too, sir."

Without so much as another word, Captain Zahlman was off, tapping Sergeant Bowvers on the shoulder to follow. With that, half the men snuck off into the night, disappearing into the high grass. Claymoore huddled in close to those who were left.

"All right, boys. Proceed quietly. That way." He pointed through the grassy field and stooped low as he took off through the weeds to the north.

The night was as dark as they could have asked for. The only visible glow of light was off to the north, presumably from Saint Peter Port. As they made their way in that direction, they stopped at the summit of a shallow knoll and took to the ground. From there, they could make out most of the town beyond the treetops. Several spotlights moved back and forth along the sky, the source of which were the high walls of the castle overlooking the harbor in the distance.

And that was their target.

Below them, a small village sat in the darkness. The thatched white-brown roofs stood out against the tree line in the distance.

"That village down there," Claymoore whispered, "is where we're going. Keep an eye on the road and stay low."

The group started back up again and slowly made its way through the vacant fields. Small farms and isolated cottages were spread all over that side of the island. They were careful to stay off the main roads, lest they run into German patrols. Instead, they leapfrogged through the fields. One man ran ahead, then covered the rest as they maneuvered the terrain. They climbed over low stone walls and pushed through hedges that squared the properties off.

Narrow pathways were cut under the thick hedgerows that seemed to grow everywhere. The paths weren't wide enough for someone to, say, push a cart through, but they were wide enough for the half-dozen men of Unit Two to move through the countryside. And they were sunken low enough that none had to expose themselves above the landscape. Though the darkness made for excellent concealment, the island seemed to crawl with sheep, which scattered at the approach of the strangers. Their distinctive moaning and bleating were as good as any alarm. If a German patrol went by, it could draw unwanted attention.

Willoughby looked off to his left and right. Across the gently rolling hills were small cottages. Some of them were piping smoke from their chimney vents, but some others appeared empty. Though no doubt some were still inhabited by civilians, it was also likely that some had been billeted to soldiers of the garrison. Either way, they were best avoided.

Lieutenant Claymoore, who was on point with Private Dodd, held his fist up, followed by an open hand to the ground. The line came to a sudden stop and crouched down. Willoughby looked around in the dark for any sign of a German patrol, but saw nothing. Lance Corporal Wallace inched up to Claymoore. The lieutenant drew his map and retrieved the poncho out of Wallace's kit bag, then threw it over himself. The faint click of a hand torch followed.

"What's going on?" Van Dekker whispered. Willoughby just shook his head.

Half a minute later, Claymoore emerged and tucked the map back into his breast pocket. He waved two fingers to the northeast and signaled for the men to move on.

"Five hundred meters," Willoughby could hear Claymoore whisper to the lance corporal. His hand gestured again, and the column started forward. Up and over an elevated embarkment into the tall grass, they crouched low through an empty field. Only the crows seemed to have any clue they were there.

The tiny village was just ahead. Cobblestone walkways weaved between the small houses. A simple lamppost was right in the center of the maze of paths, but no light was on. A small sign hung underneath, with the name of the village painted: **St. Martin**.

Ahead was a small thatched roof hut with a brick walkway that ran from its front door around the side and down a dark path toward a line of homes. Some faint flickers of candlelight could be seen in the windows of two of those houses, but everything else was dark, except for the starlight.

The unit moved low, letting the tall, wispy grass cover their approach. They finally stopped again just after reaching the first house. In the dark, beyond the line of houses, they could see movement. Claymoore waved a hand down, and the men went scurrying behind a line of thick shrubs.

Willoughby laid down behind the bushes, looking out from under the thick leaves. Out of the dark, he could make out figures emerging from down the pathway between houses. There were two of them at first, then a few moments later, several more. Each of them carried rifles and walked slowly down the cobblestone walkway. He could hear the light clinking of tin against tin as they approached.

On the wind, he could hear the voices of German soldiers carrying across the field. They moved slowly along the path. Their gray uniforms barely stood out in the night. Had the unit moved up quicker, they might well have been spotted by the patrol before any of them even knew they were there.

The six men remained still behind the line of shrubs, between the pathway and the house. At the intersection along the path, the patrol tarried for a minute in front of the village. Willoughby watched them through the thickets. One or two of them lit up a cigarette, and some words were exchanged between them. There were eight of them in total. If one of them spotted any of the team hidden in the brush, they'd have no choice but to take them out.

Nearby, Claymoore leveled his gun and slowly chambered a round. A dull click echoed. Others took the same precaution.

"*Warte auf mich!*" one of the Germans shouted to the others. The single soldier walked over toward their position, his rifle gripped with both hands.

"Shit," Willoughby whispered. He leveled his gun at the approaching man, just feet away.

The German came to an abrupt stop in front of the bush and stood there for a few seconds. He was so close Willoughby could see his boots just under the shrubs and hear the man's breath. He was half-afraid he was going to have to shoot him. A moment later, a stream of piss crossed the earth a yard ahead of him as the man relieved himself. Willoughby sighed at the sight. A ripple of laughter erupted from the patrol, and a minute later, the man finished. He kicked sand on the spot he'd wet, some of which hit Willoughby's face, before returning to his comrades.

Then the Germans moved on down the path. The last one tossed his cigarette and then continued on. Willoughby watched them as they passed out of sight. After they were sure the patrol had moved on, Lieutenant Claymoore gave the signal for the rest of them to wait while he moved from behind the bushes. Once the Germans were out of earshot, he waved them the okay to start moving again.

They snuck down the pathway, staying clear of the center of the village, pressing against the houses and trees as they moved. The lieutenant stopped them when they reached the third house, then took them down a small alley that went right through the backyards of the cottages. The walled-off yards were vacant as they made their way down. Not so much as a soul was outside.

Willoughby looked around, saw a tiny shaft of candlelight beaming through a crack in someone's rear window, and thought it ironic. They were sneaking through a village that was, for all intents, part of Great Britain, but not one of those people would ever know they'd been there. Not if everything went as planned.

Finally, they came to a small wooden door in the back alley. The door was a thick oak, with two lamps on the outside. One of them was crooked. Willoughby kept one eye on the other end of the alleyway. Claymoore leaned up against the wall to the right of the door and rasped his knuckles on a small window just above him. Across from him, the rest of the unit fanned out, keeping an eye on the approached and the other houses.

On the inside of the window, there came three soft knocks, followed by three more a moment later.

Willoughby covered the oak door with his gun as it slowly opened. A small, porcelain-white face peeked out, and then the door swung open. A small woman stood in the doorway, illuminated only by the starlight. She wore a white and blue dress and had a shawl hanging over her shoulders. The woman looked suspiciously at them for a moment and then opened the door for them.

"Come," her feminine voice said.

He lowered his rifle as the lieutenant ducked inside, followed one by one by the rest of the unit. The woman softly closed the door behind them as the last one entered the dark apartment. The apartment was as scantily decorated as the young woman was dressed. She had a petite frame, with dark black hair draped over her shoulders. And she was strikingly beautiful. Willoughby thought so anyhow. He could smell the slight fragrance of French perfume.

"This way," she whispered and took the men into a small bedroom. There was a small table next to the door, and half a bottle of red wine sitting on it. A small iron stove was against the wall. Above the stove hung pictures of people. On the opposite wall, there was a small window, with the curtains drawn closed, and a messy bed under the window ledge. The woman walked to a small table to a burning kerosene lamp and turned it up enough to light up the room.

"Galahad?" she asked, looking around.

Claymoore stepped forward and nodded. "Merlin?"

"*Oui*," she whispered and released a breath. "I was not expecting so many," she said. Her accent was French, which explained the perfume.

The lieutenant looked the woman up and down. "I didn't expect..." He shrugged. "Well..."

"A woman?" He nodded. She sighed. "I understand, *monsieur*. I confess that I too was expecting someone else. A knight, perhaps." She smiled at Claymoore, who almost seemed to blush under the black and green face paint. "So, *Monsieur* Galahad, are you all there are?"

Claymoore looked at her for a moment, then nodded his head. "Afraid so."

"Hmm. Well, you are either very special or very...how do you say—insane?"

"You have something for us?" Claymoore asked her instead of answering.

"*Oui.*" She walked to the stove and took a small box of matches off a shelf above it. She opened the matchbox and upended its contents on top of the stove, then dug her fingers into it, pulling out a folded-up paper. She began to unfold it and held it out for Claymoore to take.

The lieutenant took the paper and unfolded it completely in the dim light. It was thin, almost like onion skin. He held it up against the light. There was a drawing on the paper. Willoughby watched the young woman as Claymoore studied it for a few moments.

"It's accurate?" he asked without looking at her.

"*Oui.*"

"How can you be sure?"

"Because, *monsieur*, I have been inside the fort. I go there frequently. I know my way."

Claymoore gave her a questionable look. "You've been inside?"

The young woman adjusted the shawl back over her shoulders and nodded. "Many times."

"The Germans let a young Frenchwoman into the fort?"

"Half-French," she told him. "My father was English. That is why I'm here. He passed before the war, and I came to claim my inheritance."

Claymoore studied her for a moment or two. "Half-French. Your mother is still alive?"

"*Oui.* She and my sisters live in Cherbourg. My brother was killed in the fighting in Belgium." Her voice choked, and her lips pursed. "Since I cannot get back to Cherbourg right now, I stay here. I do what I can do to help."

The lieutenant nodded and began to fold the small map back up before putting it into a buttoned pocket on his jacket. "Why do they allow you into the castle?"

She hesitated for a moment, looked embarrassed, and then dropped the shawl from around her shoulders, exposing red and blue bruises on her skin.

"A sergeant there uses me." Her tone was blunt and full of shame. "I let him do what he wants, and he tells me things when he's drunk. He thinks I'm just a stupid girl." She covered her shoulders back up.

Willoughby looked the girl from head to toe. She was like a small doll; tiny and petite. Despite her small stature, she had some strength in her face, no doubt born of anger and hate. But despite that, he found her strikingly beautiful. He shook the thought from his mind.

"I see," the lieutenant said. He looked self-consciously down at his feet. "Well...thank you for your help. If I could do something for you, I would."

She stepped close to him. "You can, *monsieur*. When you get to the fort and you see a fat sergeant with a broken nose and an ugly face, please kill him for me." Her face was like stone, and Willoughby could see she was dead serious. "I don't think I'd be able to sleep right knowing he's alive."

Claymoore stared at her blankly for a few moments, then finally nodded and touched the tip of his beret. "Ma'am."

He gave the signal for the men to turn around and head out. Willoughby gave the girl one last, long look before bringing up the rear. Before he left, he swore she muttered something in French that sounded like a prayer. He softly let the door click shut behind him and followed the men down the path and out of the tiny village.

CHAPTER ELEVEN

Captain Zahlman kept his head flat against the brick wall he was hiding behind and slowly peered around the corner, down the narrow-paved road between buildings. The only light that shone came from the distant single orange lamp that hung over the village well at the very end of the street.

He looked around slowly, saw no signs of anyone moving, then stepped around the corner, followed by the rest of the unit. His mind flashed with images of photographs taken of the parish. He'd familiarized himself with those photos before leaving England and could easily spot the building he was looking for. It was a white, three-storied structure with a dark roof, surrounded by clumps of trees. It was away from the rest of the village, by maybe three hundred paces, which they traversed by ducking behind hedgerows and squat stone walls.

From a nearby house, a rusty-hinged door creaked open, and the entire unit dropped to the ground in fear of being spotted. A single older woman stepped outside, illuminated by a shaft of light through the open door, and emptied a bucket into the street. Zahlman watched her as he lay flat on the ground, not twenty paces away. The old woman looked around in the dark before retreating into the tiny house, locking a bolt behind her. He gave it a handful of seconds before giving the gesture to continue on.

The building across the field was a dilapidated old church. Its high steeple rose above the trees. A newer structure had been built into the church. The newer building, he knew, housed what was left of the church staff. As with all other structures around, the windows were blacked out, except for a single window on the third story. The flickering of a kerosene lamp grew brighter as they approached in the dark.

The captain stopped the unit twenty paces from the rear of the church. It was a miracle they hadn't spotted a single German since splitting up. Hopefully, Claymoore's team was having the same luck they were.

"Sergeant," he whispered to Bowvers, "Hold here. Ashford, with me."

Zahlman and Private Ashford crouched behind one of the thick trees, then sprinted across the yard. There was an archway built into the stone church that covered a thick oak door, and the two men pressed their bodies tightly against the stone walls as they snuck toward the rear doorway. Zahlman gave two soft knocks against the door, then two more a few seconds later. He gripped the hilt of his knife, ready for the unexpected. A few seconds ticked by, and they seemed to wait for what felt like forever.

Inside, two soft knocks came in reply, and then the sound of a pair of bolts being unlocked. The thick door slowly opened, and a shadowy figure stood just inside, illuminated only slightly by a flickering candle behind him. Zahlman's heart beat quickly as a single man emerged in the doorway. He wore the black attire of a priest. His head was bald, and his belly hung out over a tightened belt. The whites of his bulging eyes stood out, even in the dim light. The priest looked them up and down for a moment before finally visibly relaxing.

"Praise God," the priest said. "Come. Come."

Zahlman pushed Ashford in first, then went through the door. The heavyset priest quietly closed the door behind them and bolted it shut again. The hallway inside was softly lit by candles in small recesses built into the walls. Modest wooden tables and benches adorned the hallway for as far as the candlelight would allow.

"Lancelot?" the priest asked Zahlman, who replied with a single nod.

"Gwain?" The fat priest let out another relieved sigh and nodded.

"Yes. Thank God." He took a lamp off a small table and indicated for the two to move down the dark hall. "I wasn't actually sure if you'd make it through." His voice trembled with nervousness. "This way, please."

"Yes, well, it wasn't easy, but here we are." He looked the man up and down as he led the two through the church. They reached a modern door, underneath which light spilled out. He kept one hand on his knife and the other gripped his machine gun.

"These are uncertain times," the priest went on. "I'm sorry if I seem nervous. I didn't recognize your uniforms. If you'd been German..."

The priest, Gwain, opened the door, which took them into a larger room behind the nave. It was the church office. Against the lefthand wall were a pair of desks facing each other, and a large rectangular table was set in the middle of the room, covered with old books and church ornaments.

Gwain put the lamp on the closest desk and extended a hand to Zahlman.

"I'm glad you're here. As you can imagine, it's been difficult these last few weeks. Very difficult."

"I can understand." He looked around the vacant room. When he was satisfied no one else was present, he sheathed his knife. "Are you the only one here?"

Gwain shook his head. "There are very few of us left. There are two brothers and some nuns in the dormitory. Nobody comes down here. Not for a while anyhow."

"Your flock?" Zahlman asked.

The priest shrugged and sighed. "Gone, I'm afraid. Most of the people left on the island are frightened to leave their homes. The Germans have clamped down on groups congregating together. They allow us to leave the church for Mass. Of course, it's held under guard. Some of the German officers are Catholic, so they allow it. The only thing we're allowed to do in the church is hear confession."

Zahlman only nodded. He couldn't imagine the sight of the British townspeople sharing in communion with their Nazi occupiers, but he'd seen stranger things in Palestine.

"They've given you no trouble, I hope?"

Again, the priest shrugged. "At the beginning, yes. But it relaxed as the weeks went on. Some of the others have given us problems, though. Not the German Army soldiers, but the ones from the continent. They wear black uniforms."

"SS?" Zahlman asked him.

"A handful came here following the occupation and took some people away. Jews, I think. A few Poles as well. Nobody has seen them since. I pray for them." He hung his head sadly.

"When was the last time you saw the SS on the island?"

Gwain's eyes widened. "Some came here just a few days ago. The ferry in Saint Peter Port is still there, so they must still be here. It's probably the fourth or fifth time they've come in as many weeks."

Zahlman's forehead creased in intrigue. "Still here?" he whispered, rubbing his chin. "Do you know what they come here for?"

Gwain shrugged and shook his head. "I only know there isn't much love between them and the garrison commander. Colonel Hoth is a devout man. Not a Catholic, but he holds no care for the SS. That much is obvious."

"How do you know this?" Zahlman asked.

"One of his subordinates confesses to me, and it's easy to read between the lines."

The captain's eyes narrowed. "Confession? Really?"

Gwain mirrored the look. "Yes. Why?"

"Seems strange that a German officer would confess to a British priest. What does he confess about to you?"

Gwain's demeanor changed slightly. "I cannot speak of that. Rest assured, however, that it is of no military importance. I am still a representative of the Holy See. I must accept confession, even from those who occupy us."

Zahlman considered his words, then nodded in acceptance. "Forgive me, Father. It's just strange to me that a man of the cloth, a British man, is being confessed to by the enemy. That's all."

"God has no enemies, my son." The bald priest's face curled back with a caring smile. "One day, this war will pass as so many others have. However, as much as I abhor killing, I can't sit by and do nothing. I'm no fool. I've seen the face of war before, and I know full well what happens in occupied territory. I was in Lithuania, years ago. The Russians came and, well..."

Zahlman studied the man for a few moments and decided against pushing the issue any further. Instead, he reached down into the large pocket sewn to the outside of his trousers and produced a small black book. He held it out for the priest to take.

Gwain accepted it. His face crinkled as he looked at it. "The Holy Bible?"

"With a few notable alterations. I think you'll find Exodus to be particularly interesting." Gwain thumbed through the pages in the dim light. "I believe you have something for me?"

"Yes! Oh yes!" Gwain opened up the top drawer of the desk and handed Captain Zahlman a book of his own. "It'll need to be translated."

Zahlman opened the book. It was an old leather-bound. "Translated indeed," he said after reading the few words he could see. "Latin?"

Gwain nodded. "Any good Catholic church would have such books lying around. The Germans searched through our library and took many of the others when they occupied the island." He paused. "Hebrew is outlawed."

Zahlman bit his lower lip and nodded sadly. Reports he'd read from occupied Europe were painting a miserable picture of those who clung to the Jewish faith, among other groups.

He tucked the little book under his vest.

"There's one more thing," Gwain said. "Your route for getting off the island is in that book. There are some small fishing huts to the north that will provide you with what you need. They should be empty this time of night."

"I see. And the other civilians on the island? Should we be made aware of anyone?"

"You mean are any of them working with the Germans?" Zahlman nodded. Gwain sighed heavily. "That would be troubling indeed. I can't think of anyone who might turn you in. But all the same, best to avoid contact."

"How do we know we can trust you?" Private Ashford asked. Zahlman gave him a brief look, then turned back to the priest.

Gwain pouted and considered his words. "All I can say is that there wasn't a squad of German soldiers here when you came through the doors." Ashford grumbled, but nodded.

Zahlman summed the man up before giving him an accepting nod. "Very well. Thank you."

"You should be going now," Gwain told him and put a gentle hand on his shoulder. "I pray to God for your safe return home."

"Thank you." He looked at Ashford and gave a single nod. Gwain grabbed the lamp and walked the two out of the office and back down the dark hallway, where they parted ways.

"Good luck," were the last words exchanged between them before Zahlman and Ashford rejoined the unit holding position under the thick trees. "Let's move," he told Sergeant Bowvers. The group stealthily made its way off into the night, just as silently as it had come.

* * *

Willoughby fumbled around in his side pocket and pulled out a small pouch of dried beef. He put a cut in his mouth and offered one to Van Dekker. The South African gratefully accepted, and he put the pouch back into his pocket. He looked around the small knot of trees, surrounded by overgrown gardens, and in the night waited. They'd been waiting there for what felt like an anxiously long time. The small grove was the rendezvous point for the two teams.

The men were lying on the ground in a wide circle, watching the approaches. Lieutenant Claymoore and Lance Corporal Wallace were in the center, scanning through the dark off to the north and northwest; the direction they were expecting Team One to be coming from.

The small, isolated wood they were hiding in was just to the east of the village of St. Martin and just off a road that curved around the side of the island. To the west, a knee-high stone wall hemmed in a herd of sheep. Their incessant bleating and crying were the only sounds in the night.

Now it was a waiting game. To the east, Willoughby could hear the gentle lapping of waves against the rocky shoreline. To the northeast, the lights of Castle Cornet were brighter than before. The beams from the spotlights scanned the skies, and he could swear he heard the faint voices carrying across the water. As a fisherman, he knew sound traveled over water better than it did on land. The noise of the waves made him think of his grandfather's boat and the youth he'd spent hauling in a catch. All things considered, he felt quite at home there on the island with the scent of the sea in the air.

"Heads up!" a deep voice whispered, and instantly, everyone went deadly still.

Willoughby looked to the west for anything moving. Beside him, Private Dodd tapped his shoulder and drew his gaze to the northwest. It was hard to make out at first, but after a few moments, he caught the movement of bodies coming down the main road from the north. They marched down the roadway in two single-file columns.

"Patrol," he whispered to Van Dekker on his left, who in turn alerted the man to his left, and so on.

The dark gray of their uniforms, combined with the lightless night, made them almost invisible as they emerged from the clump of trees and abandoned homes along the roadway. The gentle stomping of their boots along the concrete occasionally broke the noise of the sheep as they marched toward them. Even concealed in the small wood, no one moved so much as an inch. It wouldn't take much to draw unwanted attention to themselves.

The patrol came down the road in such a leisurely manner that it didn't seem like a patrol at all, really. It was almost too careless. If they had been British soldiers, they might have sent someone to check out every single clump of trees, every animal pen and every square foot of island along the way. It's when you think nothing is wrong that something usually goes wrong. But these Germans had been on the island for weeks with no trouble. Perhaps they'd just patrolled those parts so many times they'd gotten into a routine. Either way, not one of them deviated from the road.

There were perhaps ten of them meandering down the path, and every eye was glued to them as they slowly paced by. Across the road, the herd of sheep shuffled around in the field as the patrol went by. A single, loud *baa* went out among them, but the soldiers barely took notice. One or two may have paused for a second, but moved on with the rest of the group.

"Sir," someone muttered. Willoughby swung his head around toward the voice.

LC Wallace was looking hard across the road, his finger raised toward the stonewall. Claymoore followed his finger. On the other side of the road, emerging out of the field of sheep, five bodies crept over the stone wall. They moved slowly and methodically.

"Friendlies," Claymoore muttered.

One man dropped over the wall, followed by another, until they were all over. Two covered the road to the south where the patrol was disappearing out of sight, another covered the north. One at a time, they each crossed and dashed into the wood.

"Sir," Lieutenant Claymoore said as Captain Zahlman slid across the ground under the shadow of the treetops.

"Lieutenant. Report."

Claymoore tapped his jacket pocket. "Mission accomplished."

"Good work. Any trouble?"

"No, sir. That's the second patrol we've spotted. Last one was perhaps thirty minutes ago. They seem to be well-timed."

"That's good." Zahlman looked around at the men, counting heads, then back to the north. "Castle Cornet should be a kilometer and a half. Let's hope our luck holds."

The captain signaled for the troop to move out. The knot of trees was part of a series of public areas along the eastern shore of the island. Each area was separated by open spaces that allowed access to the beaches. One man would run across the open areas to the next clump of trees, followed by the next individual, then the next.

Half a kilometer up the shoreline, they stopped behind a walkway wall that led down to the beach. Across the water, a small clearing jutted out to the open sea, and there were a good dozen or so German soldiers pacing around a single 3.7 cm flak gun position. A pair of bright lights illuminated the position and everything within a hundred feet.

"Damn." Zahlman snarled as he looked over the wall at the flak gun and the men around.

The area to the north was a long stretch of bushes and squat, thick trees that followed the coastline. Under the distant lights, Willoughby could make out a thick, white surf breaking against a point of rocks a few hundred meters distant. Beyond that point was the castle. But between them and that point, the light from that gun position spilled out across the road for fifty feet.

"We have to go around that," Zahlman said.

"There's a village to the west, just beyond those trees," Claymoore said.

Willoughby hunkered down behind the wall, just feet from the two officers. Under the bright lights below, the Germans were walking around the anti-aircraft gun and a small hut just steps above it. Behind them, the road stretched back for fifty paces before disappearing behind the last group of trees they'd hidden in. If a patrol happened back up from that way right now, they'd be stuck between the beach and the road, and there would be no way to stay concealed. The last thing they could afford was a firefight.

"All right," Zahlman said, "take Dodd and go through that field."

Claymoore made his way to the front of the line, tapped Private Dodd and the two set off across the road, into the trees to the west a moment later. Captain Zahlman and Sergeant Bowvers had some hushed words, after which the sergeant half-turned down the line, hugging the shallow wall.

"We need to cross the road, lads," Bowvers muttered, and the word went down. "Two more men. Mansfield, Pendleton, you're next. Willoughby and Van Dekker after that. We move until everyone's across."

They stayed low and moved in brief intervals. On the opposite side of the road, a thin line of trees concealed several homes arranged in a cul-de-sac. They emerged into a dark field behind the homes.

Lieutenant Claymoore and Private Dodd were pressed up against the wall of a single house, and the others assembled against the house opposite from them. Across from him, Claymoore gave the hand signal to Corporal Mansfield to watch to the south and for Willoughby to go north.

He tapped Van Dekker on the chest. "Wait here," he said before dashing across to where Claymoore was pressed against the house wall. In the field to his right, the next two men came out of the wood, followed by two more. Zahlman and Bowvers brought up the rear.

"Take point," Claymoore whispered to him.

Willoughby let out a deep breath, then snuck quietly around the corner, rifle covering his advance. He held up the signal that they were clear, then moved forward slowly. He passed one house and was halfway across the second, when something suddenly stopped him.

In the dark, a cat jumped up onto a low fence and startled him. The small animal let out a friendly meow and strut across the top of the fence. Willoughby swore inwardly at the damn thing. The brave little cat walked toward him, meowing louder. He stopped for just a moment, trying to push the thing away with the tip of his rifle, but the cat rubbed its face against it instead and gratefully purred.

"*Ssst*," he hissed at the cat, trying to get it run off.

Willoughby took several steps forward again, then came to an abrupt stop. Feet to his left, a door hinge squeaked, and a figure emerged out of the back of the home. His heart skipped a beat, and he jumped toward the figure.

A face took form out of the darkness. Willoughby reached out for it, grabbing the person by the throat with one hand and pressing the muzzle of his rifle against him with the other. If the house was occupied by a German, things could become dicey quick.

"Oh!" the voice eked out. He instantly squeezed, and the voice cut short.

Willoughby pinned the figure up against the darkened wall and pushed his rifle up to his throat. Ten fingers wrapped around his wrist, but they were small and feeble.

"Oh, please," the voice choked out under his grip. In English.

Willoughby cautiously loosened his grip. Behind him, Lieutenant Claymoore came around the corner, standing just over his shoulder. Willoughby's eyes examined the figure and realized it was a woman. A small one too. He loosened his grip a little further, but kept his hand just below her larynx.

"Easy," Claymoore whispered over Willoughby's shoulder. "Just be easy."

The woman slowly recovered and eased her grip from around Willoughby's wrist. He released his own grip on her. Willoughby could hear the lady make a sharp inhale, and her breathing became relaxed.

"*Shh*," Willoughby told her silently, covering his lips with a finger.

"You're English?" she muttered. Her voice was full of disbelief. She exhaled noisily, and he could almost make out a faint smile on her darkened face. "You're here to rescue—"

"Ma'am. Quietly, please," Claymoore told her. "Are you the only one here?"

"In my house? Yes. But two German soldiers live in that house there." She pointed across the cul-de-sac at a small yellow home. "I heard my cat, and..." She shook her head. "Have you come to rescue us?"

Willoughby sighed. "I'm afraid not." He shook his head. "What's your name?"

She stuttered. "J-Jenny. Jenny Fairbanks."

"Miss Fairbanks, go back inside. Forget you saw us. It's for your own good."

"But—" she began, then cut herself off. She nodded reluctantly, then turned away to go back inside, but stopped herself. "Are you ever coming back? Is England still free? We hear things."

Willoughby put his hand on her shoulder gently and gave her a light shove toward the door. "Yes. England's still free. And we'll be back." He told her that, but he wasn't sure if it would ever be true. "Now go. Lock your door. And say nothing. We were never here. Do you understand?" His voice had turned harsh.

The woman nodded and retreated into the house. The tiny cat slipping in between her feet along with her.

"Let's go!" Claymoore told him, and they were off again, sprinting across the backyard, toward the distant lights beyond the trees.

CHAPTER TWELVE

"If there's only a company over there, then I'm the damn King of England," Captain Zahlman said within earshot.

Next to him, Willoughby could see Sergeant Bowvers nod his agreement. The captain had his monocular out and was viewing the fortress across the bay. It was lit up with a flurry of spotlights. It could have easily been daylight, with all the beams cast across the castle walls. There were several buildings within those walls that were well illuminated, as was the main entrance and the towers along the wall.

Havelet Bay separated them from Castle Cornet. Small boats bobbed up and down on the gentle tide. From the southern tip of the great rock that sat underneath the fort all the way to the eastern shore, there was a thick chain. It must have been a thousand meters long and hung taut, only feet above the waterline. It was dark, but Willoughby could make out the glimmer of the boom as it swayed when the waves moved it.

"Damn," Willoughby muttered despondently.

Even now, with no binoculars, he could see men moving around from the western end of the causeway all the way to the castle and along the battlements. The fortress itself sat atop of a great rock, overlooking the sea. The old gun emplacements that lined it had been removed and replaced with several pieces of modern artillery.

Willoughby looked across the harbor and shook his head. He'd gone through hell in Norway, where he'd taken a bite out of a man's throat and survived a German attack, only to spend weeks in the hospital after being shot on the way out. Then, to complete all the training he'd gone through in recent weeks, thinking he could survive anything that followed. But now that he saw what he was facing, knowing he had to swim across the bay and somehow sneak into that, only to retrieve a small box and swim back, all he wished for was to be somewhere else.

"Infiltration team," Claymoore whispered down the line assembled along the beach shore. "You know your jobs. Get in, get out again. The time is zero one-fifty. The bombers are scheduled to hit at zero five hundred." He gave a hard look at LC Wallace, Willoughby, and Van Dekker. "This is the time, gentlemen."

The three of them unbuttoned their blouses and unstrapped their gear, leaving their arms behind with the others. Willoughby emptied his pockets and stripped down to his long-sleeved undershirt, handing his belongings to Private Darjan. Darjan was the troop's lone French Canadian.

"Damn me," Willoughby muttered under his breath. "I hope you memorized the floor plan, Corporal."

"Just follow my lead," Wallace said, tossing his blouse to Corporal Mansfield. "Are you two ready?"

"Damn me," Willoughby repeated. "As ready as I'll ever be."

The three of them got on their feet and crept down the slope with their heads low until they reached the waterline. Willoughby dreaded the thought of having to swim the distance between here and there. The idea of going in with no rifle and no backup was bad enough. Going in with nothing but a knife and his skivvies was like going in naked.

Wallace was roughly the same build as Willoughby—lean and muscular. He reached for the chain first and waded into the water, Willoughby followed, with Van Dekker in the rear with the pack carrying the fake code machine fastened around his back.

Willoughby gave one last look at the embankment before wading into the sea. He grabbed the chain and held it until the water came up beyond his waist, and then he followed Wallace into the water. With not a single gun between them, the three gripped the boom and began to pull themselves across the bay. It was tedious going. They crept across slowly, careful to not shake the chain for fear of drawing attention. Wallace set a steady pace, and they kept moving, one yard after another, across the harbor.

The opposite shore was a thousand yards away. That might have been a simple walk, but pulling oneself through water—while lugging a fake code machine in full uniform—was another matter. And as soon as the bottom dropped out from under him, Willoughby found himself struggling just to stay moving.

Off to the north, the long causeway that connected the port town to the fortress was lit up under several tall lamps, under which he could see the distant heads of soldiers walking back and forth. Ahead of them, the boom disappeared into the dark, under the shadows of the castle ramparts. The rocks along the bottom of the breakwater hid in shadow, but at the top of the wall of the fort above, bright light spilled out.

At this distance, he couldn't see any movement on the walls ahead, and it seemed like all he could do was stare at the wall as they pulled themselves across. In front of him, Lance Corporal Wallace came to an abrupt stop halfway across the bay.

"Hold!" the lance corporal whispered back.

Willoughby and Van Dekker stopped pulling and looked around.

"What's wrong?" Willoughby asked. He squeezed his grip on the boom and looked around nervously, but saw nothing. Before Wallace could answer, a spotlight lit up across the water. A tiny dot appeared on the surface just meters away and moved left and right. His fingers tightened around the chain, and after a while, he could feel himself beginning to lose his grip.

The three paused as the light from the north end of the castle wall scanned the water back and forth before finally moving away. Then they continued on again, pulling themselves along the chain at a grueling, slow pace. By the time they made it to the end, Willoughby found himself exhausted and fighting to catch his breath.

"Take a moment," Wallace told them.

They collapsed under a tall rock that obstructed the view from the wall above. Willoughby fought to catch his breath. The three huddled together, just along the waterline. He couldn't see anyone up there, but he knew they were there, blocked from sight. The top of the wall above was a good fifty feet high, and the faintest of voices carried through the air.

He looked back across the bay to the opposite shore in the distance. For a moment, he couldn't believe they'd swam across it. They'd have to do it all over again, of course, but they'd made it across without drowning or drawing attention. However, the hard part was still to come.

"The entry point is that way," Wallace told them, pointing to the northern wall. "You've got what you need?"

The hefty South African patted the pack on his back and gave him a nod. He'd just pulled himself across fifteen hundred feet of chain, and he wasn't gasping near as badly as Willoughby and Wallace were. Perhaps the years working in a South African mine had given him the endurance.

After a brief pause, they crawled along the rocks until they reached their destination. A small outfall ran through the wall, not fifty yards from the northern edge of the fort. A metal lattice barred the entrance into the storm sewer. A lock and chain held it closed.

"This is a problem," Willoughby said, examining the lock. Of all things to consider during the planning, a lock hadn't been one of them.

Van Dekker examined it, then unstrapped his bag and pulled out a small kit. He retrieved a small rod and, in the blackness, fumbled around with the lock. After a minute, there was a dull click, and the lock came apart.

"Done," the South African said, tucking the pick back into his kit.

"Good man," Wallace said with a bright grin. He pulled the lattice open and squeezed himself inside. Willoughby let Van Dekker go ahead of him. He looked up at the wall above, saw no one, and followed in behind, closing the lattice behind him.

The drain was connected to the stormwater system inside the fort. But once in, the drain was dry except for some sitting water. They'd trained sneaking through the water reclamation plant in Ayr. Those pipes had been narrow, only allowing for someone to crawl through them. This was different. The stone drain was wider, letting them move forward in a squatting position.

The drainage ran down the length and breadth of the fort's bowels. Small iron grills above allowed rainwater to move from the top through the bottom level and into the sewer. Shafts of light from the interior of the fort lit their path. They moved slowly. Too slowly, as far as Willoughby was concerned. He hated this crawling around business. He especially hated the fact that all he had on him was a double-bladed knife and his wits. He'd have felt much more comfortable with a rifle and half a dozen clips. But stealth and secrecy were the orders of the day. Charging in with guns blazing was a nice thought, but impractical.

"I think this is it," Wallace whispered. They'd reached a single grill in the center of the labyrinth of tunnels.

Willoughby gazed up. The light in the hall above was dim and distant. "You think?" he asked him dubiously. In the maze of drains under the fort, he found it hard to keep up with the turns they'd made.

"Only one way to say for sure." Wallace motioned for Willoughby to help him, and together, the two pushed up on the grill above. It took a fair amount of effort to push the metal grill out of place. Together, they stood up and peeked into the hallway above.

It was dark. The only light came from either end of the corridor. In one direction, there was light around a corner just paces away, and in the other direction, the hall intersected with another lit corridor farther away. There was no activity in either direction. Given the time of night, that wasn't too surprising. He looked at Wallace, who gave him a nod, and they slid the grill off to the side. Willoughby pushed himself up first, drawing his knife out as he got to his feet.

He snuck to the end of the corridor and peeked a single eye into the next hallway. Around the corner, there was another, shorter hallway that cut through to a wider one. That one was better lit, with bulbs running along the top of the wall. He put his ear to the edge, but heard nothing. He risked peeking around the corner, saw there was no one, and then rejoined the other two. When Van Dekker hoisted himself up from the drain, the large South African lifted the grill back into position with nearly no effort.

"Do you know where we're going?" Willoughby asked quietly.

Wallace lifted off his cap. He'd kept the tiny map drawing they'd been given by the London archives underneath. A second drawing had been given to them by the young French girl, which was only a section of the castle's tombs. He glanced down the hallway one way, and then the other. Then he gave the signal to move toward the way Willoughby had just scouted.

"That way." He put the tiny map back in and straightened out his watch cap. "Willoughby, bring up the rear."

The maze of short corridors all led into longer ones that ran down the long side of the castle. Small doors graced the corridors, and most had padlocks on the outside of them. Some had lights creeping out from underneath, but the rest were dark.

Van Dekker and Willoughby followed Wallace until they came to the main corridor. There, bulbs ran down the length of the hall. Every twenty feet, a pulsing yellow-orange light illuminated the corridor. Far to the right, the hall ended with what Willoughby knew was a stairwell that led back up to the outside. Wallace silently crept around the corner into the main hallway, then ducked quickly into a small side corridor. The larger Van Dekker followed a moment later. Just as Willoughby was about to make his own run across the hallway, Wallace held up an open palm and gave him a stop signal.

Toward the north end, voices echoed down the hallway. Willoughby peeked an eye around the corner just long enough to observe two or three soldiers moving down the hall toward him. He gripped his knife tight and held it up under his chin, ready to act if it came down to it. Across from him, Wallace was watching down the hall from the opposite angle.

The voices grew closer. His heart felt like a drum, and his breathing became heavy in anticipation. He could take one, but he certainly couldn't get two or three of them. Even if Wallace and Van Dekker came running out, one of them would scream down the corridor, sounding the alert. Either way, it wouldn't end well, and all possibility of coming out of this alive were almost nil.

The plodding of the soldiers' boots along the stone floor continued until it suddenly stopped. He froze, not daring to peek around the corner. Then he heard the noise of keys being jingled around. Moments later, a door opened. Willoughby glanced over at Wallace, hidden in the opposite hallway. He held up a single finger and gave him a reassuring nod. There was a sharp clicking sound, and the voices of the German soldiers faded away.

Wallace waved him across the hall, and Willoughby sprinted into the small corridor with them.

"It's down the hall and to the right," Wallace whispered.

Wallace motioned to him, and Willoughby didn't waste a second. He raced down to the other end of the corridor and ducked into the next right-hand turn, which dead ended. There were two doors on opposite sides of the short hallway, facing each other. Both were padlocked from the outside. Van Dekker and Wallace came slamming into him from behind a second later.

Willoughby looked at the two padlocked doors and the dead end, then gave Wallace a mildly displeased expression. "Corp?"

"It's around the corner," Wallace told him. He pulled out the diagram the French girl had given them again and nodded curtly toward the very end of the main hallway.

"Is it the radio room?" Willoughby asked him.

"How the bloody hell do I know?" Wallace said, stuffing the map back under his cap. "The room we're looking for is right around that corner."

"Resistance?" Van Dekker asked.

Wallace shrugged at him. "Expect anything. Kill. Don't hesitate." He held up the tip of his blade and nodded at them. "Understood?"

The south end of the corridor was only dimly lit. Several lightbulbs along the wall were out. Just around the corner, there was a wide double door on the left. It was closed, of course, and underneath, light spilled out of the threshold. Willoughby pressed his back against the wall opposite the door and squeezed the hilt of his blade. Van Dekker fell into place next to him. Wallace put his ear on the door, as if trying to hear what was on the opposite side.

Willoughby stood silent, anxiously tapping his fingers on his thigh. He didn't know what time it was, he just knew that he wanted to do what they'd come to do and get the hell out. A flush of anxiety began to set in. In front of him, Wallace dropped to the ground, pressed his face down on the floor, and peered under the door. Inside, shadows passed along the threshold, as if someone was pacing around. He squeezed the grip on his knife.

On the other side of the door, there were muffled sounds, like people talking and the light clicking of machinery. It struck Willoughby as suspicious that there weren't guards in the lower hallways. But it was the middle of the night, and in the buildings just above ground, there were potentially hundreds of German soldiers asleep. Behind that door, there could well be a dozen more.

Wallace straightened back up. He held up two fingers and grinned at Willoughby. Just as he did, the door in front of him opened inward, and a gray-clad German stood in the center of the doorway. His expression when he opened the door went from surprised to confused in the flash of an eye. The man looked right at Willoughby, then down at Wallace kneeling right in front of him.

"*Wer bist du?*" the man said in his native gibberish. He was middle-aged and wore an officer's uniform.

"Oh, Damn," Wallace muttered.

Willoughby's eyes went wide. Behind the German, he could see movement inside the room. The officer's face turned to panic when he realized the sight of three men in unmarked uniforms and face paint meant trouble. Without a thought, Willoughby charged forward just as the German tried to slam the door closed. He leaped right over Wallace and ran right into him, kicking past the door and driving him back toward the rear wall.

From his peripheral, he could see movement. With a quick glance to his right, he saw another man sitting behind a desk. The man's head spun around at Willoughby, and he launched up from his chair as if coming to the officer's aid. The last thing he caught was Van Dekker charging toward him before he turned back toward the officer.

He slammed the German in his grip against the wall and drove a knee between his legs in one fluid motion. By the time he realized he could've just driven his knife into the man, it was already too late. The German officer doubled forward, but drove his fist right into Willoughby's cheek. He grabbed the officer by the arm after he took the hit, swung him around toward the wall and drove the tip of his dagger right below the shoulder blade.

As he pinned the German to the wall with a drive of his blade, he spared a quick look across the room. Van Dekker had scooped the second German off his feet. The man still had a radio headset on when the larger South African got him. Van Dekker slammed him down hard on the thick wooden desk with a thud. Behind him, Wallace slid the door shut with a dull click.

Willoughby pulled his knife out of the German and then plunged it right back into him a second time. The tip drove right into the man's lung. The German officer let out a sharp cry with his last breath. Willoughby covered the dying man's mouth as he collapsed to the ground, then rushed toward the other fight, pinning the second man to the ground while Van Dekker choked the poor bastard to death. His large hands could clench the entire throat. It took seconds for the man to die, kicking as the last breath in his lungs left him.

"Bloody hell," Willoughby said.

He wiped his blade clean on the uniform of the dead radioman before looking around at the small room. The radio operator's eyes were bugged out, the headset he was wearing still squeaking out a high-pitched noise.

Willoughby just barely got the breath he'd been holding onto out when he froze in place. In the middle of the room, another door to a second room swung open. Standing in the center of the doorway was a tall, bulky German. He was hulking, with a fat face and an ugly broken nose in the center. His unbuttoned tunic flapped open.

"*Was ist los?*" the man said in a deep voice.

"Ah, fuck me," Willoughby said.

This German looked just as stunned as the officer had been when he'd opened the door to see three men not wearing German uniforms standing outside. But this man was twice his size. Willoughby charged again anyhow.

The fat German's eyes widened as Willoughby ran toward him, knife in hand. He rose his arm up just as Willoughby was about to run his knife into the man's torso and deflected the attack. With his thick arms, he pushed Willoughby away with almost no effort.

"*Alarm!*" the fat German hollered, but the sounds of his voice only echoed in the tiny two-room compartment.

Willoughby stumbled back when the German pushed him, but didn't waste a beat. He charged again, this time leaping off his feet, bringing his knife point down on him. He lightly stuck it in the German's arm, but the bigger got the best of him again. He grabbed Willoughby by the neck with his left hand and hit him in the cheek with the other. His bell rang with the first hit, and he barely registered the second one. After that, he lost his sight for a couple of seconds.

He caught only the briefest glimpse of the large man's ugly face and his broken nose. The next thing he saw clearly was another enormous fist burying itself right into the German's face. Then the German released his grip and Willoughby fell backward.

When his vision came back, he saw Van Dekker wrestling with the German. But even despite his size, the Nazi was a suit size larger, and he wasn't budging. The two hammered away at one another, but the ugly German could take a hit. And when he struck, Van Dekker went staggering back.

"Get the bastard!" Wallace said, leaping in toward the fight.

Between the two, they barely held the German at bay. Wallace had his knife in his hand, but he couldn't get any momentum. When he tried to stick the man, the German kept slapping his hand away.

"*Alarm!*" the German yelled again, his voice booming off the walls. The rooms were enclosed, and the door was shut, but within the walls, his voice bellowed.

Willoughby gripped his blade just as the German shoved Wallace to the floor. He got back on his feet and charged right toward the man, driving the tip of his blade right into the man's side. He cried out in pain, but his strength didn't leave him any. He swatted Willoughby aside like a bug, back handing him in the face.

"Jesus Christ," he said after hitting the floor once again. But this time, he shook it right off. Blood soaked right through the uniform where he'd stuck the man. With the last of his strength, Willoughby charged one more time. This time, he dodged a swing and plunged his dagger into the belly of the man, and pushed with all his strength along his gut.

"*Ahhh!*" the German screamed. His eyes bulged out as the dagger cut across his stomach. His grip released Van Dekker, and the South African covered the man's mouth with a hand as Willoughby cut him open. The German's arms flailed and flapped as his intestines spilled open. It only took three men and a couple of minutes to subdue him, but the giant dropped to his knees. He gave Willoughby one last, eerie look before collapsing forward in a pool of blood.

"Holy Christ," Wallace said. He'd been knocked down and was lying on top of the dead officer.

"You all right?" Willoughby asked him, and he nodded back. He helped Wallace back on his feet before popping his head into the next room, making sure there were no other surprises waiting. The room was empty. It was an office of some sort, with stacks of cabinet drawers.

"How the hell do we want to deal with this?" Van Dekker asked, looking down at the rubble. He was standing over the body of the enormous man they'd just killed, looking down at the three dead bodies and the blood pooling in the center of the room.

Willoughby just stood there, exhausted and out of breath. He'd expected some resistance, but he hadn't expected to be taken by surprise the way they had. That first German who'd opened the door had startled him, setting this whole thing in motion. He figured he'd have to kill, but didn't expect things to become...well, so messy. But it was going to have to be done anyhow. This wasn't going to be a bloodless operation.

"Better question is, how we deal with this?" Wallace asked.

Willoughby looked at him, following his gaze to the mess in the corner where the radio operator had been sitting. On the floor under the table where the radio had been sitting, the equipment had come down, shattering on the stone floor. The dead radioman's headset was still connected to the crackling radio.

"Must've tipped over when we scuffled," Van Dekker said, kneeling down to examine the ruined parts.

The radio was intact, but everything else was in pieces. Willoughby stepped over to the mess, pushing the pieces with the tip of his boot.

"Damn," he said. A small wooden box sat right in the middle of it. Smashed. He recognized it from the photos they'd been shown. He stooped down and poked at the mess, sorting through the dials and wires. The keys were intact, but the machinery in the back had broken on the hard floor, and half the parts had spilled out in pieces. "Bloody, God damn."

"Maybe we can …" Van Dekker began to say, but his words just trailed away.

Wallace squatted down beside Willoughby, and together, they sorted through the wreck that was their objective. Willoughby hoped against hope they might patch it together for the trip out. He tried to fit pieces together where they might have gone, but it was destroyed.

"Isn't that a bugger." He looked around and found a clock on the wall. "That's not good either." He gave Wallace an elbow. "Look." It was nearly 0330. Incredibly, it had been nearly an hour since they'd left the other shore.

"Well, that's just bloody fine, isn't it?" Wallace asked facetiously. He sighed heavily and tossed the pieces he'd been holding onto the wreck. "We need to get out of here. Now. They'll find this mess, and we'll be done before we get off the island."

Willoughby straightened back up. "Aye," he said. It was a miracle they hadn't been given away already. His mind raced. If this were a British garrison, the watch would change right about 0600, but the airstrike was well before then. *The airstrike.* Willoughby had forgotten about it.

His mind raced with a flurry of thoughts. He agreed with Wallace at heart. But that would do no good for the rest of the team. If the bomber missed the target or was shot down, eventually someone would discover these bodies, sound the alarm, and the jig would be up. The Germans weren't stupid, and it wouldn't take much for the occupiers to realize someone on the island had cooperated with the raid, forcing a crackdown. Maybe even civilian deaths.

No. That won't do. He looked at Van Dekker.

"Eh, what you got in your kit?"

"My kit?" He shrugged. "Other than the mock up box?"

"For explosives?" Willoughby said impatiently.

The South African shrugged again. "Enough composition to bring down the floor above. That was the plan."

"It's time for a new plan," Willoughby said. "You got anything that burns hot?"

"Hot? Yeah. Got some thermite."

"Will it burn hot enough to light up this room?"

"Hot enough to burn through that door," Van Dekker said. "And everything inside."

Willoughby looked at LC Wallace and grinned. "I've got a new plan."

CHAPTER THIRTEEN

Captain Gerhardt rubbed the bridge of his nose, fighting to push the away the sleepiness he was feeling. It was far too early in the morning for the nonsense Major Lentz and his companion seemed to be in the mood for. Far too early. After yesterday evening's lavish dinner, he'd assumed the two SS officers would be sleeping soundly in the quarters they'd requisitioned—a tiny cottage on the outskirts of Saint Peter Port. Apparently, he'd assumed incorrectly.

He'd barely gotten five hours of sleep when a messenger had arrived, knocking incessantly on his door. In the pre-dawn hours, Major Lentz had risen early, wishing to have a senior officer report to him so the SS official could make his inspection of the garrison's defense perimeter.

That the two SS officers had risen early enough to leave their own comfortable quarters and go halfway across Guernsey in order to rouse him from his sleep was inconvenient, to say the least. The two Reich Security inspectors had become the proverbial pains in the ass. All pleasantries aside.

He rubbed his temples, trying to push the fog of fatigue away. He'd had one too many glasses of French wine last night to be up this early.

A loud knocking came at his door again. His tunic flapped open as he stomped his boot on, then walked to the door.

"Sir!" The private in the doorway clicked his heels together as he came to attention.

Gerhardt held up a finger at the man. Biting his lower lip in aggravation, he buttoned himself up, then gave a quick glance in the mirror before putting on his cap and walking out of his room.

"Are our guests ready?" he asked the private, his driver.

"They're already in the courtyard, sir."

Gerhardt sighed. *Wonderful,* he thought. *Bad enough they should rouse me this early, but it would appear as if they're waiting on me.*

The SS had a very limited sense of humor to begin with. Field inspections such as this were even more serious. Before he stepped outside, he made sure his uniform was presentable. He didn't care for them anymore than any other *Wehrmacht* officer did, but he certainly wouldn't want his name on anyone's report for laxness either.

Lentz and Ofhoven were already sitting in the rear seat of the automobile when he left his quarters and walked across the courtyard. Lentz's gaze was straight ahead, but the junior Ofhoven gave him a disapproving look as he approached. He looked theatrically at his watch, then to Gerhardt.

"Good morning, gentlemen," Gerhardt said. Neither of them spoke. "I understand you wish to inspect the perimeter defenses?"

Major Lentz looked to him, giving only the most subtle of nods.

"Please, Captain." Ofhoven indicated to the driver's seat.

Gerhardt gazed at his watch. "It's rather early, isn't it? I thought, after your dinner last night—"

"We'd appreciate an inspection of the perimeter at this time, Captain." Ofhoven's voice was abrupt.

"Of course," he said dryly.

He circled the vehicle and got into the passenger seat, giving a curt nod to the driver. The driver put the car into gear and moved out moments later.

"We'd like to begin with the check-point positions to the north," Lentz told him. "Then take us out to Castle Cornet. That's where you have the Enigma, isn't it?"

"It is," Gerhardt said. He knew the major was fully aware of that.

He ordered the driver to head to the north side of the island. The car flew through the headquarters gate and down the dark road toward the coast.

"May I ask you what's of concern to you at the castle?" he asked.

There was a brief delay, and he could almost feel the SS major's eyes on the back of his head. The man had an unnerving disposition, but Gerhardt was well within his rights and duties to inquire about any security anxieties the inspectors might have.

"I'd just like to see the inside of the castle," Lentz said icily. "And, on the way, I'd like to bring Captain Hoff on the inspection."

Gerhardt, still half asleep, was tempted to ask him why, but refrained. He'd been given strict orders by the colonel to cooperate fully with Lentz. The two SS officers were scheduled to depart in only a matter of hours. After that, they'd be rid of the nuisance.

"Of course," he said. He gave that order to the driver as the car started off of the grounds and down the roadway ahead. The *Abwehr* officer was billeted not far away. The man had his own duties to perform, and had mostly been apart from the two SS officials. Though he too was scheduled to depart on the same ferry as Lentz and Ofhoven. No doubt, the SS major would be peppering the man with inquiries of all sorts on the trip back to Cherbourg. "Whatever you need, Major," he said. "Whatever you need."

* * *

Willoughby stood watch at the end of the long corridor. Steps away, in the radio room, Van Dekker was at work. The old mine worker was a master of his craft, methodically prepping the bricks of explosives he'd dragged with him across the water. At the opposite end of the corridor, orange light bulbs flickered, and now and then he could see bright lights from rooms where soldiers were coming and going out of near the stairway. But they were a good five hundred feet away, and nobody had yet come down toward them.

Frankly, given the importance of what was within this room, he'd thought this part of the castle would have been better protected. It seemed all that was down at this end were storage rooms and empty corridor.

Lance Corporal Wallace had sifted through the knocked over wreck that had been the code machine. The contents of the tiny wooden box had been destroyed when the radio operator had pulled it to the ground with him. After finding nothing of value, he'd begun to search the drawers and cabinets within.

Willoughby peeked around the corner, unconsciously tapping away with his finger on the side of his leg as the seconds ticked by. It had only been a few minutes since they'd stormed the room, killing the occupants, and blowing the objective of the mission in the process. From time to time, he couldn't help but glance at the shattered remains on the floor, next to the pool of blood.

Inside, Wallace finished fishing through the cabinets and stepped out of the room into the hallway.

"Anything?" he asked.

Willoughby shook his head. "They're down there, though."

He gazed around the empty halls that ran underneath the castle. That there were dozens, maybe even a couple hundred, German troops billeted just feet above him was unnerving. Right now, he really wanted nothing more than to get out and be on their way. Though Captain Zahlman wouldn't be pleased about the code machine, there was nothing to be done about that now.

"I found this," Wallace said, showing him a brown leather-backed book. "It's the code book." He tucked it away into his breast pocket. "I think."

"Make sure you give that to him," Willoughby said. Van Dekker was the one with the waterproof kit.

"I hope this idea of yours works."

Willoughby nodded. "It better. By the way, did you notice something about that German there?" He nodded back to the center of the room and the large, bulky dead man that took the three of them to subdue.

Wallace looked at the corpse, then shook his head. The dead man's eyes were wide open, and it was as though he was staring right at them. A pool of dark blood had spread out from underneath it.

"What about him?"

"Notice the uniform? He's a sergeant," Willoughby said, but he could see Wallace didn't understand. "He's fat, ugly, and—"

"And he's got a broken nose," Wallace finished for him, finally understanding. "Well, that French girl asked us to kill him if we saw him."

"For her sake, I hope that's the bastard."

"I'm tempted to just make a run for it," Wallace said. Willoughby's eyes narrowed at him. "The mission's blown, anyway."

"The mission might be blown, but we've got something to bring back. That code book must be of some use to someone. Those men in there died by our hand. If, by some miracle, the bombers can't hit the castle, we can't let anyone find those bodies intact or they'll know we were here."

"What difference does that make now?"

Willoughby grimaced and made a face. "I don't know. An hour from now, this place will be a pile of rumble if the bombers do their job. But what if they can't? All it takes is for one plane to get shot down." He shrugged to Van Dekker, still putting together explosive charges. "He came along for just such a purpose. So, that's what we do. The incendiary will torch the radio room, and the charges bring down the castle on top of it all."

Wallace listened and nodded. "Making it look like the bombers hit their target, no matter what."

"Which was the plan, anyway."

"We've still got to across that damn chain again and get off the island. The odds are against us."

Willoughby found himself chuckling lightly. "That was always the case."

Van Dekker came over to the doorway holding plastique bricks in his hand. "I've got the charges primed. The incendiary will go off inside this room. I've got to place these where they'll bring the ceiling down."

"Should you be walking around with those like that?" Wallace asked, looking at the devices in his hands.

Van Dekker grinned. "Useless without the detonator. I'll set them in place."

"How long do you need?" Wallace asked him.

"Only a few minutes. I need to time it precisely."

"And they'll go off at the same time?" Willoughby asked him.

"I'm setting the incendiary for a shorter time. The door should contain most of the blast. These'll go off shortly after that. I'll set the delay switches for an hour."

"Cutting it close," Willoughby said. "We need to be back on the other shore and be gone before they go off."

"Well then, we need to get moving," Van Dekker said. "I've got four charges to set."

"Get on with it then," Wallace told him. "I want to be out of here as quick as possible." Van Dekker nodded and went down to the end of the empty corridor with his charges. Wallace looked back at Willoughby and pointed at his head. "You're hurt."

Willoughby wiped his temple, and for the first time, felt blood trickling down his face. There was a throbbing pain in his head where the German sergeant had clocked him. He hadn't realized until now just how hard he'd been hit. Suddenly, he felt the adrenaline in his system begin to subside, and it was all starting to hit him.

"I'll be all right. Let's just get this done with and be on our way." He peeked around the corner again at the distant end of the hallway and counted the seconds off in his mind. It was getting close to 0400. Every minute they were still inside was just another opportunity to be captured, and in doing so, get their comrades captured as well. If they hadn't been captured already.

No, no, he said to himself. If they'd been captured, an alarm would've sounded, and the entire garrison would have already moved to secure the castle. It was just a matter of time now. He looked down at Van Dekker and waited.

* * *

Captain Gerhardt stood quietly by with his hands clasped behind his back, standing near the car that had brought them out to the northern shore of the island. His eyes still felt groggy from either the wine or the lack of sleep. Or perhaps both. Several paces away, the two SS officers were speaking with the local check-point sergeant about the proper identification techniques for authorizing travel for the local inhabitants.

The north end of the island was silent in the early morning darkness. Except for the sound of waves beating against the rocks and the car engine humming in the background, there was nothing. Not even the birds were chirping just yet. He looked at his wristwatch. It was just now 0400, and he was fighting to stay alert. He yawned silently, and his eyelids began to feel heavy. A warm cup of coffee would have gone a long way toward waking him up, but he'd been roused right from his bed and into this ridiculous inspection tour.

The sound of another vehicle approaching cut through the morning air. The slits of its headlights weaved along the dark road from the southwest. He watched as it drew closer and two occupants became clear. The driver and the passenger. Captain Hoff barely waited for the car to come to a complete stop before leaping out the door.

The *Abwehr* officer had been apart from the SS during this most uncomfortable inspection that had been going on for far too long. Gerhardt couldn't help but think it was deliberate on Hoff's part. Nobody enjoyed being in their presence if they could help it. Instead, Hoff had been conducting *actual* duties related to his position and had been billeted apart from them.

"Good morning, Captain," Gerhardt said. A fist hid another silent yawn.

"Good morning. Hope you slept well." Captain Hoff approached with a briefcase clenched in his hand.

Gerhardt only grunted. Bed was the first place he'd rather be right now. He spared a quick glance down the walking track at the shadowy figures speaking under the glimmer of the automobile lights.

"I imagine you're ready to depart this morning?" he asked Hoff, indicating his briefcase.

"Yes. I'll be back on the ferry." He looked at the two SS officers. "I'm sure you'll be glad to see them off." Gerhardt countered him with an inquisitive look, but said nothing. Hoff shrugged. "No one enjoys the company of Reich Security, Captain. Myself included."

"Well… hopefully, this'll be the last inspection for quite some time," Gerhardt said, putting an emphasis on the word inspection. "Did you complete your own reviews?"

"I did. My findings were positive ones. Some minor updates to the daily routines, but I trust the men under your command, Captain."

"Ah, Hoff. There you are." Lentz and Ofhoven came walking back to the running automobiles. "Hope you're ready for one last inspection tour before we depart."

"Quite ready, Major."

"I'm satisfied the local population is under control," Lentz said. "But I have some lingering concerns. Espionage, for one. The code machine is on the eastern side of the island at the citadel. Saint Peter Port is the largest settlement, and that fortress would be the first target for covert observation. How many soldiers do you have at Castle Cornet, Captain?"

"Well, there's a company of men billeted in the barracks there. Another hundred are housed in the town. With support and administrative personnel, perhaps half a battalion on any given day. That doesn't include—"

"Very well," Lentz said sharply. "I'd like to do an unscheduled inspection of the grounds. Please arrange for the post commander to meet us."

"An inspection drill at this hour?" Gerhardt asked him. Lentz gave him a sour look and let the question go unanswered.

"You can take me there at once, Captain. Captains Ofhoven and Hoff can continue along the perimeter inspection without me." He gave his SS colleague and the *Abwehr* officer a curt nod and then started toward the humming car. "The ferry leaves at ten-hundred. I'd like to get moving." He jumped into the rear of the car and shut the door behind him.

Gerhardt muffled an annoyed huff. He was looking forward to getting back to headquarters and having his morning meal. Or, to at least seeing the irritating SS major off with his colleague. The thought of spending hours with the man made his stomach twist in knots.

"Uh, Major," Hoff said, stepping toward the car. "My assignment here is done. I have nothing further to do. Surely Captain Ofhoven doesn't need me to keep him company."

Lentz probed the bottom of his lip with his tongue. His face was bland, but his eyes were as piercing as they'd become infamous for.

"Very well. The ferry leaves in a matter of hours." His head turned this way and that. "You can certainly walk back to the dock from here if you wish. I don't see any other car available for you to use."

Hoff was silent for a moment. Finally, and reluctantly, he nodded at Lentz, then he rolled his eyes over to Gerhardt.

"It seems I'll be keeping the captain some company," he said. "Can you please ensure my personal belongings are taken to the ferry, Captain?"

Gerhardt nodded. He empathized with the other man, but he didn't feel too badly. Ofhoven was the lesser of the two intruding personalities. He'd be spending the rest of his morning with Lentz.

"I'll have the sergeant phone the post commander to expect us," Gerhardt said. "Gentlemen, your driver will take you along the northern road, where you can finish your inspection business. Excuse me."

By the time he'd returned from the duty sergeant's post, Ofhoven and Hoff had left in a separate car to continue along the northern route. Gerhardt climbed into the rear seat next to the major and had the driver take them out to Castle Cornet.

Saint peter Port was quiet as they drove through; only a few lights were on in town. A few soldiers were here and there on the vacant streets. Even a quiet backwater like Guernsey still required a patrol. A show of the flag with the locals to keep them in line.

The car rolled to a stop in front of the main gate check-point at the end of the causeway bridge. A guard stepped out from the tiny hut and in front of the driver's side door. The light above the check-point illuminated the rear of the open-topped car. The guard spoke to the driver for a moment, and then looked at Gerhardt in the rear, and then briefly at Major Lentz. Enlisted men in the *Wehrmacht* kept a fair distance from the SS in all things. The guard's eyes barely rolled over the major's black uniform and swastika armband before stepping away and waving the car through.

"Open the gate!" he hollered at a second soldier.

Gerhardt returned the guard's salute as the car pulled ahead, and the gate went back down behind them. The stone walls of Castle Cornet sat at the opposite end of the causeway road. There were only a handful of men out this early. A few on the causeway, and a few more at the entrance of the castle.

The roofs of the taller buildings and structures rose above the castle walls. A tall antennae array stood atop the southern end of the castle and rose a hundred feet in the air. As the car drew nearer, Captain Gerhardt could see guards pacing along the walls above.

Next to him, Major Lentz was as silent as the grave. Which was fine, of course. The less the man said to him, the better. When the car came to a squeaking stop, Lentz flung open the door and leaped out. Gerhardt adjusted his hat and went after him. The SS major's quick stride took him by surprise so early in the morning. He had yet to eat his breakfast, and didn't have the energy to go chasing the man around.

His eyes moved around the harbor and the boats swinging silently in the distance. The very first beams of light still had yet to peek over the eastern horizon. Birds were only now beginning to stir in the early hours. The guard at the entrance straightened up as he saw the two approaching him. Behind him, the door swung open, and another officer stepped out of the castle, flanked by a sergeant of the guard. The young officer came to a quick attention and fumbled a salute. "*Heil Hitler,*" he said.

"What's your name?" Lentz asked the young lieutenant hastily.

"Lieutenant Auerbach," the officer said. "Sir."

"You're in charge?"

"He's the officer of the watch," Gerhardt told him. "Captain König is the post commander. He's in hospital."

Lentz grumbled.

"Is the garrison assembled?" Gerhardt asked Auerbach.

"I was just about to call for assembly, sir."

"You haven't done so yet?" Lentz said angrily.

"No, sir."

Major Lentz pushed past the young lieutenant and into the door through the castle wall. A wide, open courtyard was just beyond. Double story buildings were built right in the center, and rose above the castle walls. To the right, a line of administrative offices graced an open-air corridor.

"I want the alarm raised, immediately!" Lentz's voice echoed out of the hallway as he went inside.

"Hold on one minute, Major." Gerhardt chased after him. The lieutenant and sergeant followed closely behind him. Lentz kept walking. "Major!"

Inside the corridor, Lentz came to a sudden halt and turned toward him. Gerhardt casually came to a stop and looked him in the eye. He'd been under orders from Colonel Hoth to give the man whatever professional courtesy required, but those orders came down through a strict chain of command. Even Lentz had to obey a structure. And right now, the man was stepping out of line by shouting commands the way he was.

"I want the company assembled immediately, Captain," Lentz said. His voice was commanding and cold, but restrained.

"Major Lentz, I've shown you every courtesy protocol demands. But right now, *sir,*"—he emphasized the word—"you are outside the chain of command."

Lentz gave him a cold stare and Gerhardt could have sworn he saw a tiny glint of annoyance in his face. The other man made a twitching move, and for a moment, Gerhardt thought he was going to make a verbal objection. After a moment, it faded away.

"My apologies, Captain." That was all Lentz said, but his stare was unchanging.

"Lieutenant," was all Captain Gerhardt needed to say.

"Yes, sir." Auerbach nodded to the sergeant, who set off down the corridor and into a side office.

"I'll have a word with you after this drill, Lieutenant," Gerhardt told him sternly.

Auerbach should have assembled the castle garrison as soon as he'd gotten the call earlier. That alone would earn him a verbal warning, but he'd be damned if he'd let Lentz unleash his fury on the man. Auerbach was *Wehrmacht*, and that made him Gerhardt's responsibility to deal with.

Half a minute later, the inside castle grounds echoed with the winding sound of a siren. Lights inside the barracks began to snap on, and across the courtyard, he could hear the shouts of men and the stomping of boots down the wooden steps from above.

CHAPTER FOURTEEN

Major Lentz strode down the narrow corridor of the upper castle with a purpose. Within the castle walls, the alarm blared. In the courtyard to his left, under the bright lights of the interior, soldiers were assembling in the center. In front of him, staff NCOs and guards saw his approach and stepped carefully out of his way. None of them met his gaze; they just stared straight ahead. The young lieutenant and sergeant behind him struggled to keep up with his long stride.

Lentz didn't care. His job was to ensure the full security of the Reich, and he expected full cooperation. More than that, though, he took some pleasure in seeing the *Wehrmacht* jump through hoops in order to see that obligation through.

"Sir!" the guard outside the main entrance to the lower levels said. His heels snapped together at Lentz's approach.

Auerbach jumped to his side. "Open the door," Lentz said.

The guard swung the thick metal door open as the three men approached.

Lentz glanced at his watch. It was just now 0445. He barely looked at the guard as he blew past him. Just inside the door, a hallway stretched down the western length of the fort, and a dozen side doors pocketed the entire length. Inside, staff walked in and out of the small offices and rooms housed on the main level.

It was the end of watch, and by the look on the faces of the men inside, he could see the last thing they'd expected was the sight of the Reich Security inspector. A staff officer stepped out of the first office door, straightened his tunic, and stepped forward. He was another young lieutenant, barely of shaving age.

"Sir!" He gave the proper Nazi salute for addressing an SS official.

"This is Lieutenant Hahn, sir," Auerbach told him. "He's a senior communications officer for the night watch."

Lentz looked the man down before giving a nod. The lieutenant stood at ease. "Good," he said sharply. "You're in charge of all things communications, then?"

Hahn looked at Auerbach, then back at Lentz, and gulped visibly. "Yes, sir."

"Fine. You keep a full log of all communications from Rouen? Coded and non?"

"Yes, sir."

Lentz ran a finger across his forehead, wiping away strands of hair. "Good. I want to see your logbook for the last thirty days. I assume all parties with access to the Enigma are required to sign it?"

"Yes, sir," Hahn said. "Both at the beginning of their shift and the end." He looked nervously at Auerbach. "Have we done something wrong, sir?" Lentz could hear the trepidation in the young man's voice.

"No—" Auerbach said.

"That's what I'm here to determine," Lentz said, giving the lieutenant a disapproving look. Junior officers were easily intimidated by Reich Security. "Your logbook. Now!"

"Sir," Hahn said. He stepped back into the office, reemerging a few moments later with a brown leather book. He flipped through the pages and opened the ledger for Lentz.

Lentz grabbed the ledger and thumbed through the pages, carefully reading the last thirty days' worth of entries. It seemed good and proper. Only a handful of people had access to the code machine. Their names were listed in order of rank on each page.

"And everyone signs in and out?"

"Yes, sir. Every day," Hahn said. "That's protocol."

Lentz hid a slight nod. "And it appears you've followed protocol to the letter, Lieutenant." He handed the ledger back to him. "I commend your attentiveness. Now, I'd like to see the code room, please." He looked around the doors on the main level.

"This way, sir," Hahn said. The four began down the hallway. "It's this way, Major." He indicated to a side door, inside which was a descending staircase.

"Downstairs?" Lentz's eyes narrowed.

"We keep the Enigma in the lower level," Hahn told him.

"Why not on the upper level?" Lentz asked. "Doesn't Army protocol require such things to be placed under the direct supervision of the communications officers?"

Hahn gulped again.

"Necessity forced our hand, Major," Auerbach said. "We're still under strength. The upper floor is for administrative use. The room we keep the Enigma machine in is located just beneath the main radio tower. Once we repair the damage the British did before pulling out, we plan to move it."

Lentz recalled the discussion he'd had with Colonel Hoth the evening before about such a thing.

"I assure you, sir, previous Reich Security inspectors—as well as the head-quarters at Rouen—were made aware of the situation, and they all signed off on it."

Lentz grimaced slightly. He knew there had been previous SS inspections on Guernsey before. If they'd known about the variance of protocol, he wasn't about to go making a splash with Berlin about it.

"Very well." Lentz grimaced to Hahn. "Take me down."

Hahn unlocked the door and swung it open for Lentz to go first. Down a flight of thick stone stairs, he exited out into a hallway beneath the main floor. At the bottom of the stairs, there was another office. The door was open, and inside were two enlisted men. Both stood and came to attention at the sight of the officers.

"Just more administrative offices, sir," Hahn told him. "The Enigma room is at the southernmost end of the castle."

"These men have access?" Lentz asked.

"Yes, sir," replied Hahn.

"Were you men made aware of the drill going on?" Lentz asked them.

"Yes, sir," they said together.

"Who's in charge down here?"

"Officers change with the watch, sir," Auerbach said. "Sergeant Bühler is the ranking NCO. In fact, his quarters are down in these hallways. Near the code room."

"I see. Where is Sergeant Bühler now?" Auerbach and Hahn both shrugged.

"Would it be common for your ranking NCO to be absent for such a drill?" Lentz asked nobody in particular, but his gaze ultimately fell on the two junior lieutenants.

"He may be asleep still. It is early, sir," Hahn said.

Lentz gave him an unsympathetic look. "Asleep?" he said in a low breath.

"Buzz Sergeant Bühler," Auerbach told the two enlisted men without a moment's hesitation. "Make sure he's awake and have him meet us in the code room."

Lentz continued with his displeased look, shaking his head enough to let the two know of his displeasure. He blinked absently and gave the signal for them to move on down the corridor toward the south end.

* * *

Captain Gerhardt watched from the north end of the courtyard as the last soldier fell into place. Inside the fortress walls, the wailing of the alert siren was still blaring. He let it continue for another minute or two before he finally gave the order to have it cut off. The wailing fell silent a minute later. By then, the entire town of Saint Peter Port must have been wide awake.

In the courtyard, two full companies were assembled in squares. Their NCOs stood rigidly in front of either formation. From the offices that lined the walls, staff and officers gazed over at the assembly. He could see on their faces they didn't know exactly what to make of it. On top of the walls, guards kept watch to the east and the west. No doubt, all of them had seen his arrival with Lentz. The SS major's visit to the island was common knowledge, and everyone had reason to fear the man. An unscheduled inspection at this time of the morning would put everyone on edge.

A warm breeze swept through the courtyard. The men stood silently. He knew he was going to have to do something eventually. It wouldn't do for the men to see a senior officer just standing around, not doing anything after calling for assembly. It invited rumor and gossip. Besides that, it was unprofessional and bad for morale.

From out of the barracks, a tall, muscular man stepped forward. He crossed the courtyard, stopping in front of Gerhardt, and came to attention before snapping away a salute. He wore the insignia of a senior sergeant.

Gerhardt returned his salute.

"Companies are formed and ready, sir," the tall, blond sergeant said.

"Very well, Sergeant. Keep your men at attention." He scanned the courtyard for a sign of the SS major. He just wanted to get this thing over and done with so he could finally get some breakfast in his belly.

"Is this a drill, sir, or are we in some sort of trouble?"

Gerhardt gave him a curious look, but ultimately couldn't honestly say one way or another. His cheek protruded from where he pressed it with his tongue. He looked at the assembled companies and the guards on the wall.

"Just keep them at attention, Sergeant," he finally said. "I'll be back."

"Sir!" The sergeant saluted, and the captain returned it again before turning and marching off toward the offices within the walls. His patience was wearing thin. Inspection or not, there was no need for any of this ridiculousness. He'd be speaking with Colonel Hoth concerning this before the end of the day.

He walked into the passageway that housed the main administrative offices at the fortress.

"Where is Major Lentz and Lieutenant Auerbach?" he asked the guard outside the main entrance.

"Sir, the major and lieutenant went downstairs."

"Downstairs?"

"Yes, sir. I believe it was the major's intention to survey the Enigma room."

Gerhardt didn't want to go down into the bowels of the castle. He was chief of staff for Colonel Hoth. He didn't go chasing after SS officers unless told to by the commanding officer. More than that, he didn't wish to spend more time around the man than what was necessary. But he didn't like the idea of a junior lieutenant being around him either, if he could help it.

"Damn it," he muttered under his breath. He relented and told the guard, "Open the door."

The guard put his hand on the door to open it up.

"Sir!" a voice called down the hallway. From the line of offices, an enlisted man came, double-timing it toward him. "Excuse me, sir."

"What is it?" Gerhardt asked, as the man came to a stop in front of him.

"I'm sorry, sir. I didn't know who to give this to," he said. "Lieutenant Auerbach isn't anywhere to be found."

"He's downstairs with Major Lentz. What is it, Private?"

"I beg pardon, sir. We just got a communique from headquarters. I thought the lieutenant would want to know about it."

"Lieutenant Auerbach is busy right now. Is it important?"

"Yes, sir."

"Well, spit it out, man!"

"An observation post on the north side of the island reported a large plane passing overhead."

Gerhardt's eyes narrowed to a slit, and his forehead creased in confusion. "What? A plane? When did this come in?"

"Just now, sir. We had nothing scheduled for today. That's why I thought—"

"From the north?" Gerhardt cut him off. "This came from Colonel Hoth's HQ?"

"Yes, sir."

Gerhardt rubbed his lip. "Did they give a description of the plane?"

"Just a large plane, sir."

Headquarters wouldn't have reported such a thing, unless... "Can't be possible," he whispered. "Did you notify anti-aircraft positions in the vicinity?"

"No, sir," the private said. "I thought I should—"

"Alert the local area batteries. Now! Then let Colonel Hoth's headquarters know we're going on full alert. Go!" The private took off back down the corridor.

Gerhardt waved the guard away. Instead, he strode down the corridor behind the messenger. He peeked his head inside the second office on the right. Inside, another private was just pouring himself a cup of coffee. Gerhardt saw the piping brew and heard his stomach grumble. The private inside saw him and came to attention.

"Sir?"

"Sound the air-raid siren!"

The private looked at him, confused. "Sir?"

"The alarm, you fool! Sound it now!"

"But, I just—" the private began to say, but fell immediately silent.

"Sound the damn alarm!" Gerhardt hollered so loud that everyone within the sound of his voice down the corridor looked to see.

"Yes, sir!" The man put his coffee cup down and followed his orders.

He stepped back into the open corridor and stared down at the faces, looking back at him. "Get to your posts!" A moment later, the siren started up again, but it was different. It was a more piercing wail than the first alarm had been. And everyone present knew the difference. "Go! We have a possible air raid incoming!"

* * *

"Where are his quarters at?" Lentz asked.

"Uh, I believe they're up on the right, sir," Hahn said. "Toward the end of the hall."

Lentz, flanked by Hahn, Auerbach, and the sergeant who'd followed them into the lower levels, walked to the end of the main corridor. The stone walls were bland and cold. A string of lights ran along the top of the hallway. A hundred yards down, the corridor ended and turned left.

"I'm sure Sergeant Bühler was simply up late last night, sir," Hahn said.

Lentz ignored the comment. Up late or not, a drill alarm had gone off. Someone upstairs must've canceled it, as he noticed the wailing had ended and the echoing had ceased. When he returned upstairs, he expected to see the entire castle garrison assembled.

"Does nobody come down here?" he asked either lieutenant. "Why are these rooms locked from the outside?"

"Only select personnel need to come down here, sir," Auerbach said. "Many of these rooms are used for storage only. Some are used to billet personnel. We lock all doors down here."

"Well, at least you're smart enough—" Lentz stopped himself and came to an abrupt halt in the middle of the long corridor.

"Is there a problem, sir?" Auerbach asked.

"What's this?" Lentz asked. He pointed down at the floor.

Auerbach stepped closer to him. "Sir?"

"Do you have eyes, Lieutenant?" he asked him angrily. "It's wet. Why is the floor wet?"

Auerbach looked down and shrugged. "These tunnels are connected to the storm system. Water sometimes comes down from the upper level, then runs into the storm drain beneath the castle."

Lentz looked at the water and traced it all the way to the end of the corridor. He was dead silent for several long seconds. Behind him, and to his right, the corridor turned down a sub-hallway. He turned and watched the tiny wet spots disappear behind the corner.

"Storm drain?" he asked innocently. He turned and looked at Auerbach. His eyes didn't blink. The young lieutenant's face turned slightly flush as Lentz gazed into his eyes.

"Yes, sir," he said nervously.

"Lieutenant, I've been on this island for a week now. Have you seen any rain in that time?" His voice was condescending.

Auerbach's throat swelled, and he shook his head. "No, sir. I haven't."

"Then where did it come from?"

"I... I don't know, Major. I'm sorry—"

"Follow me!" he told his escort sharply. They walked down the corridor a bit more. "Wake this Sergeant Bühler up. I want him—"

Before Major Lentz could finish his sentence, the end of the hallway instantly turned a bright red. In a second's worth of time, a blast of intensely hot air moved down the hallway, washing right over the group, stealing the breath right out of his lungs. His skin tingled, and his eyes went blind for a moment. He turned his head away from the heat. There was a brilliant flash of explosive light around them, and at once, the entire group fell to the ground.

A ball of fiery flame passed right overhead, petering out halfway down the corridor. He heard someone cry out in pain. Lentz gasped to get oxygen back into his lungs, and it burned slightly as he felt those lungs fill up again with air. His face tingled with pain from the heat. The explosion evaporated after a few moments, but he froze in place, in shock.

As he lay there on the floor, staring up at the ceiling, he could hear the faint sound of an alarm going off above them. It took him a minute to recognize it as an air-raid siren. Just as it registered with him, another detonation went off. From down the corridor, a second boom exploded. It was a duller sound, and the entire castle seemed to shake under his body. It was followed by a second and a third. The last of them was the most powerful.

What came after was like the creaking an old house made, but it was far, far worse. Lentz lifted his head off the floor just enough to see the other end of the corridor collapse. The ceiling came crashing down, knocking out the lights along with it.

"Get out!" someone hollered over the sound of the crashing.

Lentz twisted his head just enough to see the sergeant and two lieutenants behind him push themselves up and back away from the ceiling as it came down above them.

"Wait!" he yelled.

There was another loud boom from the heavy stone and planks of wood coming down. His body became blanketed in dirt. He tried to push himself up, and could even feel hands wrap themselves around his arms, but they let go almost immediately. The last thing he saw was the sight of the others escaping back down the hall before the wooden beams above him collapsed.

The two companies in the courtyard broke almost immediately after the siren began. A flurry of orders were shouted by the NCOs, and the men went scrambling. Most probably felt this was yet another drill put on by an overly ambitious officer. The men standing guard on the ramparts took no action at all.

From the alcove of administrative offices, Captain Gerhardt could see the lack of response from some men walking the corridors. It was still early, and the last hour had been a series of contradicting orders and actions. He blamed Auerbach for not being prepared, and he'd be setting his subordinate straight about that.

"Do you hear that?" he shouted at the men casually strolling about the grounds. Some faces turned his way in blank expressions. "Air raid! This is no drill!"

His voice echoed across the open yard. Those who heard him jumped without another warning. He strode through the upper corridor, repeating his commands. They were far too slow moving to their posts, and he kicked himself for the delay. If that fool Lentz hadn't insisted on some idiotic breach of protocol, they might not be in this situation.

"Get those idiots to their posts!" he yelled at a sergeant standing near the main entrance.

Outside the main entrance, the causeway was alive with activity. Men were only now moving to their assigned posts. The air-raid siren was blaring as loud as could be. It was only now, as orders were relayed from NCO to NCO, that the full garrison was moving. On the other end of the bridge, lights in Saint Peter Port were snapping on as the siren whined and curious civilians looked outside to see what the commotion was. They were only on for a couple of minutes before the main power station shut them off again.

Blackout conditions applied during air raids; the island's power station had strict orders to disconnect under such circumstances. Only the spotlights of the anti-aircraft batteries would remain on, powered by generators. To the north of the harbor, those spotlights flicked on as each battery became fully manned.

At least someone was alert and doing their jobs, he thought.

He mentally counted off the minutes it had taken them to get to battle positions.

"Sir!" a voice shouted. Gerhardt turned to see the senior sergeant approach him from inside the fortress walls. "To the north!"

He turned to look, just in time to see a torrent of green-blue bolts stream skyward. A single battery had opened fire on the north of the island, followed by a second a moment later. To the northwest, there was a distant flash of light, then the crackle of heavy anti-aircraft fire reverberated across the air.

There was a thud. It came from the west, toward Colonel Hoth's headquarters. *A bomb.* The sound was over and gone with before he knew it. A second bomb resounded, this one much, much closer. The ground shook under his feet as if the explosion had gone off nearby.

There was a sudden, thunderous crash that rose straight up from the ground. He scanned the sky momentarily, looking for a plane overhead, but didn't see a thing. The ground shaking ended almost immediately, but it left him guessing.

"What the hell?" Gerhardt caught himself before he fell over. He looked around for an explosion, but didn't see one.

Across the harbor, another battery opened up. The gun flashed as each shell fired from the end of the barrel. The bolts were shot at a low angle, as if shooting at something coming in low. Something in the distance flashed in the air. A fire seemed to streak across the sky, but it wasn't moving along the horizon. It was coming straight at him.

"Take cover!" the senior sergeant hollered.

Gerhardt ran for a wall of sandbags at the very end of the causeway. To his left, a ball of fire was bearing straight in toward the fort. To his right, a plume of dust rose above the walls. He barely gave it a moment's thought before diving behind the sandbags. He turned his head up just as the plane made a low approach. The AA guns ceased their fire as it got low to the ground. Rifles fired away at it as it streaked down toward them. It was definitely a bomber. A light one, by the look of it; only two engines—one of which had fire breathing out of it.

Instinctively, he gripped his sidearm. But it was pointless, so he let it go. The plane flew directly above the harbor, where the ferry Lentz and Ofhoven were going to use to return to the French coast with only hours from now, still swung. The nose leveled out, and its bomb doors opened.

A single bomb fell from its belly, striking the ferry. It went up in a bright fireball. In an instant, a second bomb fell into an empty harbor and exploded. He saw the distinguished roundel of the RAF on the bottom of its wings as it flew overhead. Two more bombs fell out, descending into the center of the castle. His heart paused as he watched. Then the explosions came.

They were so close that they were absolutely deafening when they went off. Fire rose from inside the walls, sending a deep shock through the ground. The bomber disappeared from sight after that, and the only thing he heard were the cries of men.

CHAPTER FIFTEEN

Willoughby's legs wobbled under him as he emerged out of the water and onto the sandy beach. His wet uniform picked up flecks of sand as he kicked his feet. After reaching halfway, his knees gave out from under him and he bent down to the ground, struggling to regain his breath. Van Dekker was right ahead of him. The hefty South African was still moving, despite having just pulled himself across the bay for a second time. Wallace was coming up last, and looked just as exhausted as Willoughby felt.

His eyes glanced around at the darkened beach. Across the bay behind them, the echo of the alarm had died away. He hadn't even noticed when. But now, there was nothing but silence.

"Keep moving," Wallace told him from behind.

He put one foot under him, then the other, and lifted himself back. Ahead, the sand rose sharply and leveled out into a grassy knoll covered by trees. He looked down the length of the shore as far as he could see, but saw no movement. He'd half expected to see men rushing down to assist them, but there was no one.

Van Dekker was the first to get to the dune and staggered up the bank. Willoughby moved slowly behind him, watching to either side. To the north, beyond the trees, the lights of the town were glowing softly. Across the bay, the castle was still lit up.

"Where the hell...?" Van Dekker asked softly. He was standing atop the shallow knoll, looking around.

Willoughby pushed himself up through the sand until he got to the top, next to him. He looked around, saw no one, and his heart instantly began to beat like a drum.

"What are you two doing?" Wallace asked as he reached the dune and started up.

"There's no one," Willoughby said softly. He looked through the trees and saw that there was nobody hiding there.

Wallace crept up to meet them, and the three of them stood there for several long seconds, looking around.

"Where the hell did everyone go?" Willoughby asked.

"Must've been the alarm that scared them off," Van Dekker said.

"Can't be." Wallace stepped forward. "Zahlman wouldn't..."

The trees rustled with a gentle breeze, and the tide slashed against the shore behind them. Other than that, there was no movement that he could see.

"We can't stay here," Van Dekker said.

Willoughby nodded. He gave Wallace a gentle nudge, and the three moved toward the trees that blocked the roadway.

"Wait!" Wallace said, pulling Willoughby by the wet uniform. "Look."

Across the road to the west, three dark figures emerged from the shadows. Rifles were leveled at them as they approached. Willoughby felt the energy drain out of him as he saw them moving at them, covering them as they drew closer. A part of him felt a strange sense of relief at it. If he was going to be captured, then that would be the end of his bit of the war.

"Damn," he whispered. The three of them raised their hands as the riflemen approached.

"About damn time," one of the dark figures said. In English.

"Ah. Thank God," Wallace muttered.

Claymoore's face became recognizable, and the three lowered their rifles. Willoughby's exhausted arms fell to his side, and he let out an audible sigh of relief. Behind Claymoore were Mansfield and Darjan. The two were lugging the gear the three of them had left behind.

"It's about God-damned time you three showed up," Claymoore said harshly. He looked Willoughby and Van Dekker up and down. "We thought for sure you'd been captured. We heard an alarm go off."

"We nearly were, sir," Wallace told him. "The Jerries had us cut off for a bit. Took us some fancy legwork to get out of there. And it wasn't pretty, sir. Not pretty at all."

Mansfield gave Willoughby his rifle and Bergen sack. Willoughby felt the exhausted muscles in his back contract when he took the sack and put it around his shoulders. If he lived through this night, he was going to be sore in the morning.

"So," Claymoore said, looking at each one, "you've got it?"

Willoughby tightened the strap of his sack, then put on a painful face. All three of them were silent for a moment.

"No, sir," Wallace told him. Through the face paint, Willoughby could see Claymoore's expression instantly turn sour.

"What did you say?" Claymoore stepped close to Wallace and Willoughby. "What do you mean, you don't have it?"

"We got in, sir, and,"—Willoughby looked into his eyes and gave him the truth—"we lost it. There was a scuffle, and, well…"

Claymoore's expression became frozen, like a marble statue. His mouth hung open, and the grip on his rifle loosened, letting it fall down to his side.

"It was my fault, sir," Van Dekker said.

"What the hell happened?"

"We charged the room, sir," Willoughby told him. "The box… the machine was destroyed." The words hung out there for a moment. "It wasn't anyone's fault."

Claymoore just stood deadly still for a time. In the distance, across the water, there was a sudden dull thud. All eyes turned that way.

Willoughby tightened his gear around his shoulders and chambered a round in his rifle.

"That would be our going away present," Van Dekker said.

"We need to be out of here, sir," Mansfield said. He tugged on Claymoore's shoulder when the lieutenant didn't budge. The man was in some sort of shock. "Sir?"

"Yes," Claymoore said. "Let's get moving."

Willoughby and Van Dekker swapped glances. The South African had killed the radio operator, but he certainly wasn't to blame, no matter what he might have felt. Looking back on it, what had happened was almost inevitable, and the chances of success had been long, anyway. In all actuality, they should've all been dead by now.

The six of them crossed the road, climbed over the low wall, and ran into the trees beyond. Willoughby followed Claymoore, who was in the lead. He knew the lieutenant wasn't happy, and that Zahlman would be even less so. No one would be happy. It meant the ten of them had infiltrated onto enemy-held soil, and failed in a mission that could have proven to be vital.

"We waited till that damn siren went off," Mansfield whispered to him. "The captain took the others and went off to scout a way out. We thought you'd bought it."

Willoughby sighed. "Yeah. We did too."

To the north, he could see the lights grow brighter. Through the trees, there was the movement of lights winding along the road they'd crossed, and he could hear the faint sounds of a car horn beeping. The entire town would be awake by now, and every German on this half of the island would be out. Even if they didn't know about them, it would make getting away nearly impossible.

They made it halfway across an open field when another familiar sound blared. The mechanical wailing of another siren sounded in the open.

"Damn," Willoughby whispered to Mansfield next to him. "Air-raid siren."

The cranking sound echoed, and the group picked up the pace. Willoughby's legs were tired. Right behind him, he could finally hear Van Dekker breathing hard. Their wet boots squished when they ran. They moved through an open field and past empty homes before finally arriving at an old graveyard. A tall, cast-iron fence marked the cemetery grounds. Scores of trees grew up over the graves.

By the time the six of them got there, Willoughby was utterly short of breath. Captain Zahlman was nestled up next to a tree when they arrived, looking through his monocular at some commotion taking place just to the north. The line of trees broke there and opened up onto a road. To the west, the road rose and bent behind a low-lying hill. To the east, the road ultimately ran right into Saint Peter Port.

"Stay here," Claymoore said. Willoughby could hear the warning in his voice. The man had been with them since the get-go, and he didn't like the feeling of having let him down. The lieutenant stomped off to where Captain Zahlman was. The two held a brief conversation, and the captain came swiftly over. He had the same look on his face as Claymoore.

"We don't have much time," Zahlman told them. He looked at Wallace. "What happened?"

Wallace sighed. "We got in, then stormed the room the French girl said to go. She was right. It was in there. But, we got surprised. There was a fight, and... well, the machine was destroyed."

Zahlman huffed. His already tan features turned red under the green-black face paint.

"It was my fault, sir," Van Dekker told him.

"We don't have time for that now," Zahlman said brusquely. He pointed to the northeast. "Hear that? We only have minutes. Sergeant?"

"Sir?" Bowvers said.

"Get them up and moving. We'll deal with this later."

They started off from the cemetery, moving north toward the road. Closer to the town, more lights came on. Small houses east of the road suddenly came alive. Windows swung open, and lights shined out into the early morning hours. Dogs barked, and the sound of another dull thud echoed.

The road was empty to the northeast for as far as Willoughby could see. He had no idea where they were going, but Zahlman knew. He must have. The man was one of the most prepared officers he'd ever met. He led them to the road, then turned due north, through a hedge of thickets and on. The blaring siren became louder with each step.

It was just after they'd pushed through the thickets that the first bullet smacked against a tree nearby. A second and third one tore through the leaves, and they were followed by a sharp cry.

"*Achtung!*" a voice shouted. It was followed by the sound of a half dozen more shots.

Willoughby dove through the bush, cutting his hand along the sharp thorns.

"Get down!" Sergeant Bowvers called out.

Men dove to the ground. Out of the corner of his eye, Willoughby saw the movement across from them. They were merely outlines in the night, hidden in the dark of the opposing tree line. Only the popping of their rifles really gave them away. Lying against the ground, Willoughby could see at least ten of them taking aimed shots at from their position. Half would fire while the other half moved.

"Put 'em down!" he heard Captain Zahlman yell.

Willoughby grimaced. The cat was out of the bag now, and the fight was on. Men opened up and fired back. Three Germans, who were trying to move at them from the right, were driven back as British rifles fired. Next to Willoughby, Corporal Mansfield uncapped his scope, picked a target and fired. Across the open road, Willoughby saw one of them take the hit. The man's head snapped backward as he fell.

"Ah, hell." Willoughby took aim and emptied half his clip on them.

Half the bullets fired on either side flew wildly, not aimed at anyone in particular. The hot flashes from the muzzles of German rifles were all Willoughby could see of the enemy. They were well hidden. They couldn't have been aware of what had happened at the castle. It had been too soon. Most likely, a patrol had spotted the team moving through the field. But all this back-and-forth shooting at each other couldn't be spared. It wouldn't be long before more showed up and brought machine guns with them.

And they didn't need to wait very long before the big show began. In the skies to the west, north and east, blue-green bolts flew skyward in the distance. The distinct pumping sounds of AA guns resonated from all directions. Over and over, they beat like drums, drowning out all but the closest rifle fire. The entire island came alive in a split second. With the first burst, all of Guernsey would be awake and alert.

"Let's go!" Zahlman shouted down the line, against the firing of rifles.

One by one, they fell back and ran. Willoughby emptied the last of his clip, and Corporal Mansfield took out a second one before making a dash to the north. To the northeast, the first of several eruptions burst to life, and then the noise of a half dozen more bombs striking. Willoughby took a parting look at the Germans behind them, still firing away. But as they ran away, the rifles fell silent, and the bombs began exploding.

* * *

Colonel Hoth came jetting out of his headquarters building and into a scene of utter chaos. The alarm was sounding, and vehicles were going through the main gates at high speed. Officers were shouting orders, and everywhere, the sound of rippling AA fire resonated. Some men were half dressed. Awakened by the sound of explosions. Some ran out into the middle of the yard with nothing but their boots and trousers on, loading their rifles as they ran. By the time Colonel Hoth came striding out through the main doors, half the garrison was outside and darting toward their posts.

From the southwest came the boom of another explosion. The faint sound of an airplane propeller went by, and the colonel knew instantly it wasn't one of theirs. By the sound of it, it was a twin-engine light bomber. Hoth put his cap on and scanned the heavens. There was nothing he could see, but the scene in the distance told him all he needed to know.

"Sir!" a voice called out through the madness. A young lieutenant came running across the courtyard.

"Lieutenant." Hoth looked at the man as he stomped down the steps. "Were you asleep at the wheel?" The lieutenant came to a halt and made a confused look. He saluted, but Hoth ignored it and went right by him.

"Sir?"

"It's a British raid!" Hoth screamed, throwing a hand up to the skies. "What happened to the men who were supposed to be manning the radar?"

"Yes, sir," the young officer said nervously. "They were. We only now picked them up. They came in too low for our radar." He nervously trolled behind.

Hoth sneered. Their own aircraft detection system wasn't near as good as the British. There were far too many holes in it, and he lacked the trained personnel to operate the stations efficiently. He gave the lieutenant a considering look. The young lieutenant was out of breath from running across the headquarters compound. He was tempted to make a scolding remark, but held himself. It was no use chopping off the head of the man for something he couldn't possibly be responsible for.

"I put out a general alert as soon as observations posts reported the first plane in," the lieutenant said.

"How long ago?"

"Ten minutes, sir."

Hoth scowled. Ten minutes wasn't unreasonable, given the circumstances. A strategically insignificant backwater like Guernsey wasn't exactly teeming with hardened veterans. That the lieutenant had the good sense to put out a general alert was at least forgivable. Perhaps if Berlin had sent him the resources he'd asked for to finish the island's defenses, and the manpower, they might not have been caught so flatfooted.

"Where have they hit us?"

"The fortifications along the coasts, mostly. Saumarez, Hommet, the barracks just south of Le Marchant, and Castle Cornet." Just as he finished, another stream of anti-aircraft fire streamed skyward in the east, followed moments after by a mushrooming explosion in that direction. "Light aircraft. They came in low."

"Have you contacted General Udet's headquarters?"

"No, sir."

"Contact Rouen," Hoth said. "Tell them to get us some fucking *Luftwaffe* support immediately! Inform the general's headquarters of what's happening, and that it may be part of a larger operation."

A car came to a screeching halt in front of the building, and another young lieutenant jumped out and walked up the bottom steps. The yard beyond the gravel driveway was an assembly area for the troops stationed nearby. They were moving into position under the bright lights of the HQ.

"Find Captain Gerhardt. Have him report to me immediately."

"Captain Gerhardt is gone, sir," the lieutenant said.

"Gone? Gone where?"

"He left about an hour ago, Colonel. Major Lentz wanted him to take him on an inspection tour."

Hoth rolled his eyes. Agitation swelled up in his veins. "Do you know where he is now?"

"He could be anywhere, sir."

Frustrated, Hoth waved over to one of his company commanders standing in the yard. "Well, find him! I'm going to the port. Find him and have him meet me there. You're in charge here."

The other two officers came bolting up the steps toward him. One was a staff lieutenant, and Captain Werner, one of his company commanders.

"Werner," he said. Werner was a grizzled man; an old soldier who'd come up from the enlisted ranks. A veteran of Verdun, his face and body were horribly scarred by wounds from that war, but he wore them as badges of honor. The man stood like a bear over the others. Instead of a helmet, he wore a plain field cap, and carried a rifle. "Are your men ready?"

Werner grinned and turned half around to the sight of the company assembled on the courtyard's grass. His men were a crack company who were drilled by him daily. A few were veterans, but most were not. But regardless, Werner trained them mercilessly.

"Always, sir. Always."

Hoth nodded approvingly. He looked at the lieutenant who'd accompanied him down the steps. "Why are you still here? Contact Rouen!" The young officer paled, then nodded his head and ran up the stairs to the main doors. Hoth sighed in exasperation. He looked at the second lieutenant. "What is it?"

"We just received a report that an enemy patrol was just sighted to the west of Saint Peter Port."

"What?" Hoth asked, incredulous.

"A patrol reported encountering what they believe were British soldiers. Near the old Catholic cemetery."

"When?"

"Just minutes ago."

Hoth seethed. "Dammit! Did the report state which direction they were moving?"

"No, sir. There was a brief skirmish. The patrol sergeant reported at least a dozen enemy soldiers."

"This could be part of a larger operation." Hoth ran his tongue under his lip as he pictured the map of the island in his mind. He knew every roadway on Guernsey. "There are only two ways for them to go from there. Either south or north."

"South would take them damn close to the airfield," Werner said. "Possible that they're planning to get out in a plane. Or hit the field itself."

Hoth shook his head at the suggestion. "Not likely. The airfield will be too well secured. We'll have *Luftwaffe* cover shortly," he grumbled. "If there's an incursion, they may be linking up with a larger force. Or there may be more than one enemy unit on the island."

The two junior officers were silent, as Hoth considered the situation. There were ten times as many civilians on Guernsey as there were German troops, and the island wasn't that large. The only places for any British forces to hide would most likely have been amongst the occupied population. He knew he'd have to make a show of force after all this was over with.

But his priority was hunting down those British soldiers. He'd deal with the civilians later.

"Get your men moving," he told Werner.

"Where, sir?"

"The crossroads. From there, you can go either south or northeast. The garrison in Saint Peter Port will have cut off any escape to the east and all the way down the coast. I want them cut off from the north."

"Yes, sir."

"Once you get into position, I'll have a company from the port move north and west. If the British go that way, they'll be corralled right to you. Understood?"

"Understood."

"You." He leveled a finger at the second lieutenant. "Alert the airfield to be on the lookout for the enemy." He waved at a car coming around the driveway perimeter. The car pulled up to the bottom of the steps and idled. "Get them moving, Werner." Hoth gave him a curt nod, and Werner turned and started off toward his men assembled on the grass.

"Oh, and Werner." Werner turned back. "I want prisoners. I don't care how, but I want prisoners for interrogation."

"Sir."

Hoth jumped into the passenger seat of the car and looked at the lieutenant behind him. "Coordinate the air defenses. I'll be at the port." He tapped the driver. "Go."

Dust flew up in the car's wake, and it was off, beeping its horn as the driver drove through the lines of soldiers and vehicles now lining the sides of the road.

CHAPTER SIXTEEN

Colonel Hoth's car didn't even bother to slow down as it approached the check-point guards at the end of the causeway bridge. Three guards tried to ward off the driver, but they fell away when Hoth stood up in his seat and waved them off. The gate lifted, and the car sped through.

The causeway was smoking from a bomb crater. Just meters from the base of Castle Cornet, a bomb had fallen, taking part of the northern wall down with it. In the harbor, the ferry was burning, and men were racing to extinguish the flames before the entire dock caught fire. To his right, a giant cloud of black dust hung above the castle. One building in the courtyard inside had a gaping hole in its roof, and the entire southern end of the castle wall had fallen inward.

His eyes searched around him. The scene was as chaotic as he'd seen on his drive from his headquarters. Bodies were lying along the causeway, and wounded were being carted away on stretchers. To the south, beyond Havelet Bay, the sea was on fire. Petroleum was burning on the water's surface, adding to the smoke in the air, and the tail of a large plane was standing straight up from the water.

The car brakes screeched to a halt. In front of him, two men carried a wounded man across the causeway near the castle entrance. Hoth looked at the burned face of the wounded man as he went by, then looked around for any sign of command. There was a sergeant barking orders to men at the entrance. A platoon of soldiers were tugging at hoses and water tanks, trying to get the pumps going to extinguish flames inside the walls.

"Sergeant!" Hoth yelled. He jumped from the car and ran over to him. "Sergeant!"

The senior sergeant saw him and approached. "Sir."

"Report."

The sergeant ceased giving orders and wiped his sweaty forehead with the palm of his hand. His face was filthy. "It was a British bomber, sir. We took it out, but not before it did this. The castle took direct hits."

Hoth looked around at the efforts playing out. "Casualties?"

"Minimal, actually. They got the barracks itself, and the radio tower. But the men had been assembled in the yard. Only a few men were still inside when the bomber hit." Just as he said that, the sound of a building collapsing came from inside the walls. "Captain Gerhardt had called for assembly—"

"Gerhardt. Where is he?"

"He's right there, sir," the sergeant said, pointing to the end of the causeway. A medic was there, putting bandages around a man's head. "Carry on." Hoth walked across the graveled bridge. On a bed of sandbags, Captain Gerhardt was bent over, holding a blood-soaked press against his face. He saw Hoth's approach and began to stand.

"As you were," Hoth told him.

The medic cut the bandage and pinned the wrapping around Gerhardt's head. He had drops of blood on his tunic, and his face was as dirty as the sergeant's had been.

"Sir," Gerhardt said, his voice shaky.

"The British have hit us all over the island," Hoth told him.

"We saw the explosion, sir. We got the bomber, but..." He coughed slightly and waved a hand at the collapsed wall of the castle and the plume of smoke hanging above.

"You're all right?" Hoth asked him.

"I'll be fine. Just have some smoke in my lungs." The medic finished his work and went off for the other wounded.

"How many men do you have here?"

Gerhardt looked around and shrugged. "Maybe two hundred, sir. The men in town make three."

"I'm taking your sergeant there," Hoth told him, pointing a thumb at the senior sergeant at the main entrance. "We've got a British force reportedly nearby."

"On the island?" Gerhardt asked, disbelievingly. Hoth nodded.

"Werner's company is moving in from the west. I want some men here to move up the coast." He looked back at the sight of soldiers working to fight the fires. "This could be part of a larger incursion."

Captain Gerhardt sighed. "I can have a company assembled—"

"No," Hoth said. "I'll take that sergeant. You're to remain here for now. If more British forces are on their way, I want you in charge of the port. The sergeant said you ordered an assembly?"

"Yes." Gerhardt nodded, pressing the gauze against his bloodied face as he stood up from the sandbags. "Major Lentz wanted an inspection of the grounds. It might have been the only thing that saved the lives of those men."

"Where is Lentz now?"

"Last I heard, he'd gone into the lower levels of the castle, sir. He wanted to inspect the code room." He shook his head in vain. "I don't know what happened to him. The bombs hit the castle. I've been told that level has collapsed."

"Hmm." Hoth bit his lip and grumbled. If the major was dead, then someone was going to be demanding answers in Berlin. He'd deal with that if and when it came. "Keep the recovery effort underway. The *Luftwaffe* should be here shortly to provide air cover. I'll have any resources I can spare shifted to you. Dig those men out if you can."

"If we find Lentz is dead?"

Hoth considered it for a moment, then lightly shrugged. "Then he's dead. Did his companion go down there with him?"

"No, sir. Ofhoven and Hoff separated from us. Last I saw, they were out on the northern route."

"Fine then. At least we'll have one SS officer to send back to Berlin." Hoth turned and hollered for the senior sergeant, still giving orders to the relief workers. The tall man ran over to them. "Assemble a rifle company, Sergeant. You know the map of the island?" The sergeant nodded his affirmation. "We have a force of British infiltrators. I want them hunted down."

"Yes, sir," the sergeant said with a grin.

"Captain Werner's men will be coming from the west. You're to take half your men and push from here to the crossroads. The other half is to follow the coast road north. Cut them off from any retreat. Do you understand?"

"Yes, sir."

"Cut them off, then Captain Werner can surround and capture them. I've given orders to Werner to capture as many of them as possible. Those orders apply to you as well."

"Understood, sir."

"What your name?"

"Strehler, sir."

"Very well, Sergeant Strehler. There are some vehicles at the end of the bridge. You have my authority to take what you need. Go now. Captain Gerhardt will put together a backup force and send them along after." Strehler saluted and took off running, shouting for his men to fall in behind him. Hoth turned back to his chief of staff. "Coordinate here. I'm going back to headquarters. Lock the town down. Not a single civilian is allowed out of their homes."

"Yes, sir. What if we find the civilians have taken part in this?"

"I expect some have. I will deal with them after this. But first thing is first. I want those British soldiers captured."

* * *

Willoughby spared a quick look back the way they'd come. He couldn't see any signs of pursuit, but he knew that wouldn't last. By now, the Germans would at least have an idea that a British force was on the island. Once word of it spread, they'd be moving in from every side, cutting them off from the coast. That hadn't been part of the plan. They were supposed to be at their extraction point already. But plans were only good right until the moment they met with reality.

To the north, the anti-aircraft guns had ceased, but everywhere else, it was still quite alive. The sound of rippling fire and bombs hitting the ground filled the air. The guns around Saint Peter Port were particularly active. To the east, he could just barely make out the shadow of a plane descending across the horizon. There was a burst in the air, and the sound of a plane winding out of control. It was followed several moments later by a hard crash slamming into the ground.

Poor bastards, he thought and kept on moving. There was no time to dawdle in grief.

So far as he could tell, they were somewhere in the very center of the island. All that had to happen was for another patrol to hold them up for a while, and half the garrison would be on them like flies. Frankly, he was surprised half a battalion hadn't already come charging in from every direction. Perhaps the Germans had their hands full dealing with the bombing runs. There had been more than enough explosions to suggest the bombers had hit most of their targets. He'd hoped Castle Cornet was one of them. Not that it really mattered anymore.

At the head of the line, Captain Zahlman brought the troop to a halt in a shallow pathway that sat at the edge of an open meadow. He moved down the line, to where an old, overgrown brick wall began and wound down the path. He called for Sergeant Bowvers and Corporal Mansfield to go with him, and the three disappeared without a word through the bushes at the end of the wall.

"What's going on?" Wallace whispered to him. Willoughby just shook his head.

Claymoore had some words with the surrounding others and caught up with Willoughby and Wallace afterward. He kneeled down next to them and looked around in all directions before coming back to the two of them.

"So what happened in there?" he asked them. There wasn't a hint of displeasure in his voice anymore.

"We got in there, sir, and we got surprised," Wallace told him. "Some damn German officer walked right into us. It was over before we really knew what had happened."

"It could have been worse, sir," Willoughby said. "But bottom line, we lost that damned machine. We don't have any excuses. I'm sorry, sir."

Claymoore pouted and looked away from him. He let out a small sigh, then nodded. "I'll admit, I always had some reservations about the whole damn thing," he said. "It's nobody's fault. Probably a fantasy we could have ever pulled this off."

Willoughby looked at him. Claymoore was younger than he was, but he was tough. Hearing him speak this way sounded almost defeatist, but he knew that wasn't the way of it. The lieutenant was inexperienced, but like everyone else, the stress of events might simply be bearing down on him.

"I thought that way in Norway," Willoughby told him. "Damn objective was lost anyway, and we thought we'd all be winding up in a prisoner camp." He shrugged. "We fought our way out of it. We'll fight our way out of this too, sir."

Claymoore's mouth twitched, and he could swear he saw a slight grin on him. At that moment, to the right of the line, the shrubs parted and Captain Zahlman came crashing back through, with Bowvers and Mansfield right behind.

"Sir?" Claymoore asked.

Zahlman bent down. "We've got an enemy platoon coming this way from the east." Willoughby instantly chambered a round. "Wide front."

Willoughby looked in that direction and listened. He realized he had heard no further bombs exploding off in the distance. Not a single AA gun within earshot was firing. It was over. The bombers had done their job. The Germans would be coming for them next.

Nearby, birds in a tree were chirping their morning song. Daybreak was almost upon them.

"There's a crossroads just to the north of here," Zahlman said, getting to his feet. "We need to be beyond it, quickly."

He didn't need to say another word, and the troop was back on their feet and following Zahlman into the empty pasture. A cottage sat on the east end of the field, with its lights on. Even this far away, Willoughby could see the curtains open, and faces looking out into the early morning. The bombs had dropped, and the entire island had been awakened. Adding another obstacle to their escape: curious onlookers.

The pasture ended at a V-shaped wooden rail that ran southwest to west. After that, the landscape opened back up to open country. The view went on for a kilometer, and Willoughby could just barely make out faint lights in the distance. The lights of the city behind them had gone out, and the glow to the north were only that of spotlights scanning the skies.

Three roads converged to the northeast. One ran back toward Saint Peter Port. Another went southwest and the other to the east. The road there was elevated above a drainage ditch. They stayed off that road, moving instead along the shrubs that lined the south side of it. They got about half a kilometer from the fork in the road when Zahlman took a chance and crossed the men over the road and into the ditch on the other side. Claymoore and Mansfield brought up the rear and watched out as the rest crossed over the road. Willoughby just barely made it over the roadway when a call when out.

"Lights!" Mansfield shouted across the narrow roadway. The men on the other side of the road dove into the shallow ditch. Mansfield and Claymoore stayed hidden on their side.

Willoughby laid down next to Sergeant Bowvers and watched as the headlights of an automobile came winding down the narrow road. It was moving slowly, with no signs of a larger escort. It was driving so leisurely, he thought maybe there was a civilian behind the wheel. But, as it came closer, he realized it was a German Army vehicle.

"What the hell?" Bowvers whispered as the car drew near.

As the car was bearing down on their position, Willoughby could make out tiny pennants flapping on the front fender. Usually the sign of a commanding officer of some sort.

"What the devil?" Bowvers muttered. "It's an officer's car, sir," he called down the ditch.

In that moment, Captain Zahlman jumped up from the ditch and rushed out into the middle of the roadway. Willoughby's eyes narrowed in awe as he watched him stop in the road and raise his hands up in the air for the car to stop. The headlight beams shined on him, and the car began to slow down.

"The hell's he doing?" Bowvers asked aloud. But Willoughby only shook his head.

The brakes squeaked until the car came to a complete stop. The driver stood up from his seat and shouted something at him in German. In the seat behind him, two others were sitting. Not riflemen either; there were no helmets on their heads. Instead, they wore officers' caps. One wore a jet-black uniform with a swastika armband. The other was younger looking, dressed in the usual German Army gray.

In the lights, Zahlman's green uniform must've been visible. Willoughby couldn't believe his eyes. His first concern was that one of the Germans would recognize he wasn't one of them, and gun him down. But that didn't happen. Instead, the driver put the car in park.

"Let's go!" Willoughby shouted and got up, running toward the stopped vehicle.

Out of the roadside and from the bushes, the rest of the men came out and surrounded the car. Willoughby and Bowvers covered the driver with their rifles. In the rear seat, the black-clad officer stood up. His face was flush with confusion.

"*Was ist los?*" he shouted, looking around angrily. He pointed his finger around at each of them. The driver looked at the guns aimed at him and put his hands up slowly. The shouting man in the rear kept saying the same thing over and over, apparently oblivious to who was surrounding the car.

"Is he daft?" Bowvers asked.

"*Was machst du hier?*" the officer in the rear said angrily, but nobody understood.

After a few seconds, the second man in the rear seat said something and put his hand on the other officer's arm. After finally realizing they weren't German soldiers, the man's facial expression changed from anger to fear. He looked around the car nervously, and his right arm slowly reached down to his side.

"Ah, ah, ah." Private Ashford leveled his rifle at him, then stepped toward the car, reached in and snatched the man's sidearm. "Don't be clever now."

"Up!" Claymoore shouted at them, twitching his rifle. "Up. Now!"

"Get them out of the car, Lieutenant," Zahlman told him. "Sergeant."

"Sir?"

"You have something to bind their hands?"

"Yes, sir."

"Get them squared away, then. We're taking them with us."

The three Germans got out of the car slowly. They were bound behind their backs and gagged, their side arms taken.

Bowvers patted them down harshly, searching their pockets, even under their hats. "This one's SS, sir," he said, tugging on the collar of the black-clad German.

"Good. He'll be our consolation prize. The other?"

Bowvers checked the other officer's uniform, pulling out a small notebook and some credentials from his breast pocket. "Don't know, sir. But he's got this." He tossed the credentials to Lieutenant Claymoore.

"I think he's *Abwehr*, sir," Claymoore said. "Intelligence."

"Excellent. They'll be most useful. Headquarters can interrogate them if we get out of this."

"We need to be on our way, sir," Claymoore said as the captives were secured. "Those patrols will be coming this way."

The captain nodded. "Step back," he ordered everyone, then leveled his machine gun and blasted away at the car, flattening the tires and killing the engine.

"Sir?" Claymoore asked him, before even the echo of the gunfire had dissipated.

"They already know we're here, Lieutenant. Now, they'll just think we're some failed attempted raid that got lucky and grabbed some prisoners." He stepped closer to Claymoore. "Before we leave, cut the driver loose. He's no use to us, and he can testify that he saw a British force well north of the castle, capture some officers, and retreat into the sea."

"Right." Claymoore and Pendleton took point, with Sergeant Bowvers and Private Ashford and the three captives right behind them.

Zahlman whistled and swirled his finger around in the air. They hadn't made it fifty yards when something caught Willoughby's eye. To the east, a squad of German soldiers came rushing from the trees. Behind them, rifles fired. Enough of them to sound more like a light machine gun than Mausers. Darjan was to his right, and Willoughby took to a knee, waited for him to clear his line of sight and leveled his sights. He squeezed the trigger three times successively, enough to bring one of the Germans down and keep the others from approaching any further.

"Get moving!" Zahlman's voice bellowed.

Behind Willoughby, they began a fighting withdraw. On the other side of the elevated road, the Germans were pushing out of the bushes. Their muzzles flashed from the ridge of the roadway, and they were damn good shots. Too many of them came close to Willoughby's position, pelting him with tiny showers of earth.

He moved half a dozen paces, then dropped to the ground. Corporal Mansfield, the crack shot, was right next to him. One shot was all he fired, straight through a German's chest. The impact took the dead man right off his feet, knocking his helmet off and sending it rolling down the into the ditch.

"Nice shot!" Willoughby said.

The other Germans on the road took the two kills as a warning, and didn't proceed any further into the field. He and Mansfield took the brief lull to make their own escape, dashing through the tall grass after the others. Dodd and Belafonte covered them. German bullets whizzed by Willoughby as he ran. He kept his head low and his legs moving. Just behind him, there came a sharp cry.

"*Ah!*"

He stopped and whipped his head around just in time to see Corporal Mansfield fall forward into the grass, curled up in a ball, cradling his leg in pain. Dodd and Belafonte kept up their cover fire, and Willoughby crept back to Mansfield. He'd dropped his weapon and was holding his right thigh with both hands.

"Corp?" Willoughby asked him. He looked at Mansfield's leg, pulling his hands away ever so slightly to see. The bullet had gone into the rear of his leg, but Willoughby could find no exit wound. "I've got you."

He slung his rifle around his torso and wrapped his arms under Mansfield's armpits. Dodd jumped forward and gave him a hand, and the two dragged the corporal through the grass. Mansfield kept his grip on his bleeding leg as his boot heels dragged into the earth behind him.

"Behind you!" Willoughby looked up just in time to see Captain Zahlman running back toward them. He was gripping his American-made Thompson with both hands. "Get down!"

Willoughby and Dodd hit the ground, and Zahlman opened his gun up on the Germans now crossing the elevated road. The quick succession of rounds cut them down like blades of grass. Bodies fell forward into the ditch. He ceased his firing, and they began moving the wounded Mansfield again.

The road fell away behind them, but the sound of rifle fire continued. It didn't register with Willoughby just how far they'd gone until he looked back. The Germans had stopped their advance in the field. Along the road, several vehicles were arriving, their headlights gleaming over the open field.

The pursuit took a pause long enough to make it beyond the reach of their rifles. But now they were coming in with vehicles, which meant they were going to make every attempt to move in on them.

"How you doing, Corp?" he asked. Mansfield stifled a cry and gave him a firm nod. He wasn't looking good. His leg was bleeding heavily. "Lay him down. We need to stop the bleeding."

He unbuckled Mansfield's gear, cut the strap of his Bergen sack and wrapped it around the leg. He pulled it tightly, drawing a cry of pain from Mansfield, then tied off the end.

"Let's move him," Zahlman said.

Another dull crack of a Mauser broke the short-lived silence. A single shot was fired from a ridge to the west. The first rays of morning sun illuminated a broken wooden rail fence at the top. Behind the fence, a tall German soldier was standing with his rifle aimed toward them. He fired again. This time, the bullet found its mark. Lance Corporal Wallace, surprised by the first shot, had turned into the path of the second. His hand instantly gripped his left shoulder as he fell to the ground.

Belafonte turned and fired back at the man who'd taken the shot. Zahlman fired toward the ridge, where a score of Germans came running around the fence line and down the sweeping slope that now stood between them. Two of them fell under his Thompson, but the rest kept coming. Willoughby and Dodd pulled Mansfield over his objections to be left behind. Wallace picked himself back up. Blood was coming from his shoulder, but at least he could move.

Van Dekker put his hand on Willoughby. "Let go," he told him. "I'll take him."

The thick South African picked Mansfield up by his arms and scooped him right off the ground, tossing him over his shoulders and carrying him off. Willoughby snatched the rifle off his back and joined Zahlman and Belafonte in firing at the German soldiers coming down the ridge. The force from the road was now running through the field. On the road itself, another squad was leaping off the back of a truck. A pair of machine guns waved around in the air as they ran toward them.

He emptied the last of his clip at the soldiers charging down the ridge, then reached down to pull his last magazine out and slapped it into place.

"Get moving," Zahlman said.

Another burst from his Thompson took down another German. After that, the ones coming down the ridge side slowed their approach. But from one end of the open field and atop the ridge, the rifles continued firing on them. They were drowned out a minute later by the sound of a machine gun letting loose. The rapid fire of which cut a tree to pieces just as they disappeared through the leaves.

CHAPTER SEVENTEEN

The sun was coming up over the sea to the east, and daybreak was spilling out across the island. Ahead of him, Van Dekker had taken a surprisingly wide lead, even with Corporal Mansfield slung over his shoulder. He seemed to have found his speed, and Willoughby couldn't help but find himself laughing on the inside. He'd moved so slowly during training exercises.

Willoughby, Zahlman and Belafonte brought up the rear. One would fire at the separate groups of Germans, then turn and run again. The enemy, in contrast, were slogging across the fields from both the west and the south. Headlights in the distance were moving along the road toward the eastern shore to cut them off.

It wasn't going to be pretty if they were successful.

The rearguard reached a downward slope that ran into a small hamlet. There were homes on either side of a narrow retention canal. As he ran past, Willoughby saw the faces of civilians peeking out from behind curtains. Most shut their blinds as soon as they saw what was happening. It was impossible to not know what was going on, with the ferocious exchange taking place outside their homes, coming right after a bombing strike.

Smoke was still rising around the island from where the RAF had struck. He didn't know how to feel about that. Hopefully, those pilots were good at their craft and had dropped their bombloads on the right targets. The idea of their own civilians being killed in the raid didn't sit well with him.

A single house door squeaked open, and he leveled his rifle at the doorway. A little blond-haired boy in brown trousers and suspenders stepped outside to watch the action taking place. Willoughby cursed and lowered his gun as he ran by. An adult reached out and snatched the child back in, slamming the door shut behind.

Bullets fired from behind. He stopped a moment, turned, and emptied his last shots into a German soldier a hundred feet away. He collapsed dead, and Willoughby continued through the narrow streets between houses. There was a walking bridge in the center of the houses that crossed over the canal. Belafonte and Zahlman got across first. Willoughby came charging across behind them. Zahlman fired off a quick double burst into the ground as a warning to the people inside their homes.

"I'm out!" Willoughby said as he got to the other end.

Zahlman was putting a new magazine into his Thompson. The three took cover behind a small house on the canal. On the opposite side, the Germans were moving cautiously down the street. Dodd and Darjan were holding on either flank.

"Willoughby, go that way," Zahlman told him, pointing two fingers in the direction Van Dekker and Wallace had taken. "We'll hold them up."

"Sir?" Willoughby couldn't hide the concern in his voice.

"I'm not dying here, Willoughby," Zahlman said. "We'll delay them, and we'll be right behind. Get to Claymoore. Tell him to get ready to shove off. Those blasted officers are as valuable to us now as any code machine." He pulled back the bolt of his gun. "We'll slow them down and be right behind you. *Go!*"

Willoughby left them behind. He spared a quick look to his left, down the length of the canal. It ended about a hundred paces to the north, and the Germans coming down the ridge would probably know that and come across there. He didn't like leaving Zahlman behind like this, but he was no use without ammo. The gunfire began again almost immediately after.

Van Dekker was moving a lot slower when Willoughby caught up with him. The extra weight of the corporal slung over his shoulder had finally slowed his pace, and Wallace had simply disappeared. Willoughby could hear the other man's labored breathing as he ran toward the coastal road. A single-wide dirt road curled around the knots of trees that dotted this part of Guernsey. It was a grueling three-hundred-yard dash to make it there.

"Wait," Van Dekker said to him. He stopped at the road and let Mansfield fall away from his shoulders. "I can't..." His breathing was hard, and he fell to a single knee. Corporal Mansfield let out a tiny whimper as he set him down. He'd fallen unconscious during the run. "I need a breather."

He was tempted to tell Van Dekker there wasn't time, but he also knew lugging an extra thirteen stones couldn't have been easy. It would have taken longer if they'd had to drag him.

"Wait here," he told Van Dekker.

Willoughby dug into Mansfield's belt and took a magazine off him. He slapped it into place and dove through the knot of trees. The other side opened up to the northern coast. A blast of warm sea air hit him in the face when he got there, and he briefly stopped to look at the dark blue water beyond. It was a beautiful sight, and he lost himself in the moment of it.

The reverie broke at the sound of a harsh, unfamiliar voice shouting, *"Englischer Soldat!"*

To his left, a single German was standing just fifty feet away, between himself and what looked like an aerial observation bunker. He was unarmed. Willoughby had nearly forgotten that he was. When he went to raise his rifle, the German took off back toward the bunker, screaming and yelling at the top of his lungs. He was tempted to let the man run until he saw three more men coming out of the concrete box with rifles charging right toward him. Then he pulled the trigger. He fired a single shot and then hit the ground.

The first two Germans stopped and leveled their rifles at him. Bullets whizzed overhead. The closest of them came to within twenty paces away when he suddenly stopped in his tracks and fired. More bullets flew above him. In the air, a grenade lobbed over Willoughby's head and bounced along the ground toward the attacker. Upon exploding, the sound of a machine gun opened up, turning the German into broken flesh.

Sergeant Bowvers came running past him, stopping only to level his Bren toward the two Germans still in the open. The surrounding ground erupted in a hail of bullets, tearing their bodies to pieces. The single unarmed soldier kept running, and Bowvers let the man go.

"Willoughby!" He jumped to his feet at the sound of his name. The sergeant and Private Pendleton were alone. "Where's the captain?"

"Back in the hamlet. They were holding up the Jerries. Where's Claymoore?"

Bowvers pointed a thumb over his shoulder. "Over that there hill. There's a cove. You alone?"

"No. Van Dekker's over there. Corporal Mansfield's been hit. He was carrying him."

"Fine. You two get him over there, then. We're going to back up the captain."

Bowvers and Pendleton went running off toward the hamlet and the sound of guns. Willoughby went back to find Van Dekker hovering over Corporal Mansfield. His leg had bled profusely, and his skin was turning pale.

"Let's get him—"

"He's dead," Van Dekker said before he could finish.

"What?" Willoughby gasped. "But..."

"He must've bled too much."

Willoughby stooped down to feel Mansfield's neck. He couldn't get a pulse. "Damn," he said sorrowfully. "Let's get him out of here, then. Lieutenant Claymoore's not far. Help me."

Van Dekker took Mansfield's torso and Willoughby his legs, and together, the two lifted his body and carried it away.

Claymoore was right where Bowvers said he'd be. There was a small cove just beyond a shallow hill. Several cottages and shacks dotted the shoreline, and there wasn't a single enemy soldier anywhere to be seen. There was an empty cottage nearby, with a tiny outbuilding just beside it. The front door of the cottage swung open and closed on the breeze.

The lieutenant was standing next to the outbuilding along with the three prisoners they'd taken. The two caught Claymoore's attention as they carried Corporal Mansfield's body toward the outbuilding. Out of the main house, the disappeared Wallace emerged with his arm in a makeshift sling that looked to be cut from someone's bed sheets.

Beyond Lieutenant Claymoore were two other buildings in the distance. The first was a small structure with a flat, sod roof. The second was just beyond that, and twice the size of the first. It had windows on either visible side. Down further were several small row boats stacked on top of one another in the open. Private Ashford was wrestling to get one of them detached from the others.

Out to sea, waves crashed into a sandbar between the shore and some tiny tidal islands. One way or another, this was the end of the road. Their escape route might well become their last stand. The sub was only supposed to tarry until daybreak. Well, that time had long since come.

"The captain's holding them up, sir," he told Claymoore. "But they're coming up right behind us."

"How far?" Claymoore asked. He looked at the body of Corporal Mansfield. "How is he?"

"He's dead, sir," Van Dekker said.

"And they're right behind us," Willoughby said. "I'd say two full companies. The captain's holding them up, but we won't have long." He looked down at the three Germans tied up and leaning against the wooden building. The one in black was making no attempt at trying to hide a smile.

Claymoore sighed at the news of Corporal Mansfield, but shook it right off. "Van Dekker, help Ashford get a couple of those boats free. Willoughby, go search those buildings there for something useful."

Willoughby took the last magazines off Mansfield before running down to the small building near the shore. It was little more than a beat-up shack just yards from the water. He kicked the flimsy open door. Inside, large barrels were stacked along the walls. He could smell the odor of fish inside. He pried open a barrel with his knife, finding it filled to the brim with salted fish.

He looked around the space. He was just about to leave when he saw the face of a man looking at him from behind one of the barrels. He drew his knife back as if he were about to strike.

"Whoa, whoa," the man said. He put his hands up in the air. "Easy, lad."

Willoughby exhaled and blinked hard. He was an Englishman. He was squatting down behind one barrel, his arms held out.

"Jesus Christ," Willoughby said. The man was shaking visibly. He had wispy white hair, and his face was bright red. The tip of his nose was bulbous, like someone who spent his life drinking hard. "What the hell are you doing in here?"

"We're hiding," the man said. He burped, and Willoughby could smell the liquor on his breath from feet away. Another head popped out from behind the barrel and put his hands up as well. "We heard guns."

Willoughby shook his head at the man. "Stupid, dad. Very stupid. I could have killed you." He sheathed his blade.

"Dan," the man said.

"What?"

"You... You called me dad. It's Dan. This is Tom."

The other man held a half empty bottle in his hand. It was obvious the two had been drinking from it. Willoughby grabbed the bottle and took a good, long swig.

"Hey! That's gin right there," Tom said. "Difficult to come by these days."

"And it tastes good," Willoughby said, handing back the bottle. "You two came down here to drink your sorrows off, did you? Bit early, isn't it?"

Dan and Tom just shrugged at the question. They stood up, with their hands still in the air.

"Put those down," Willoughby told them. "I'm an Englishman if you couldn't already tell. You shouldn't be here. You should go home."

"Out there?" Tom asked nervously. He shook his head. "There're Germans out there."

Willoughby smiled. "This is a storehouse?"

"Aye. We keep our stock in here."

"What about the other building?"

Dan shrugged. "Just supplies for the boats. But not much need for that these days. The Boche don't let us off the island."

"What kind of supplies?"

"I dunno," Dan said. "Rope, sails for the boats. Just stuff."

"Any motorboats around here?" Willoughby asked.

"Motorboats? Aye." Tom laughed. "But not a drop of petrol. Germans took it all when they came here. And you can't run a motor on kerosene."

Willoughby's eyes narrowed at the word. "Kerosene? Where? Up there?"

"Aye."

"Thanks, Tom," Willoughby told him with a smile and a wink. "Do yourselves a favor and stay in here. We'll be gone shortly." He shut the door behind him and double-timed over to the larger of the two storehouses.

There was a bolt lock on the outside, which he knocked off with the butt of his rifle. The sound of gunfire echoed over the hill, and it was getting close.

Inside, the larger structure was filled from top to bottom with boating supplies. The floor was filled with baskets of oyster shells, each stacked on top of one another. Cans of kerosene sat on the top shelf of a long bench, and bundles of coiled rope hung from nails off the beams. His eyes drifted around the room, and suddenly, an idea came to him that could only have come to the mind of a native fisherman.

He bolted back to where Claymoore was. Wallace had rejoined him and was holding his rifle at their captives over his wounded arm. Beyond the hill, the echo of guns rippled again.

"Willoughby!" Claymoore said. "Get down there and help get those boats in the water."

"I've got an idea, sir," Willoughby said, ignoring the order. He laid out his idea, but could see Claymoore had no clue what he was talking about. And he didn't have time to spell it out for him.

"You want to do what now?" Claymoore said, confused. "How is blowing up some damn storehouse going to help us? You'd be better served getting those boats in the water. I don't have time for this, Willoughby."

"I can't explain it all to you, sir, but trust me. I know what I'm talking about. Van Dekker has some incendiaries left. We use those, and we can cover our retreat."

Claymoore's expression didn't budge. He had a doubtful look on his face, but after a moment, he simply nodded. "Very well."

Van Dekker was pulling a boat down to the water when Willoughby got to him and took him back up to the storehouse, snatching up his kit on the way. The South African smiled broadly when Willoughby told him what he wanted to do.

"Oyster shells make lime?" Van Dekker asked inquisitively.

Willoughby batted the question away. "We need it to burn hot. Very hot. Can you do it?"

"Of course I can do it," he said, holding up his kit. "By why don't you just have me blow the damn building up? I've got what I need to blast it to bits."

"We want the smoke. I don't want it to catch the other building."

"Why?"

"There're two perfectly good old men hiding in there."

Van Dekker nodded an understanding and took the last of the thermite from his bag. Willoughby took the coils of rope and placed them on the floor around the baskets. Half the cans of kerosene were used to douse the oyster baskets and floor underneath. Anything and everything that could burn was put in a pile together.

When Willoughby came back out again, the fighting was already on the hilltop. He heard the distinct hum of a half-track vehicle approaching. German rifles fired incessantly at the shrinking number of men trying to fend them away. Lance Corporal Wallace had taken two of the three prisoners to the boats, leaving the driver tied up next to the outbuilding. Dodd was coming down to the cove with a wounded Private Darjan leaning on him for support. His right arm was snug against his rib, and blood was pouring from an open wound near the elbow.

"This had better work," Van Dekker said to him. He squeezed the detonator with pliers, stuffed the bomb back into his kit, and placed it on a shelf above.

"It has to," Willoughby said. "It's the last trick I have in my hat." He tried to put as much conviction into his words as possible. Out of all the ideas he'd ever had, he felt as good about this one as any other. Audacity had worked for him well enough in Narvik when he'd run into a pitched street battle with naught but a Molotov cocktail and a barrel of petrol. "It'll work."

"Well, in five minutes, we should know," Van Dekker said sourly.

Sergeant Bowvers emptied his rounds at the enemy, then ditched his Bren and pulled out his sidearm. Captain Zahlman hotfooted it down to where Claymoore was. There was a brief conversation between them, then Zahlman called for a general withdrawal.

"Willoughby." The captain approached him. The look on his face was the same that Claymoore had made when he'd told him what he had cooked up, but Zahlman never asked him about the details. Instead, his demeanor felt like something else. Trusting, perhaps. "You have this, Private?" Willoughby only nodded a reply. "Very well."

Zahlman whistled and rounded up all the others but Lieutenant Claymoore and Private Belafonte. A half dozen Germans were cresting the top of the hill now, crouching low and firing down on them. The heads of a score more were moving along the ridge in either direction. In a minute, they'd be sweeping down on them from all sides.

Van Dekker spilled the last of the kerosene onto the walls and oyster shells in the storehouse, then reached into his kit for a match. He looked at Willoughby one last time, waiting for a nod. Willoughby gave it to him, and the struck match fell on the soaked rope. It instantly began burning. The blue-white flame of burning kerosene spread like wildfire.

"Let's go," Willoughby told him.

A single half-track moved into position at the crest of the hill. On top, its shooter aimed the gun down on the force below. Claymoore and Belafonte pulled back in good order, keeping their fire on the advancing Germans. Willoughby took the opportunity to run back down to the smaller of the two shacks where he'd found Dan and Tom. Behind him, the banging sound of a loud gun began going off, and the shack ahead was pinged by heavy rounds. The tiny wooden structure took half a dozen shots fired through the top of it.

Around him, Van Dekker and Pendleton were sprinting for the water. Captain Zahlman and half the men had already arrived at the boats and were even now pushing the one with the prisoners out to sea. Van Dekker and he locked eyes for a moment, and he saw the South African begin to run back toward him. But there was one last thing Willoughby had to do.

The two old men were huddled in the corner of the dilapidated storehouse. Holes punched through the old wooden walls where the half-track's heavy gun had blown a hole through, and the light from the sun outside beamed through. He gave the old men a sorrowful look and hesitated for a second. His fist balled up, and the look on the other's face saw what he was about to do. The red-nosed man, Dan, looked up at him, and gave him a dutiful nod. His eyes were bright white, and the old fisherman reminded him of his grandfather for a moment.

"Go on, son," he told Willoughby, and smiled. "It's all right."

Willoughby hesitated. He hated the idea of what he was about to do. He drew his arm back and balled up a fist. "Sorry, dad."

Old Dan looked away as Willoughby's fist landed on the side of his face. He pulled his punch, of course, but that didn't make it any easier. The old man went down like a sack of grain. His face was red from where Willoughby knocked him out. He did the same to Tom. The younger man needed a little more force to go down, but in the end, they both were out and lying in the middle of the shack. If the blasted Germans didn't blow the building to pieces and kill them, they'd hopefully think the two had simply been in the wrong place at the wrong time. Which they had. Only Willoughby would know they'd helped them to escape.

"Come on!" Van Dekker said. He grabbed Willoughby by the collar and pulled him out of the shack and the two took off running toward the water.

As they moved, German rifles fired, hitting the rocks along the shore nearby. But not a single round found either of them. Willoughby discarded his rifle into the water before diving in and swimming out to the boat now paddling out to sea. It just got beyond the outer sandbar when he reached for the prow. Dodd leaned forward and helped to pull him in. It took both of them to haul Van Dekker out of the water, and the boat rocked hard when they did.

Ashore, there was a series of loud popping sounds, like firecrackers going off. Willoughby looked to see the large storehouse set ablaze. The incendiaries burst to life, catching the vats of kerosene immediately. Fire quickly consumed the building. Flames licked out between the wooden planks and the sod roof.

Willoughby watched as the large storehouse went up in flames. On the other side, shadowy soldiers were advancing toward the beach. The two vehicles parked there had ceased their fire on the tiny shack, and German infantrymen were crossing the field toward it. He worried they'd find Tom and Dan lying inside and just shoot them. He hoped that wouldn't be the case.

Driven by the sea breeze, the thick smoke billowing out of the burning storehouse drifted toward the Germans. Willoughby laughed aloud when he saw the storehouse burning like a torch. The Jerries weren't going to have any idea what was about to hit them. It didn't take long for a thick smoke to blanket the entire area around the cottage. Between the burning fuel and the incendiary explosives, the entire storehouse blazed like a volcano.

"Bastards," he muttered.

The storehouse burst apart at the seams in a flash of fire just as the first Germans stormed by. The thick, lime-laced smoke churned out. Those too close were either caught by the expanding fireball or cloaked in the smoke. Either way, they wouldn't be any more trouble. The gunfire ceased, and the enemy became lost from sight.

"So, what's the deal with oysters?" Dodd asked him, grabbing an oar and helping to row out beyond the tidal island.

"It makes lime," Van Dekker said, as if anyone should know that.

Willoughby chuckled. "It burns if you get it on your skin or in your eyes. Usually, it takes hours to burn them down. We used to do it back home in Portrush to make cement." He shrugged. "Best I could come up with."

"I hope you didn't anger those bastards too much," Dodd said. "Chances are we missed the ride out. We may have to spend the rest of the war on that island."

They drifted out past the group of small islands just offshore. The extent of damage done to Guernsey became clear as they went further out. Spires of smoke were rising from half a dozen different places. To the south, a large plume darkened the port and Castle Cornet.

Several more minutes went by before the first sign of a periscope was sighted.

"Guess the Jolly Jacks stuck around for us," Dodd said happily.

The sub surfaced not a hundred feet from the boat carrying Captain Zahlman's party. By the time the second boat hit the hull, a pair of German fighter planes showed up, circling around the island to the west.

"Best we get out of here," Claymoore said as a trio of sailors and an officer came above deck to assist. "Brought back a couple of fish for you." He pushed the two Germans up the ladder of the conning tower.

The first bullets from the German fighters just barely erupted in the water. By then, it was already too late. The hatch sealed shut behind the last man, and the sub dived beneath the waves like a rock. And that was the end of that.

CHAPTER EIGHTEEN

Willoughby held the burning cigarette up to his lips and inhaled gently. The tension he'd felt seemed to slip away, and the exhale felt just as good. He'd never been a smoker. In fact, he'd despised the habit in others. He'd always felt it was a dirty compulsion that served absolutely no purpose. On his grand-father's fishing boat, everyone had smoked except him. But now, with the burning butt and the taste of decent tobacco, he could understand its appeal.

He stood near the top of the gangplank. His face was wet with perspiration, his uniform was soiled, and his muscles ached from head to toe. But the tension seemed to ease with each draw. Just feet in front of him, the corpse of Corporal Mansfield was being carried off the deck of the sub that had brought them back to England. It was draped with a white sheet, save for the dark red stains that soaked through. He stared at it for a fleeting moment before turning his attention back to the group of men crawling out of the sub and onto the deck above.

The day was overcast, but it felt good to see the sky again. He was tired, though. They all were. The berthing compartment was a clustered, cramped space in the sub's bow where the crew was housed. This morning, they'd made it available for the commandos to use to sleep on the way home. The berth had been quiet as a tomb, but it had given him the chance to get some sleep on the way back to England, however brief. The crew had offered tea, but he'd shrugged it off. He was filthy from head to toe, and his skin felt raw. All he wanted to do now was get out of his uniform and take a long shower.

He knocked off the ash at the end of his cigarette and took one final, long drag, then flicked the butt into the water. Ashore, there was a group of curious onlookers. The sight of a Royal Navy sub was common enough, but the men getting off might have looked out of sights. Berets and face paint were hardly the norm in the British Army, and he saw the people staring at them strangely.

Two sailors carried Corporal Mansfield's corpse down the plank and onto the dock, where they slid it into the rear of an ambulance. Willoughby grabbed what gear he had and followed in line as the troop made their way down the swinging walkway. Each man walked in silence.

A pair of military police guards and an officer were at the end of the gangplank. The two Nazi officers they'd brought back with them were brought above deck. They meandered down the walkway and were taken into custody. The black-clad SS officer spat contemptuously on the dock before a guard took him by the arm and escorted him into the rear of a lorry.

In front of Willoughby, Wallace nursed an arm in a sling. Darjan was next to be carried down the plank on a stretcher. The bandages wrapped around his arm were soaked in dark red-brown blood. He was unconscious and had developed a severe fever on the way back to England. He was placed inside the ambulance next to Mansfield.

Three wounded and one dead was almost nearly a fair trade under the circumstances. Wallace and Ashford's wounds weren't that bad, and had been dressed by the steward on board the sub. Though he didn't like the feeling of the losses, he imagined that back on the island, more than one person living there might be added to that loss count. He hated the idea of that even more. He'd heard stories about innocent civilians on the continent being the victims of terrible crimes. The image of the young French girl came to mind.

"Fall in, lads," Sergeant Bowvers said. His normally deep voice seemed strained this morning.

The men lined up on the edge of the dock. Willoughby couldn't keep his grip on his gear any longer and let it slip to the ground. Zahlman and Claymoore were met by several officers at the other end of the wharf. Willoughby barely gave them any notice, or paid attention to Sergeant Bowvers as he droned on about some such thing. Handing out congratulations on a successful return. Willoughby didn't hear any of it. Instead, his gaze drifted aimlessly around the gray harbor and at the people watching.

"Wonder what they're saying down there," Wallace whispered next to him.

He nudged Willoughby gently in his side and nodded down at the conversation going on between the officers. Instead, he watched the ambulance that was pulling away with Corporal Mansfield and Private Darjan inside. He didn't know Darjan, but had known and liked Mansfield. He'd been someone of good character.

Lieutenant Claymoore came walking down as the ambulance drove up the ramp. There was a slight limp in his step. He spoke with Sergeant Bowvers for a few moments.

"Very well, sir," Willoughby heard Bowvers say. "All right." He turned and told the assembled, "Take care, lads. Lorry there'll take you to your billets." He tried to grin through the face paint and failed. "There's some hot showers and food waiting for you. Get some rest." His back snapped straight. "Dismissed."

They broke without another word, and the lorry drove them from the dock to a triple storied boarding house in the center of Falmouth. It took everything in him just to keep his eyes open on the drive, and he barely registered the hot shower he took afterward. All he knew was that it felt good to be back.

Each of them had been given their own rooms, which was a welcome bit of news. Upon his return to his room, he noticed the woman who ran the boarding house had come in while he'd been showering. His kit had been placed neatly in the corner, and a fresh uniform was waiting on a chair. He collapsed on his bed and, before his head even hit the pillow, he'd fallen asleep.

The next morning had brought a summons for Willoughby to report to Captain Zahlman. He'd barely gotten half his breakfast down when Sergeant Bowvers had found him. He'd pushed aside his morning meal and tea and gone straight to Zahlman's temporary office.

He had taken little in the way of food since returning to England yesterday morning, and found himself strangely with little appetite. The thought of food and drink had no appeal for him right now, anyway. He hadn't felt that way following Narvik, but he'd also landed himself in the hospital right after that. He tried to shake the feeling away as he left the boarding house and made his way through the town streets. The captain had been set up in an empty office in a municipal building in Falmouth for the time being, close to the boarding house that the rest of the troop was billeted in.

There'd been no shortage of military personnel around the tiny seaside town these days. Many had returned from with an expeditionary force in

France and Belgium. Sullen souls whose morale had been beaten out of them facing down Hitler's panzer divisions in Northern France. It showed on their faces as he walked down the cobblestone streets. Half of them didn't even bother to look up at him as he gazed at them, or else their eyes were staring off into nothing.

There had to have been a thousand foreign fighters as well. Hundreds of French soldiers, in their thick blue trench coats, sat along sidewalk benches. Most were still waiting to be repatriated back to France, following last month's armistice with Germany. Here and there were Dutch and Poles, and others whose languages were completely foreign to him.

The white stoned building that Captain Zahlman had set up his office in was just a block from the harbor. An officer was exiting as Willoughby came in. A clerk's desk sat right inside the foyer, but no clerk sat there. Lieutenant Claymoore was standing just inside a tiny side room. He saw Willoughby enter, dropped a handful of folders onto a nearby table, and stepped toward him.

Willoughby was just about to come to attention, but Claymoore waved a hand at him first. The young Claymoore looked as exhausted as Willoughby probably did.

"Willoughby. Here for Captain Zahlman, I imagine?"

"Yes, sir."

"Hmm. Well, I wanted to have a quick word with you. It concerns your actions on the island."

"Yes, sir?"

"I... I..." He fumbled like he was searching for his words, then let out a heavy sigh and visibly relaxed. "What you and Wallace and Van Dekker did was, well, it was quite extraordinary. I know how you and the others might feel about the outcome, but that shouldn't detract from what the three of you did."

"Thank you, sir." Willoughby nodded gratefully.

"I also wanted to tell you that your quick thinking was what saved us. I can't imagine how you devised such an idea, but it showed some real ingenuity." Willoughby smiled at him.

"I appreciate it, sir."

"That was my first action, you know."

Willoughby knew that, but played coy anyway. "Was it, sir? I wouldn't have been able to tell."

The ends of Claymoore's mouth twitched in a quarter smile. "Well, I just wanted to say that to you." Surprisingly, he held out his hand, and Willoughby shook it. "Hopefully, we'll be put back together in the future."

"Hopefully, sir?" Willoughby asked. He had given no thought to what was coming next. In the back of his mind, he'd just assumed the men who'd come back would be thrown right back into the mix together.

"What do you think they're doing behind that door?" Claymoore gestured toward the oak door at the end of the hallway. Captain Zahlman's name was written on a piece of tape. "Assignments aren't permanent, Private."

Willoughby grimaced for a second. "No, sir. They're not. May I ask you whether you've heard anything about Private Darjan?"

"Might lose his arm." Willoughby sighed. "But word is, he'll survive."

"I see. Thank you, sir."

"Well, go on then." Claymoore craned his neck toward Zahlman's makeshift office. They saluted one another and then Claymoore left through the door.

There wasn't a soul left in the room but him. He knocked gently on the thick door and waited for permission to enter. The door swung open, and he was surprised to see that it was Zahlman holding it open for him. Inside, there was a second person in the room, sitting behind a wide desk.

"Come in, Willoughby," Zahlman told him. As usual, the captain's appearance was immaculate. His No. 2 Service Dress uniform was freshly pressed, and his thick black hair was perfect. One would hardly have known the man had been on a mission into enemy territory just a day and a half before.

Willoughby took three long strides forward and came to a sudden halt in the center of the office. His right foot stomped the floor, and he came to a swift attention, snapping his hand upward in a proper salute. The man sitting on the opposite side of the desk returned the salute and then leaned back in the wooden chair. He was a middle-aged man with slightly graying hair. His uniform could have just as easily belonged to a private, but for the insignia of a full colonel on his shoulders. Unlike other British Army officers, he wore no ribbons or devices on his uniform. Nothing except the patch of the Royal

Warwickshire on his shoulder. The colonel struck a match and puffed his tobacco pipe to life. The cherry aroma of it filled the office.

"At ease, Willoughby," he said out of the corner of his mouth as he drew on the stem.

The colonel was a sinewy man. His body was lean, and his skin was like toughened leather. Despite his small stature, the fact was that anyone in the brigade would instantly recognize him as someone who knew his business inside and out. He knew Colonel John "Jungle Jack" Devereaux was one of the masterminds behind the Special Service Brigade. His experiences surviving the frontier of northwest India and the jungles of Malaya were practically legendary. To those in the regular forces, the demure man might easily be mistaken for just some paper-pushing administrative type. But looks could be deceiving.

Willoughby relaxed his stance, holding his hands behind his back. Next to the colonel, Captain Zahlman stood with an approving grin on his face. Unlike the colonel, Captain Zahlman was in full-service dress, with all the articles.

"So," Devereaux said, opening up the folder in front of him. "Captain Zahlman's after-action report on the Channel Islands operation made for quite interesting reading. I had to do it twice just to make sure I'd read it correctly. Seemed like something more out of a novel than a military report." He skimmed through the pages. "The original plan went south just after arriving at the target. The book would have had your unit withdraw immediately, scrubbed the operation and headed straight for the extraction point. Leaving behind whoever couldn't make it. According to Captain Zahlman, and I quote, 'Lieutenant Claymoore and half the team would've been left for dead, or captured by the enemy. Quick thinking and a unique ability to improvise spared them that fate. Private Willoughby's actions showed an ability to consider unforeseen options and to execute a plan that not only saved lives but, in the end, secured enemy prisoners that may prove vital to the war effort.'"

He ended the report and looked up. "Mister Willoughby,"—the colonel's voice became softer, almost friendly—"it's these kinds of things that make the case for units such as this one. Officially, the objective was a failure. However, I can tell you right now that headquarters looks very favorably on this mission, and in particular, your actions." He smiled broadly. "Unofficially, objective failure or not, I say well done, Private. Lives were saved that might not have otherwise been, and two highly valuable assets are now cooling their heels in interrogation cells. I spoke with MI6 just this morning. They've already identified one of these men as an SS officer, partially responsible for the execution of Polish prisoners of war. I'm sure, under threat of handing him over to the Free Poles, he might start singing. It might interest you to know, the other prisoner you took is a German Army intelligence officer. Both are high-level captives. They'll make for excellent substitutes for the lack of a code machine." He closed the file and smiled.

"His Majesty's Government is very pleased with the outcome, regardless. With those things said, I want you to know that I've put a letter of commendation in your file. This report is circulating through Westminster even now. So don't be surprised if a few MPs hold you up as a shining example. Don't let it go to your head."

"No, sir," Willoughby said modestly. As if he would.

Colonel Devereaux looked at Captain Zahlman and gave him a nod. Zahlman reached into his pocket and held out a small black box.

"Private Willoughby. Between your actions in the Channel Islands and those during the Narvik evacuation, the Army has seen fit to advance you to the rank of lance corporal." Zahlman handed Willoughby the white box, which he opened. A single chevron was inside. "Congratulations."

"Thank you, sir," Willoughby said.

Colonel Devereaux stood up from his chair, extended a muscular arm, and shook his hand, followed by Zahlman.

"Well done, son," Devereaux said.

"Thank you, sir," Willoughby said. He fumbled the chevron around in his hand. "May I ask a question, sir?"

"Go on." Devereaux nodded.

"On the island, sir, some people helped us. A French girl, for one." He hesitated. "I was wondering..."

"What will happen with them?" the colonel said, and Willoughby nodded. Devereaux sat back down in his chair. "War is a bloody business, Willoughby. We hope for the best, but are prepared for the worst. Our sources on Guernsey, and in other places, are putting their lives on the line. Truth is, I don't know what will become of them. This raid will probably be seen as an internal security disaster for the enemy. But that's not our problem, Lance Corporal."

Willoughby was slightly taken aback by the callousness of the colonel's words. But after a moment, his blood settled. He knew Devereaux was right.

"Your next assignment awaits you," Zahlman told him, holding out a sealed envelope. "The Number Four battalion is being formed near Weymouth. Your orders are in there. You're to report there a week from tomorrow."

"A week, sir?" Willoughby said, and instantly kicked himself for the breach of protocol.

"The war doesn't wait for you, son," Devereaux told him.

"You'll find some familiar faces when you get there," Zahlman said. "I believe you're friendly with Private MacAvoy?"

Willoughby smiled at the name. "Yes, sir."

Zahlman nodded. "Good. Then, you're dismissed, Lance Corporal."

"Sir!" Willoughby saluted, then spun around on his heels and marched out of the office. Colonel Devereaux was just relighting the bowl of his pipe when he marched out, leaving the sweet aroma behind him.

"That's one we'll want to keep an eye on right there," he could faintly hear Devereaux tell Zahlman. "Indeed. A few hundred more like him and we'd win the war within a month."

He didn't dawdle any longer. It wouldn't be proper to get caught eavesdropping on an officer's conversation. He adjusted his beret before stepping foot outside. The salty sea breeze out of the east was fresh, and the sun was bright in the sky. Suddenly, it felt good to be outside and on his feet. He stood just outside the building and opened the envelope in his hand. He had a week before he was to report to Weymouth, and now he knew his friend MacAvoy would be waiting for him when he got there.

He also noted the name of the CO he was to report to when he arrived. Captain Saul Zahlman's name was typed in large, bold letters.

Things were looking very good. Very good indeed.